candice y. johnson

EVERY BLACK GIRL DANCES

BLACK
ODYSSEY
MEDIA

WWW.BLACKODYSSEY.NET

Published by
BLACK ODYSSEY MEDIA

www.blackodyssey.net
Email: info@blackodyssey.net

This book is a work of fiction. Any references to events, real people, or real places are used fictitiously. Other names, characters, places, and events are products of the author's imagination, and any resemblance to actual events or places or persons, living or dead, is entirely coincidental.

Library of Congress Control Number: Applied for.

First Trade Paperback Printing: January 2024
ISBN: 978-1-957950-08-2
ISBN: 978-1-957950-09-9 (e-book)

Cover Design by Ashlee Nassar of Designs with Sass
To the extent that the image or images on the cover of this book depict a person or persons, such person or persons are merely models and are not intended to portray any character in the book.

All rights reserved. Black Odyssey Media, LLC | Dallas, TX.

10 9 8 7 6 5 4 3 2 1

Manufactured in the United States of America

Distributed by Kensington Publishing Corp.

*Dedicated to everyone who's been told
they can't dance. Turn on the music...
the floor is yours!*

Dear Reader,

I want to thank you immensely for supporting Black Odyssey Media authors, and our ongoing efforts to spotlight more minority storytellers. The scariest and most challenging task for many writers is getting the story, or characters, out of our heads and onto the page. Having admitted that, with every manuscript that Kreceda and I acquire, we believe that it took talent, discipline, and remarkable courage to construct that story, flesh out those characters, and prepare it for the world. Debut or seasoned, our authors are the real heroes and heroines in *OUR* story. And for them, we are eternally grateful.

Whether you are new to Candice "Ordered Steps" Johnson or Black Odyssey Media, we hope that you are here to stay. We also welcome your feedback and kindly ask that you leave a review. For upcoming releases, announcements, submission guidelines, etc., please be sure to visit our website at www.blackodyssey.net or scan the QR code below. We can also be found on social media using @iamblackodyssey. Until next time, take care and enjoy the journey!

Joyfully,

Shawanda Williams

Shawanda "N'Tyse" Williams
Founder/Publisher

ONE

"GIRL, YOU ARE black as hell."

That's not exactly what the woman perched in the aisle seat says to me, but it's what I hear as our plane hits a second round of turbulence in half an hour. Even heaven seems annoyed by her incessant yapping about all things relevant to only her. Thank God, this flight only has a little more than two hours to go.

My row-mate is too cheery for six in the morning. I should be taking my first pee, not listening to a complete stranger with zero sense of boundaries or discretion, chattering about social media and current events while casually tossing in how pretty I am for a dark-skinned girl. Make that *extra dark*, as if I'm not already aware. Her thin lips latch onto the rim of her Styrofoam coffee cup as she flips her bright red curls, utterly oblivious of how insulting her backhanded compliment really is. Somehow, my blatant snub and wide-eyed silence isn't the effective deterrent I'd hoped it would be. Now, she's circling from waxing about visiting her elderly grandfather for a spell in Frisco, Texas, back to her fascination with my skin.

God, I don't have the strength to speak laymen's right now.

"I hope you don't find this rude, but your skin is simply luminous to be so . . ."

"Dark?" There. I finish for her. She knows it's rude before she alludes to it. My submissive face takes over as I lean against the

1

window, observing her green eyes grow into saucers and soak up all this darkness in awe. "Makes you want a Snickers, huh?"

Her paltry giggle in response to my direct jab is a staunch reminder of the harsh scrutiny my particular shade of black forces me to deal with every day: she just doesn't get it. She chirps her name as if I care enough to register the pointless syllables in my memory bank. Sandy. Penny. Chrysanthemum. Hell, who knows what she just rattled off? For the rest of this flight from Los Angeles to Dallas, all I want to hear is my playlist while I catch a few zzz's.

What's-her-name blinks, taking a brief respite from her irrelevant musings to breathe. Facing me, she rests an elbow on the armrest and perches her head on top of her hand, curiosity etched across her heart-shaped face. Seriously, if she doesn't stop staring, I will invoice her for a counseling session. Sis acts like my skin's giving her third-world healing.

"Your braids are so . . . unique," she sings loud enough to provoke the passengers occupying the rows in front of and behind us to indiscreetly investigate for themselves as if I can't see them squirming in their seats just enough to judge whether her assessment's on point.

"So different," she mutters, intent on eliciting the response she didn't squeeze out of me the first time. One of her wiry hands gestures as if to reach across the empty middle seat between us to fondle my tailbone-length braids, regarding them with the wonder of a mythical creature she's discovered is actually real. A scowl replacing the excruciating smile I've managed to maintain this long prompts her to draw it back quickly. She darts an index finger toward them instead. "The colors weaved across the middle—I've never seen that before."

"Jamaica," I eek out as pleasantly as I can on the strength of the sigh which carries it.

"Your name's Jamaica?"

I giggle. Not because there's humor in the situation, but because I'm tired. These types of cultural interrogations are seemingly barren but never easy to birth. I'm a realist: no response I give this woman will make her see anything other than my skin. Her creepy gaze almost makes it impossible for me to restrain my snarky attitude, which is two seconds from reaching: *I wish you would.*

"No, ma'am, my name's not Jamaica. The color in my hair represents the Jamaican flag. Where my dead father's from."

"Oh."

She's uncomfortable now. One, because the bitter taste of ignorance isn't so tasty on her tongue. And two, I have yet to give up any useful intel on myself. Not even my name, which sis has been patiently waiting for since we strapped in for takeoff. But as long as I've mastered the resting "B" face—which I'm about to switch on effective immediately—silence shall ever be her portion.

"What did you say your name is? What is it that you do?" *See how intrusive she is?* When I saw our flight wasn't crowded, I expected to snooze all the way home to Texas. But instead, I got stuck with . . . her.

Maybe if I respond, she'll back down and stop leering at me like a puppy begging for a treat. Keeping my cool, I flash the smile the dental hygienist I hired to fix my teeth with my first Hollywood check and blurt, "I write and direct films."

"Oh yeah?" She perks up under the false impression that a bond is forming between us. "What kind of movies do you make? Anything I've seen?"

"Probably not," I hark a laugh as insipid as our wordy transaction. Obviously, there's no way this suburban duchess, who's probably never tasted a swear word, has been exposed to my gritty dramas. If she had, this conversation would've already detoured to mute.

"I make films exploiting Black trauma," I go on to explain. "You know, pimps, domestic violence, drug trafficking, crack babies. Real entertainment." I pull my denim jacket closed and lean closer to her, mimicking her pose on the other side of the armrest. "I write the real rough stuff. Families killing each other, men who can't keep their junk in their pants, silly, trifling baby mamas, and female doormats. Hood stuff like that. But I'm flying to escape the set of my latest film, *Crack Dreams*, because I'm sick of profiting off my brothers' and sisters' pain for the appeasement of people like you."

And just like that, sis turns away with a 'tude, reclines her seat, and pushes out a fake yawn. When she squeezes her eyes shut, I jam my earbuds in and press play on the first song in my playlist. Guess our meet and greet is over.

You've only got one reason not to love me,
But I can give you a thousand more
It's amazing how you hate me
Because my future's far from yours . . .

The jazzy tune by my best friend, Tati Ko, blares through the earpieces, and I recline my seat. Tati's being positioned to be the next queen of R&B music, but I'm flying back home to Parable to help celebrate her million-dollar win on *Battle Exes*, a wilderness-style reality competition show pairing ex-lovers and pitting them against their rivals from past seasons. Even though her ex helped secure Tati the win, she kept the entire bounty for herself. The Twitter crowd and I couldn't be happier that she got her revenge against the narcissist who's still threatening her and her family with violence over her selfish decision.

I peer out the window. The skies seem friendlier than the universe has been to me lately. Not that I'm anything close to a singer, but I can hum a mean tune, so I do it along with "Redeemed by Me," the song Tati wrote for my debut film, *Flogged*. *Flogged* chronicles the life of 16-year-old Nas, who was sold by her mother into the sex trade for drugs, and later convicted of murdering both her kidnapper and her mama. Like I told sis earlier, warm fuzzies. Hard to believe, but a week ago, the same tune I'm jamming to now almost got me killed. Okay, maybe I'm being dramatic. But the incident was enough to make me come close to soiling the yellow sundress I planned on returning after sporting it at my girl Olivia's bachelorette party. Just because I have a few dollars tucked away in savings doesn't mean I'm not cheap.

Olivia's party was so lit, I stayed way longer than I originally intended. In my defense, *pole dance karaoke* far exceeded my expectations, killing my self-imposed curfew. But when the bride's mother slides from the top of the pole to the bottom in slow motion while killing the best of Whitney Houston in mezzo-soprano, you don't move. If nothing else, it helped me forget the crap day I had in preproduction for my next movie.

Anyway, I was zooming down the side streets on the way back to my loft, belching the remnants of the mini-mountain of mimosas I drank, feeling too good to notice I was pushing my red convertible Lexus well over the speed limit by 20 miles an hour. Didn't even see the police car waiting to catch an unsuspecting lawbreaker like me slipping until I flew by him, and the lights started chasing me.

"Great, just great. Hudson, I'll have to call you back," I told my boyfriend, who'd been on speaker the entire hour-long ride, to help keep me awake.

"What's wrong? Everything okay?" The slight panic in his voice did nothing to ease the fear swirling in the pit of my stomach as I eyed the wailing lights behind me. The way the flashes of blue and red intermingled with each other felt like a threat and made my stomach sink. Immediately, I wished I hadn't guzzled so many drinks.

"I'm not okay. I just got pulled over," I explained as I pulled to the side of the road and put the car in park. My trembling hands outshook my quaking voice. Minutes ago, the air was so cool; now, a trail of sweat immediately formed around my edges.

"Is that all?" Hudson chuckled. "Just comply with whatever they say, and you'll be fine." The amusement in my man's voice shook off any buzz threatening to keep me from walking a straight line if I was issued a sobriety test. Not to mention the one word that would ban my ovaries to him for the rest of our tenure together: *comply.*

What the entire hell?

"I have to go. I'll call you back." Ignoring Hudson's unsolicited advice, I reached to the dash where the phone was mounted and hung up. Then I started my video recorder and rested my hands on the steering wheel like my father taught me.

Breathe, girl, breathe. You're going to be fine.

Spying the officer creeping toward my car in the rearview, I was suddenly aware that my braids were secured in a bun at the nape of my neck. What if he mistook me for a man? Would it make a difference? Was there just a matter of minutes before I became a hashtag swimming in a pool of my own blood? Would there be protests in my name, or would I be quickly forgotten by the next day's news?

Would I be awarded a posthumous Oscar?

I won't lie. The officer's brown skin was a relief when he appeared at my window. After chronicling some pretty damning scenarios involving the boys in blue in my films, at least I was being stopped by a cop who looked like me . . . right?

"Good evening, ma'am. Do you know why I pulled you over?" His baritone thundered through my spirit. His broad chest heaved, and his badge issued a silent dare. *Try me.*

"I guess I was speeding," I said, not that my misdemeanor needed confirming.

"You were." His head tilted to the side, then quickly upright. "Hey, aren't you Hudson Pyke's girlfriend?"

No, I'm JC Burke, the dummy who let my blue-eyed lover get famous off my scripts while I literally became his shadow. But yeah, I'm her.

Eyes ahead, hands on the wheel. "Yes, Officer. That's me: JC Burke."

"Uh-huh."

I hesitantly allowed my head to inch left, scanning for the officer's name in case I needed receipts later. In the meantime, Officer Riggins's eyes darted past my face to the phone mounted on the dash.

Smile . . . You're this close to becoming viral.

"That last movie of yours - the cop was acquitted of attempted murder for shooting the kid in the back, right?"

I knew it. "Yes, he was, sir. I mean, the girl was running away after being suspected of shoplifting a T-shirt. And there was no excuse for swinging at the boutique owner when he tackled her, even though no stolen goods or weapons were found on her. At least she was only paralyzed, right?" I pressed my lips closed, bottling the rest of my opinion inside.

"Right. What was the name of it again? The movie?"

"*First-Degree Melanin.*"

His brows pinched together, broad shoulders hunched. "Yeah. The wife didn't care for that one too much." His low voice dodged my cell's audio as his fingers tapped against his ticket pad, which I preferred instead of on his holster. "She said the plot was unrealistic."

. . . in spite of the real Wisconsin news story I based it on?

"Look, it's hard to see out here. We don't want you having an accident, do we?"

You mean by car or bullet?

Without relaxing my tightened jaws, I peeled my stoic glare away from the badge, staring ahead. "No, sir, we don't."

"Good. Slow down," he warned. Taking a quick second to assess my threat level, he must've determined my 135-pound frame wasn't too menacing because he jammed the pad back into his pocket and exhaled the tension from his body. "Be safe out here."

The lump obstructing my throat didn't dislodge until Officer Riggins hopped back into his patrol car and left me reeling on the side of the road. How long had I held my breath? I slumped over the steering wheel in tears, trying to coerce my spirit to climb back into my mortified flesh, all while Hudson's instructions burned my chest.

Comply.

I slammed my hands against the dash until I swore I'd drawn blood. Without a shred of empathy, the rearview mirror gave me a glimpse of my runny mascara and snotty nose. *Comply* rang in my ears, breaking me down worse than the actual traffic stop.

After a few minutes, I turned the key in the ignition and pulled back onto the main road at a much-slower pace. Without bothering to call Hudson to give him an update, I powered off the phone. Let him worry whether I had *complied* for the rest of the night while I tried getting some sleep.

Once I got home and climbed in bed, I slept better than during the six weeks we'd been working on *Crack Dreams*. The next day, I powered through Olivia's wedding, then hit the reception with Hudson at my side. It was a grand affair of excesses and sparkle, so I didn't need to bring up his prior night's infraction until after the bride and groom's first dance. I think I did a pretty good job presenting the thousand other ways Hudson could've handled things better when I told him I got stopped; however, he made a conscious effort to misunderstand while *white-splaining* me instead.

"What's the big deal, JC? The drinks are flowing, and everybody's happy. There's no reason to walk around here with your face all twisted up." Hudson spun me as the other couples slow danced around us. His eyes were hidden behind his signature red frames. Tousled brown hair mussed from yanking it every two seconds while I patiently walked him through the source of our latest fight.

Hudson dipped me, but I locked my back to protect my breasts from spilling out of the strapless eggplant bridesmaid dress barely containing them. When he pulled me up, I pushed into his chest, hoping to feel the same security in his arms that I felt on our first date.

Nothing.

"At least you didn't get a ticket." Hudson's nonchalant assertion harbored dangerously close to amusement.

I backed away, dishing a death glare. "Have you heard *anything* I've said? I could've had my head blown off last night."

"Sure, in an imaginary scenario, which has absolutely no bearing on here and now." He smoothed a hand over my braids. "All I'm saying is don't waste your energy on something that didn't even happen. You've had 26 years to understand how traffic stops work. All you have to do is—"

"Don't you *dare* say, 'comply'!"

That word transported me back to the playground in elementary school when my bullies forced me to eat dirt pies.

Know what my teachers said when they gave me a spit cup to rinse the dirt out of my mouth in the bathroom? *"No one likes a tattler. Next time, walk away."*

What kind of a gutless waste of skin says that to a child who soiled her panties because she got jumped? *Code: comply.* Same disrespect, different recipe. And every time the man who rarely says he loves me outside of the bed brushes off my concerns with the standard refrain that I'm "just being emotional," it tastes like one of those disgusting dirt pies.

Hudson gently tugged me by the rhinestone belt cinched around my waist, pulling me closer. "Can we have one day without you swiping your black card?" As soon as the question dropped, his pale skin turned crimson when he noticed my lips pulled in a tight line. "I'm sorry."

"I am too."

Two minutes later, it wasn't hard convincing Olivia I wasn't feeling well and had to exit the celebration early. Hudson didn't call my name when I walked away from him. Didn't reach for my arm to hold me back or match my steps so I couldn't lose him on the way out of the gargantuan hall. By my estimation, he had at least 20 steps from where we were dancing to the parking lot to right his wrong.

But he didn't.

"Oh my, I didn't realize I'd fallen asleep." Sis is awake now, blowing stale air up my nostrils, which I quickly cover with a hand. Judging by her restored cheery demeanor despite our earlier exchange, she's still not woke, though.

"Just in time for landing." I grant her a smile, my fleeting apology for getting fly when she's only trying to make this trip pleasant for us. That's one thing I've hated about myself since I was a little girl. Being bold enough to buck, then too quick to nurse the wound when 'ish gets uncomfortable. I'm brazen on film, but I'm scared of being muted if I hit the wrong note.

Once we've landed and been given the go-ahead to exit the plane, sis stretches, then peels herself from the seat to retrieve her bag from the overhead. She grins and maneuvers into the aisle, pushing her way through the other passengers, all trying to get off the plane at once. "Enjoy your trip."

"You too." I don't follow behind her.

My backpack seems heavier when I hoist it over my shoulder, waiting for row after row of passengers to empty the plane. When there is finally nothing but empty seats in front of me, a kind gentleman allows me to squeeze into the aisle ahead of him. I'm praying the nice gesture will be indicative of my week at home.

Maybe.

People scurry past me as I slowly make my way to the baggage claim. By the time I get there, sis has already grabbed her stuff and is heading off. We lock eyes for a moment, and she waves like we'll see each other again in this lifetime. I wave back, thinking how at some point in our lives, every Black girl dances to someone else's expectations. It's about time I choreograph for myself.

TWO

"I CAN'T BELIEVE I have the JC Burke in my car! When my kids find out, mind blown—just like mine. And my wife, she's never going to believe I had you in the back of my sedan!"

As long as I don't end up in the trunk.

The remnants of scraggly strands of hair form a crescent moon on the back of his sunburned head as the middle-aged driver transports me from the airport to the skating rink where Tati's hosting her party. Probably from miming his brain exploding every time something surprises him. The unforgiving August sun has baked his round head until it resembles one of those old-school Red Hot Links my mother used to feed me when she wasn't on the road because she was too busy touring to learn how to cook. If I were cruel, I'd snap a picture of it and post it to see if anyone agrees with my assessment. But he's so cute the way he's gushing over me. What's not to love about the man who skidded in front of the passenger pickup, jumped out of the car, and announced to the general public he was there to scoop up the *female Spike Lee*? His gold star for the day.

So while my biggest fan alternates between heaping praise and trying to pry exclusive information he promises will stay "between us" (did the actresses who played mother and daughter in *Flogged* really get into a fistfight on set?), I'm exhausted. The

20-minute ride can't be over fast enough. *Please, Lord—don't let that gas hand keep inching toward "E." I'll die if he runs out.*

"We're just a couple of minutes away," he informs me.

I owe You one, God.

I shove empty fast-food paper bags and balled-up burger and taco wrappings aside to get more comfortable. Judging by the family of Barbie dolls and toy guns getting squished under my classic yellow Converse, his tribe can't be old enough to be fans of mine.

"So, your kids have seen my movies?"

"Every darn one of 'em," he proudly announces in a stiff Southern twang. "My 10-year-old has seen *Flogged* a hundred times. Quotes every line with the best of 'em." His eyes glint in the rearview.

Bet she cusses with the best of them too. This is getting gooder and gooder, as I'm sure he'd declare if I give him time.

"So, what do they like best about my movies?"

"Huh?" he asks.

"Your kids—what do they appreciate most about my films?"

He harks, biding time to think about it. "The grit," he says. "Anything down and dirty, my kids are with it."

Interesting. I lean back in my seat and spend the rest of the time listening to this guy wax on about how my films have made his heart more sympathetic to people like me, while inwardly, I'm begging to come across a weapon to gouge his eyes out so he'll stop leering at me like I'm a sideshow.

We finally pull up in front of Skateland. He parks and helps me get my bags out of the trunk of the car, still chattering on about how his family's going to die when they find out he's been in my presence. I grant him a selfie, and he hops back in the car and skids back down the dirt road, leaving me to ponder the sketchy cinematic legacy I'm leaving his kids to devour.

Bags secured, I lumber inside the skating rink, praying the air-conditioning will expel the musty demons that have attached themselves to me from my biggest fan's dank car. I step one foot inside, and my eyes immediately rivet on *him*: a giant drenched in terra-cotta. Sharp jawline tinged with the slightest bit of scruff. Closely cropped, precisely edged hair, and an unyielding presence not to be wasted on *what-if's*.

Within seconds of spotting him, the writer in me mentally sketches a storyboard that ends with our happily ever after. Not necessarily in matrimony because I do have a man and don't even know this Adonis's name. Still, I imagine a beginning starting with whatever's lurking beneath the black T-shirt clinging to his broad chest and ending wherever he wants it to.

A few feet closer, and I'd be able to hear the witty banter emerging from his scrumptious mouth that has the mini-entourage of kids surrounding him doubled over in laughter. Feels like I'm missing out on something. I want to laugh as hard as the elderly man clinging to this guy's stout frame, knowing he has no business being on wheels in the first place. Should Adonis let go, the elderly cutie will find out just how brittle his old bones are.

The two men are perfect before and after shots of each other; I'm assuming grandfather and grandson. Every time the silver-haired fox wobbles, Adonis nonchalantly holds him up as if it's part of their normal routine. God, I've been around my share of fine brothers, but there's no explaining why this one's got me so weak in the knees. He's more beautiful than my virginity thief. Only with darker eyes that hold a bunch of secrets I inexplicably want to uncover for myself. And familiar. I've seen that expression alternating between fervent and flirty somewhere. Television? Social media? Adonis and I have crossed paths before, I'm positive. But we've never met.

"Finally, the love of my life escapes the clutches of Hollywood to grace us small-town folk with her celebrity vitality. Hope you brought your Black girl glitter with you." Tati invades my thoughts and hoists me in the air, accidentally knocking my oversized, floppy white hat to the floor when she spins me around—our greeting since we were kids. I'm taller; she's stronger. I clench my sweaty legs tightly around her exposed midriff to keep her from dropping me and mush my face smack in the middle of her short, springy mix of kinks and coils dyed a funky shade of light pink since the last time I saw her. She smells like Bath and Body Works comingled with weed. Hopefully, she's lucid enough to play hostess tonight.

"I've missed you like crazy; you have no idea how much."

"Liar," Tati chastises above her bouncy single, "Drop It on Me," blaring through the speakers. She cautiously lets me down on the floor. My legs wobble with the instability of a toddler learning to balance. "If you missed me so much, then explain why I've only seen you on video chats for the last two years. You even missed my blackberry pie for Christmas."

God still works miracles.

"Well, I'm here now." I squat to pick up my hat, brush it off, and replace it with a tap on the brim. "Hudson's folks are obsessed with gathering the entire family on major holidays, significant others included. The Hamptons for Thanksgiving, Calabasas for Christmas. I couldn't get out of it."

"Right. Don't want to disappoint the future in-laws by skipping out on green bean casserole and mac-n-cheese topped with bread crumbs." Exasperation seeps through the pores of Tati's bronze skin. She thrusts her hands on her hips. I'm about to get lectured.

"Go easy, all right? Mrs. Pyke's trying harder to get along with me." The lie claws its way up my throat, but I spit it out and continue justifying. "She's stopped blurting whatever comes to her mind, then asking me if it's offensive, doesn't run down her list of Black friends, so I know she's *down*, and even took the initiative to add greens to the menu last Thanksgiving."

"Turnip or collard?"

"Turnip."

"Mmm-hmm." Tati slams me with the scowl she reserves for topics she hates. Hudson and his family fit the profile. "Mother Pyke should've taken the initiative to find out which green veggie would get her invited to the barbecue." *Strike two.* "Did she at least put ham hocks in it or bacon grease . . . any form of pork product for extra flavor?" *Invite rescinded.*

Confirmation via omission fastens my face.

"Thought so."

I reach forward, grip Tati's hand, and lace my fingers between hers. "The menu's beside the point. It's a start, even without swine." I pause a second and let my eyes plead for empathy. She's not biting. "Listen, it's taken years, but at least the woman's finally started calling me by my name."

"She may be calling you Jonica to your face, but trust—what your man's mama calls you behind your back starts with *N* and ends with *R*. You fill in the rest."

I bit my bottom lip—Tati's right. Too many of us—myself included—have extended Mrs. Pyke a *"that's just how she is"* pass for her cringey commentary aimed at people of color. It's amazing how old money and pedigree supersede good ol' human decency.

My eyes waft past Tati's pronounced cheekbones, heart-shaped lips, and anime-crafted eyes to the sheer red sundress draping her fit body. A rainbow of colors spans across her arms, chest, and neck. In the midst of all those tattoos, I notice she's added some new ink to the last available space along her neckline: *Invite your enemies*. She catches me gawking and clamps her left hand over her right shoulder to block my view, fidgeting the entire few minutes we've shared—either Tati's smoking too much or slipping into one of her episodes in front of my face.

"Full exposure?" I use our code for transparency.

"Go ahead."

"Something's off. You good?"

Tati's breezy chuckle sails through the air on the heels of a mischievous grin. Her guests are starting to roll in; the curtain's about to close on our heart-to-heart. "If by *good* you mean is suicide attempt number seven coming after the party, then I'm great. Solid. You have nothing to worry about." Doubt contorts my face like a strong filter.

"Seriously, life's good, JC. At least for the moment. Nothing but happy thoughts, I promise. Philippians 4:9." We've known each other since we were six. Tati randomly inserting a Bible verse into the conversation proves she's full of something other than hope. It'd be more believable if every word weren't strung together like she was threading a needle. I don't want to capsize our reunion or ruin her big night, so I let it go.

She's here to live another day.

Live.

Live.

Live.

I'm silently commanding her.

Live.

I snatch my hat off and fan with it. The bodies piling into this 50-year-old rink make it feel like the devil's crack. If I were wearing foundation, it would've melted and be streaking the front of my white halter by now.

"Do me a favor." I'm not asking; I'm telling. As a mama-friend.

Tati's attention is waning. Her hips sway to the beat of her own music, ready to skate her problems—and lecturer—away. "What's up?"

"Don't pretend to be the strong friend who doesn't leave behind clues something's wrong until they're gone." I crane my neck, making her look me in the eyes to keep her from lying. "When life isn't so good, if something's wrong—*anything* at all—no more hysterical calls from Mama Ko saying you're in ICU bleeding out from your wrists. You'll call me?"

An angry gust of air bursting through Tati's flared nostrils is my answer.

"When was the last time you cried, T?"

"Probably the same as the last time you peed." Tati clucks her tongue, and eyes slam the ceiling. "You all have got to stop worrying about me."

"Then stop giving us stuff to worry about! I don't want to wake up one day to the news that you're gone."

Tati embraces me as if I'm the one coddling fragile emotions. "When all of you concerned citizens take the time to find out why I don't want to wake up instead of making me feel bad on the days when I'm not feeling it, maybe I can come to you. And until any of you can listen without judging, leave it and me alone. I'm not afraid of the dark; I'm ashamed of it."

The tears welling in her eyes are a surprise. The trembling lips and ugly cry face she tries to smile through . . . none of it typical Tati behavior. I bump her thick hip with my narrow one. "Hey, we're here to celebrate, right? Let's not turn this into a fight—let's party." Tati huffs her cigarette breath in my face. "Listen, I don't mean to upset you on your big day. I just want you to care as much about yourself as we do."

"Jonica Burke, I'm messy and mixed-up, but I have a million reasons to find out if money makes you happy. And until I figure out if that's my remedy, stop tripping." She backs away from me and spins on the custom, blinged-out skates with her picture airbrushed on them. "I sank a lot of dough into this victory/break-up party, so let's get into it. We're here to have fun, all right? Besides, my therapist says death isn't good for my health."

I laugh. Not because any of this is remotely funny, but because what other response is there? I look past Tati, fixating on Adonis again. He's skating toward us.

"Someone on your mind?" Tati rubbernecks to peek at him too.

"I wasn't looking."

"Yes, you were, but it's fine. Look all you want because he's my welcome home gift to you."

"A who? What?"

"Trust me," Tati laughs long and drawn out like she's reaching for the show-stopping high note at the end of a featured solo. "You're going to *want* to talk to him."

So, I hate Tati.

Because of her, I've been sitting across from who seems to be the most incredible human I've ever met for the last hour. Turns out *Adonis* is actually Lucas Favors, media technology teacher at my Alma mater, H.E.C. School of Performing Arts. But to the world of social media, Mr. Favors is known as *The Hottie Professor*.

Luke (that's what he asked me to call him) moved to Parable a year ago, has a deep, throaty voice that carries the rapture, and is trying his hardest to remain chill, even though he's totally fanning out over me. All the attention he's giving me is almost as endearing as his outlandish grin that I pray doesn't stop.

We're shacked up in a corner booth, where I won't be bombarded with selfie and autograph requests. My gaze refuses to stay committed to either Luke or his silver-haired twin, doing his version of skating with the gaggle of kids holding him up and performing tricks around him.

"I still can't believe I mistook *Big Luke* for your grandfather."

Luke turns his head left to look at his father, giving me a chance to admire the soft stubble grazing his chin and cheeks under the rink's red strobe lights. "It's all right. We get that a lot. That's what happens when men wait until their fifties to have children." His deep chuckle forces the baby hairs on my arms to stand. An involuntary laugh pushes from the pit of my belly in exchange for his. "What's so funny?"

I shrug, giggling a little more. "The fact that you and your Nikon camera went viral in a Polo shirt and khakis with the caption, *Who wants to help me shoot?* I knew I recognized you from somewhere. Total thirst trap."

"Did it work?" Luke lifts his glass of Pepsi, slowly sipping with his eyes lassoed to mine.

I'm quenched.

"Maybe for the single ladies who don't have boyfriends back home in LA."

Luke doesn't mask his disappointment at the reminder that this conversation is temporary. Can't say I'm offended that he's let down, especially with the sneaky way Tati's trying to set us up. The real question is, why am I turning to jelly over a guy who probably has less than 15 percent battery left before his social media notoriety goes dead? He is marvelous to look at, though.

"So, none of those kids are yours?" I nod toward the group of youngsters enthralled by Tati burning circles into the floor with her wheels. The louder they hoot and holler, the more animated she becomes, dropping low to the floor and popping back up to prove she can still hang. *I could never.* I can barely keep my balance walking, so there's no way I could stay upright on wheels. Big Luke stands a better chance of not busting his tail than me.

Luke shakes his head. "They're more like my payback kids. You know, paying me back for all the grief I gave my teachers when I was their age. But, I have to give it to them -those kids are extremely talented and brilliant, even if they are making me prematurely gray." Luke's explanation comes with a chin massage as he sinks his teeth into his bottom lip.

Hello, lover.

"Hey, I have an idea!" Luke tramples my thoughts. "There's no way God's giving me this much time with you, without me being able to shoot my shot—"

I interrupt him with my *I'm so flattered* face, and a raised palm. "Let me stop you right there. Since you claim to be a praying man, I know God has told you I already have a man. Don't be weird." I let my hand down, pick up my cup of iced tea, and sip real quick with my pinky finger turned out. "Besides, you don't know me to be asking me out."

Amused, Luke's brown eyes wave me off. "That's good. For *you.* But I wasn't asking you out." *My face—I can't feel my face.* "I have a proposition for you. *Professional* proposition."

"Oh, I see." *If there's no feeling in my face, does it at least have color?* I pick up the cup again and swirl the liquid around, assessing where I just landed on the scale of idiot or narcissist. Considering I just accused this guy of hitting on me with little more than circumstantial evidence, I'm going with the latter just because I wanted him to want me.

"What you got for me?" I croak.

Luke's easy grin forgives my infraction. "You know the *Students in Film* competition, right?"

"Of course. I entered the original version of *Flogged* my senior year."

"You mean when you won the competition after entering *Flogged* senior year. Don't be so modest."

Is it warm in here? I stop playing with the cup and take another sip of tea.

"Anyway, my class spent the entire summer filming a documentary to enter in the contest. It follows the resurgence of recreational skating, and we focus on the Heal on Wheels club the kids started. That's them over there." I follow Luke's proud gaze to the kids challenging each other to battles on the floor. Everyone deserves to be seen with that kind of reverence.

The way Hudson used to look at me.

"Sounds interesting. Where do I come in?"

Luke glances down at the table like he's checking for something, then shifts his focus to me. "School starts Monday, and I was thinking it would kick the class's year off right to have the new blueprint for Black Hollywood give a quick lecture, check out our work, and maybe give the film a basic critique?" While Luke wrings his hands together like he's waiting on bended knee for a response, I shake the visual of us on a honeymoon from my imagination by killing the rest of my drink. "Since we're about to hit August, there's not much time to get it ready. The winners will be announced on Halloween in LA. We can really use your help."

Please stop looking at me like that.

I drum a sporty French tip against my cup, willing my giving heart not to yield under the influence of Luke's thick brows or the way his mustache crinkles like he's singing a lullaby when he speaks. *Give me something to sleep on.* Look at him, sitting there like he came to America to find his bride. And since we're clear this isn't a date, how can I turn down that face? That body. That . . .

"Why not?" my mouth confirms before my brain does. "I'm in town for a couple of weeks, so I'll do it."

"You are a lifesaver." Not really sure Luke means to come off quite as enthusiastic as he is, but if it gives me the opportunity to admire those straight teeth of his, keep smiling, baby. "I can't wait to tell my kids."

"Anything for my alma mater," I say. "When do you want me there?"

"Eight o'clock, Monday morning." Luke extends a hand so we can shake on it. "You just made me the hero of H.E.C. before the first day of school. I can't believe you said yes!"

"They're only kids," I say. "How bad can it be?"

THREE

AIN'T NOTHIN' LIKE mama.

Except those who call their daughters at four in the morning to pray and intercede, as if God doesn't hear folks praying at a decent hour.

"Seriously, Mom, can't we tell Jesus all about our troubles a little later? I'm on vacation." Snatching off the bonnet that's already slid halfway off in the middle of the night, I roll over on the cushy mattress in the guest room upstairs at Mom's house, burying my curses in the plush, satin-covered pillows. I'm grown, but not adult enough to cuss in front of Temper Burke, gospel superstar, known to her legions of fans as "The Pearl of Gospel." I pinch the sky-blue dragonfly dangling from the end of the platinum chain hanging around my neck while I listen to Temper go on and on about what the Lord has done for me.

"Did God take a vacation when He sent His only begotten son to die for the pardon of your sins?" Temper melodically sails her rebuke through the line in the patented soprano that made her famous. "Maybe Calvary was a day at the spa? I suppose the nails they put in His hands and feet were mani-pedis? Surely, 'The Cross' was nowhere near as cushy as that mattress you're too lazy to get up from and spend time in God's presence."

24

I bolt straight up and slam my back against the king-size bed's headboard, resigned to the fact that I'm about to get as much sleep as a honeymooning couple getting it in.

The electric clock on the nightstand says *4:03*. I bite a flake of white polish from the tip of my pinkie nail and spit it out, waiting for Temper to finish her speech and climb off the Cross with Jesus. After another minute of listening to her chastising, I double Dutch my way back into the conversation with, "I'm sorry, Mom. I've been working a lot, and I need my rest."

"The word says there's no rest for the weary."

"That's because the weary don't get rest." I hoot out a halfhearted chuckle with my eyes squeezed shut, hoping to reclaim the lucid state I was in before Temper interrupted the best part of the sleep—right before the drool hit the pillow.

I'm surprised I was able to get any sleep at all before Temper's disruption. Since there were kids present, Tati's party was dry, and I was involuntarily sober. Not a stitch of beer or alcohol to numb me to the fact that I have to crash in Mom's seven-bedroom house alone while she's on tour. Don't tell her I prayed all the way through downtown to prepare myself. That girl will swear up and down all those scriptures she's forever quoting are rubbing off on me.

Last night when I got here, as soon as I turned the key in the front door's lock, I missed my daddy. Crossed the threshold, and the flood of burdens that kept me away from this house for the last six years came rushing back like a depressing love song.

"I should've booked a hotel room," I fussed at myself.

I dropped my bags in the foyer and climbed out of my sneakers to uphold Temper's no shoes on her plush ivory carpet rule, then pressed my way through the gargantuan living room with its brazen black-and-white country-chic décor, sprinkled with hints of sunflower yellow here and there. Slowed my steps as I got closer to my father's study, then stopped at the door. The name plate was the first thing my eyes landed on. **Pastor Christopher James Burke.** Folks called him CJ; me in reverse.

When I saw Dad's robust smile bursting from the 20 x 24-inch painting hanging on the wall above the cherrywood desk where he did his Bible study, all six feet of me shriveled to barely five. My chest caved under the weight of two simple thoughts racing through my mind: One, my handsome father looked more like a male model than a man of the cloth. And two, I wished he wasn't dead.

Graduation day, Cox School of Film. I'd just fastened the royal blue gown and fitted my cap over my relaxed, bone-straight, shoulder-length tresses, double-checked my flawless makeup for the tenth time, and was spinning in the full mirror of my dorm room for one last inspection when my cell chimed.

"Hey, Mom!" I answered without waiting for Temper to speak. "Can you believe today, for the first time, I finally see why everyone's always calling me Dad's twin? You should see me! I don't know if it's all the excitement or finally straightening my hair or getting my braces off or what, but when I look in the mirror, all I see is Pastor CJ. Girl, I look like I'm about to preach." I paused a quick second to laugh, then went right back in. "But enough about that. I'm so nervous I don't know what to do, Mom. Now I know you and Dad thought I wasn't going to finish school because of last semester's disaster, but we won't bring up old stuff right now. The point is I did it, Mom! I did it! I'm going to be a filmmaker!" I didn't notice Temper hadn't gotten in a word. The biting silence on her end of the line should've indicated something was wrong.

"Where are you guys?" I kept chattering, oblivious. "I want to get some pictures in with my wonderful parents before the ceremony. Without you guys, none of this would have happened." Temper cleared her voice, but I was intent on getting everything out I wanted to say. "And are we still going to Chow-Chow's to eat later? I can already taste the Mediterranean fried catfish with red beans and rice. And the

jalapeño corn bread . . . Girl, I've worked hard for these calories I'm about to pile on!"

I laughed. Temper didn't.

"Baby, I need you to listen to me," Temper's voice hit a vibrato reserved for the bridge in her upbeat songs. "Your father—"

I blew a kiss at myself in the mirror. "Yes, Mom? Please don't tell me you guys missed the plane. Not today of all days. It's too important."

Temper sighed. Sniffed. Sighed again. "Your father was picking up your graduation gift from the jewelry store, and . . ."

I stopped prancing around and froze in the middle of the cardboard boxes coming back to Texas with me. My entire life was packed away in those boxes. What I didn't know was that a few minutes later, my spirit would die and climb inside with the other stuff. "You're scaring me, Mom. Say something."

Temper's breathing grew throaty—the news she was avoiding delivering caught in a single breath. "Your father's heart gave out, baby. Right there in the store. It just . . . stopped." The moment she granted me to digest the bomb she dropped seemed like an eternity. The scream I felt coming on balled into a fist and blocked my air passage. I slumped on the floor against the boxes, silently begging God to stop my heart too. "They called an ambulance, but by the time they got to the store, your father passed away. He's gone, baby. He's gone!"

I never heard Temper sob the way she did when my father died. It sounded like she was being operated on without anesthesia. I've never heard such a wail like that again in my life . . . except the one that came from me.

Dad was Mom's best friend, but I was his favorite girl. Being in this house without him doesn't seem right, so I've stayed away until now. All I have left of my father is the dragonfly pendant he died buying for me—the one I'm wearing now.

"I'm so sorry I couldn't be there with you last night, sugar. But you know this tour isn't over until a few months from now," Temper says.

"As nice as it would be to see you in person without filters and FaceTime, it's all right, Mom." I eek out a loud yawn. "Where are you again?"

"Memphis, my love."

"That's right. Don't know how I forgot that."

"A flower in a gorilla's hands doesn't make sense."

I laugh. "What does that even mean?"

"It means you're still grieving, darling. It's been six years. Don't you think it's about time to start moving forward?"

"Grief isn't on the clock, Mom. I heard one of those therapists on television say that." Temper doesn't believe in therapy. She thinks gospel music and church are all we need to get better, which would make sense if church folk weren't so messed up. The pauses between her short breaths open a gap wide enough for survivor's remorse to pick at my veins. But she's not ready for that discussion.

"Hey, Mom, I need to go. I'm speaking to the Media Tech kids at H.E.C. tomorrow, and I need my rest if I want to look like I know what I'm talking about."

"Sounds like fun, baby love."

"At the very least, it'll be a nice diversion before I fly back home."

"LA is home now?" she pouts.

My pores crave the climate.

Sushi and mimosas for breakfast.

My pay grade keeps me from being easily offended, even when I'm being corporately ushered through the colored entrance.

Being treated to the sunrise kissing the mountains in the morning makes my soul happy.

. . . Yes, that's home.

But if I don't change the subject, I'll never get back to sleep. "Do you think you'll be back here anytime soon, Mom?"

"I'm not sure, baby love." Temper's drawl grows thicker by the syllable. "The promoters have added some dates to the tour, and it's terribly hectic. It's causing utter chaos on my skin too." She draws in a breath like she's doing vocal exercises and whistles. "As much as I miss you, I've got to give the people what they want. And it looks like the people want a little more Jesus. And your mother too, of course."

I'm disappointed. Haven't seen Temper in a couple of years, and now I'm in her house alone. I'm starting to feel like an orphaned child. I rock against the headboard, and my dragonfly beats against my chest. Maybe I should've stayed in LA.

"Well, let me go so I can pray and make myself presentable for my glam squad before they arrive, mi amour."

Great. Way to make sure I'm wide awake while you get dolled up. "Hey, Mom?"

"Yes?"

"Before you go, can I ask you something?"

"Yes, you may." Pre-gospel, Temper was a fifth-grade English teacher who never resisted the urge to correct my grammar.

"My movies. Do you actually watch them?"

"Why, darling?"

"Because I'm not sure God approves." Temper doesn't say much about my career directly to me, but since the first time she saw my name scroll across the opening credits in my first film, she's bragged about her famous daughter's cinematic success. Still . . .

"Haven't missed one, and I love them all. Why?" Temper lies in soprano; her second alto confirms that even with all the obligatory F-bombs in my scripts, she sits through both hours, although the frog in her throat suggests she doesn't love them like she claims.

I pick up the bonnet lying next to me and wave it in the air, picturing Temper in her weekend wig, named LaChelle. Jet black, severe bangs in the front, big body waves flowing down the tawny back she loves showing off. The saints hate it when she shows her bare back. Jesus doesn't approve of skin, I guess.

"Am I going too far with my movies?"

A heavy sigh precedes Temper's response. "Since you're asking, must there be so much sex integrated into every other scene? Why are the pictures so dark and gloomy—do drug addicts and thugs disintegrate in the light or something? And for the love of Christ, can't any of your characters speak vocabulary higher than four letters?"

"Okay, not exactly the point of reference I'm looking for," I cut Temper off to block the shrapnel of her disapproval. "Last night, I came across a Twitter thread accusing me of being shortsighted and ignorant when it comes to *us*. Someone even insinuated that I'm setting us back, when I do all I can to push our narrative forward."

"Then why are you holding the narrative hostage where it is? The last time I checked, kings don't wear grills, dear."

"But the King of Kings did wear a crown of thorns."

Temper's laugh rumbles through the line. "All I'm saying is, for someone who posts so much about Black royalty on social media, your movies don't reflect the same reverence."

"Jesus wasn't dripping in three-piece suits either, Mom. So explain wearing our *Sunday best* in service?"

Temper's most glorious faults are that she's aggressively affectionate, utterly oblivious to boundaries, and knows when she's caught on the ropes. But I give her credit for being perpetually armed with a good scripture. "Baby, Romans 12:6 says, '*Having gifts that differ according to the grace given to us, let us use them.*'"

"Can we discuss this in English, not King James? I'm having a real crisis here, Mom."

"I'm saying do what you do, baby. We're here to serve our function. God graced you for this." Temper slips into the mama I grew up with. "Have you ever known me to change the lyrics to my songs, loosen up the gowns that hug my curves in all the right places, or dim my light for the saints who aren't ready for all this sparkle?"

"No, ma'am."

"You know what they say about opinions and buttholes—but what they don't tell you is, the ones screaming the loudest don't wipe well."

"I don't get it," I mutter.

"In other words, don't let broke folks' opinions stop you from getting paid, baby. Do what you do. Just don't get mad when it's time to pay the bill."

On my first day of junior high, my feelings were crushed when an eighth-grader said I must be eating raw coffee because I'm so black. After that, I wore nothing but ivory and white (even on my heavy menstrual days) for the next six months and drenched myself in bleaching cream at least five times a day to lighten my skin.

At first, my parents didn't notice anything had changed with me. Not even the strong medicinal odor streaming from my pores . . . until patches of skin literally started burning off my body from using too much of the bleach. When Temper made me confess what I'd been up to, she was livid. "*Tell Jesus you need some new skin because you messed up what He gave you!*" she hollered right before she grounded me and proceeded to throw my bleaching cream in the trash. She was so pissed that she even banned me from wearing white for a spell.

"You don't understand, Mama. There's no such thing as light-skinned issues," I argued.

"If all you see when you look at me is the shade I am, then I haven't done a very good job as a mother."

From then on, not a day goes by without Temper reminding me how beautiful I am—dark skin and all.

Temper finally lets me off the phone, or maybe I let her go. No matter how I situate myself, I can't fall back asleep. Behind my closed eyes, I see Dad. The more relaxed I get, the more intense his essence grows. If I were in LA, I'd go right to Hudson's. He'd rock me in his arms until the ghost is gone, and I fall asleep. When we aren't fighting, that's the good part of him. The side I wish everyone who wants me to break up with him so bad could meet. I wish I were at Hudson's place now instead of alone in this room.

Actually, I wish I was with my daddy.

FOUR

"SO, YOU'RE LEAVING me here alone with a completely blue body to play school with a bunch of hoodrats for another week? I need you, baby." The sunrise has yet to appear in Hudson's sleep-deprived voice. He doesn't like waking up before noon, but I'm on Texas time.

"This isn't about sex or you, Hudson. I'm doing a favor for a friend."

"What friend?"

"You don't know him."

Ten minutes into our conversation, and he's violated my peace in a thousand different ways. I thought a few days of separation would force me to crave him. Maybe be desperate to see him. But every conversation feels like we're hurling wineglasses at each other. Even though my gut said to let my sleeping dog continue lying while I waited in H.E.C.'s parking lot, I called Hudson, thinking he'd encourage me before I delivered my speech to the kids. I was wrong.

". . . and they're not hoodrats," I snap. "Don't disrespect them like that."

"My bad. Underprivileged, inner-city youth in underserved communities." Hudson's snarky response makes me rethink my New Year's resolution to quit smoking cold turkey. I mean, it was only for a month when I was 16 and felt like since my boobs came

33

in, I was grown, but when my good pastor-father caught me firing one up in the back of Christ Central Church . . . Let's just say I had help getting delivered from the habit. But sometimes, dealing with this man makes my nerves feel like limp noodles.

My lips form an "O" the way I used to do when I was blowing smoke. "I'll have you know the students you're degrading are from exceptionally affluent homes, babe. They are sons and daughters of designers, beauty pageant winners, publishers . . . even the mayor of Parable." I let Hudson rest on that lineage for a second. "These kids are scholars and budding filmmakers. Far from the ghettos you like creating."

Hudson's stiff chortle blankets me like a sheath. "You and I make a lot of money off those imaginary ghettos we create together." He laughs again, more irritated than amused. "No one's degrading these kids, and I'd hardly call pulling stunts for social media clout as viable evidence of them being the future of cinematic glory."

There's a loud clicking noise. I picture Hudson with his hands gripped around the remote, gaming in the middle of our argument or whatever this is we're getting into. His way of dipping a toe in the shallow end of my concerns without committing to diving into the deep end. "Hold on a second, *Hot Chocolate*—I have to take this call real quick."

Hot Chocolate. The latest nickname he tags me with based on food. I hate it as much as I hate Hudson putting me on hold instead of calling me back, but I'm stuck with the hip-hop hold music plucking my ears when he clicks over. 7:45 in the morning is way too early for this much bass. Oh well. I recline my car seat, thinking about how he and I met at Cox.

Hudson was the only white person in my Defending Oscar Micheaux: The Libel of History's First Black Filmmaker course. Instead of taking one of the gazillion unoccupied seats in the room, Hudson and his geeky, red-framed glasses, mussed hair that stuck straight up, and a constellation of brick-colored freckles sprinkled across the perimeter of his nose plopped right next to me. He was an adorable dork with an impossible grin that helped him get away with being the token white boy who was either trying to prove he didn't see color to his one Black friend or a serious, aspiring filmmaker whose movies wouldn't be whitewashed.

Like Hudson, I was dressed down in a simple sweatshirt and joggers to prove I was serious about learning the craft, not partying and hooking up with random guys I wouldn't remember five years after graduation. That's the vibe I was throwing, yet Hudson dropped pens and notebooks on the floor, dry coughed, and created every other minor disturbance he could to get my attention. When I didn't budge—not even a peripheral glance, he popped a piece of gum into his mouth and smacked. Loud. The peeve that struck a nerve.

"That gum must be good," I whispered while our professor scribbled on the whiteboard, and the students around us pretended to be busy writing notes.

Hudson played right along with me. "What makes you say that?"

"Because you're tearing it up like vegans canceled red meat, and this is your last chance to eat it."

Hudson grinned and yanked a page from a spiral, spit the gum in the paper, and crumpled it. "It's good, but I'd rather have a steak. Maybe you'd like to grab one with me later?"

WHERE DID OSCAR MICHEAUX FAIL? *The professor pointed to the question he scribbled across the whiteboard. His thick, graying brows rose, daring one of us to answer.*

"He didn't," Hudson called out. Every eye flew to him, shocked at the nerve. Unfazed, he took off his specs, cleaned them on the front of his hoodie, and kept talking. "Micheaux provided Blacks in films with jobs, told compelling stories his way, and gave the Black plight dignity, despite what much of Hollywood and his disgruntled peers thought."

Hudson's empathy and arrogance were intriguing, if not somewhat condescending . . . in my opinion. "Micheaux also fed into unspoken colorism that still plays throughout the film industry today," I countered. "The darker the berry, the lesser the role. Ask me how I know. I always pay the highest price for being the darkest berry."

"The darkest or the finest?"

Oh, you charmer, you.

Before I made it back to the dorms that day, Hudson and I enjoyed T-bones and potatoes at Rancher's Steakhouse. And when we shared our first kiss at the front door, I knew he would be mine. That's what I get for hooking up during cuffing season.

A cluster of kids whizz past my rental, a covey of them on skates. All right, time to get into it. Last night, I wrote out the plans for my *Ted Talk* today:

First, I'll list some of my creative influences—Alice Guy-Blaché (the first female director), Spike Lee—the first Black director to make America collectively uncomfortable, and Ava DuVernay, the modern wildfire who beats the brakes off conformity. Then I'll talk a little bit about the filming process, throw out some technical terminology here and there, and open the floor for questions. Simple, right? I wish my upset belly would fall into formation.

"You there, Hot Chocolate?" Hudson clicks back over.

I realign my seat to the upright position to gain some control over the anxiety slapping me in the face. "I'm here."

"So, that was Skye Falling on the other line," Hudson mentions casually.

My eyes involuntarily toggle to the back of my head. Skye's an adult film actress trying to rebrand herself as a serious Oscar contender. It was Hudson's idea to dress her in some real clothes instead of sprawled out on an air mattress in Victoria's Secret knockoffs and give her a role with some real meat for a change:

Quita, a recovering addict trying to rescue herself and her six kids in *Crack Dreams*. After the first table read back in January, I wasn't impressed. Now that we're filming, I'm still not. But my honey thinks Skye's got the goods, so I'm rolling with it. For now. However, I don't invest much in her numerous complaints and suggestions about *my* film. She's a self-anointed diva, trying to call the shots with no ammunition.

"And what new demand is Madam Falling making now?" I don't try to hide my aggravation.

"More changes to the script and a table read this weekend." Hudson ticks off her requests like he's seriously giving them some credence. "Skye says there's no way a real Black woman from the hood would react like Quita does in the situations we put her in, and her dialogue needs sharpening to be more realistic." A gush of animated music in the background alerts Hudson that he's the game's high scorer. "Bottom line, Skye only signed onto this film for the accolades, and it needs to be darker. It's not gutter enough."

"Gutter? What the hell does she mean, 'gutter'? I'm the queen of gutter! No, not gutter. Grit, I mean grit. My films have grit." My arm flails in the air, picturing our lead's overinflated lips in front of my face. "You call that tragic piece of plastic back and explain to her how it cost triple for us to insure her because all the fake elements in her body make her a fire hazard! And furthermore, please inform Ms. Falling that no woman whose name reeks of triple X ratings will make me alter a single word of my script."

"Our script," Hudson grunts. "Don't forget who's financing this thing."

Right. With the fortune your father won in the lawsuit against his supplier for getting himself addicted to opioids. "Your money, my words." More kids pass by. Part of me is getting eager to meet them, even if my speech is a total blank. "Just tell her we'll talk when I come back from vacation. In other news, I miss you, babe."

Crickets.

Charmer and instigator. Perpetually poised to simultaneously get in my pants and piss me off at the flick of an attitude.

"You may want to look into drawing a few boundaries for the talent, yeah? Don't give everyone so much access to you." Hudson's remote clicks louder than he mumbles. I picture him relaxed on the brown leather recliner he's always trying to beat his personal best from while he shirks his end of our deteriorating relationship. I pinch the bridge of my nose between my fingers.

"Are you sure you don't want to come on back home now, Blackberry? We need you here." *Of course. You and your hungry member feel neglected.* "We have a lot of work to do."

"So, not because you miss my hugs or kisses or anything." I state it instead of asking to keep my face from getting broken.

"I'm barely awake. I don't want to think about that right now." Hudson tethers our small-boned relationship, taking it for a stroll through my whimsical fantasy of our forever making it past year eight.

"Hey, the magazine cover came out." I try lightening the mood. "Have you seen it?"

He hitches his last nerve to a sigh. "It's just a picture, JC. I'll get around to it."

In my mind, I scream, *There's always just something when it comes to me! I'm not your woman—I'm your livelihood.* I would remind my man of these things, but the cute, royal blue Kia Sorento parking next to me keeps my chapping lips pressed closed. I lean over and snatch the nearest gloss from my open leather saddlebag, then crane my head to get a peek at the driver.

Luke.

"Hey, I have to go." Not that my hanging up first matters to the one who's always first to break our hugs. In the meantime, I duck my head so Luke won't see me and swipe the clear balm over my lips.

"Yep."

Luke waves from his car, then hops out and locks it. Short-sleeved, red plaid shirt, relaxed jeans, and blue Jordans. Fresh trim. *If my teacher looked like that in high school, I would've graduated with a 4.6.* He strolls to my driver's side and waits.

"Call me later?" I ask Hudson.

"I've got some stuff to do, but I'll try." Hudson's monotone doesn't shift.

"Hey, I love you."

"Uh-huh. Bye." He hangs up.

Usually, I'd drop a frustrated tear or two behind Hudson's Jekyll and Hyde mood swings. But Luke's bright smile reminds me how I've had all the stray hair eviscerated from my body, teeth whitened, and put a pop of color on my face to match the sheer black-and-white polka dot shirt draped over me like the perfect date. I check my top knot in the rearview, then hop out and join Luke at the front of the car.

"I almost didn't recognize you." Luke's energy matches ten cups of coffee.

"Excuse me?"

He holds up a copy of *Limelight Magazine*, with a sexy shot of me gracing the cover, then flips to the five-page spread inside. *JC Burke: Leading the Pack of the 50 Hottest Millennials Behind the Lens.* "I was kind of expecting something different." Luke's eyes measure the picture of me in fitted red slacks highlighting my high booty and yellow pumps, making my thick calves pop.

"Different?" I lock the car a third time, biding a few extra moments to take in Luke's amazing scent. He pushes his hands forward with a deep chuckle. "No offense. I just mean the article made such a big deal about your makeover that I assumed you'd be glammed up and high maintenance. You know, full face of makeup, mink bundles hanging from your eyelids."

The schoolgirl in me takes over with a giggle. "I think you mean mink lashes, and I don't wear them." A soothing breeze cools the heat from my conversation with Hudson. "That *makeover* was just a pop of color on my face and getting my hair braided." I tap the top of my crown and shove my hands into my pockets. "You know how mesmerized *they* are when the stuff we've been doing for hundreds of years finally hits their radars. Conveniently appropriated."

Luke swipes a hand over his mouth, grins with his eyes, and watches my lips like I don't notice.

"As far as maintenance goes, all I need is a clean body and deodorant," I tell him.

"Minimalist and hygienic. My type of woman." That hearty laugh and his dazzling smile make it hard to divert my eyes when Luke flirts. His presence is nothing short of a four-course meal, complete with dessert. "Obviously, your natural beauty canceled candidates two through forty-nine. Look who landed the cover."

Luke catches his bottom lip between his teeth on the tail end of his compliment, reeling me in as he slowly releases it. His reassuring tone makes me feel like I don't have to shrink. Like, I can say what's on my mind without worrying about backlash. He checks the birds flying overhead like they're serenading us and cocks his head to the side. My ego follows the wind to his muscular arms. He closes the space between us and reaches out, resting a hand on my shoulder as if we've been connected for years. His thick brows angle me in. It's 100 degrees outside, but I'm a chilly mess under his touch.

"JC?" Luke startles me from the stupor I've fallen into.

"Huh?"

"I was asking if you're ready for this." My shoulder immediately goes limp when he takes his hand away to gesture toward the hundreds of students congregating on the lot before the first bell of the year sounds. "We might discover the next JC Burke in my class."

". . . or possibly the next whomever they are."

"Sorry, didn't mean to imply anything."

I wave him off with a forced smile. "It's fine. It's just that my entire career, I've been called the next Spike Lee. Or the next somebody." I clutch my bag to my chest. "Kids should be free to simply create without feeling the pressure of someone giving them an identity instead of cultivating the one they have. That's how I've gotten this far. And as soon as I can get Hollywood out of my purse, I'm sure I'll get even further."

"Duly noted."

"I appreciate that. Not everyone understands individuality, you know? Especially when it comes to kids." I glance to my right, seeing we're feet from Heritage Hall—my old stomping grounds. "Without teachers like you, the world may have never known my name. I'd probably be holed up somewhere drawing sketches and talking to myself."

"Thankfully, you have me to talk to instead." Luke holds up a fist, which I dap with mine. "These kids can be merciless monsters, but they'll love you. Just like I do." Luke realizes what he said when my face twists into a question mark. "I mean, I love your work."

"My *work*. Okay."

"So, you ready?"

"Why not?" I breathe in the clean air and exhale. "Like I said before, it's just a bunch of kids. How bad can it be?"

FIVE

I SHOULDN'T HAVE asked.

Every minute hitching itself to the half hour since my introduction—"*Hi, I'm JC Burke,*" has felt like a noose tightening around my neck. See, this is why I'm not into the whole bondage thing with my boyfriends. I can't. I just can't. One yank, tug, pull, or pinch in the wrong place, and I'm out. And by the way, these kids have been stomping all over my "spot" (*nee: ego*) instead of soaking up all this glitter and anointing of me, their honorary big sister. I should've said no.

Listen, I'm no punk. But all these peepers honed in like they just witnessed me giving Jesus the fatal peck on the cheek have me quivering in my pumps a little. *Drops mic, no applause.*

These tiny geniuses have got my head exploding before the floor's been opened for questions. I'm standing here looking a fool when what I really want to do is hightail it out of here, go rustle up the biggest, juiciest, gut-busting triple patty cheeseburger, extreme chili-cheese-fries piled with jalapeños, and a raunchy root beer float I can find, then pretend I never got out of bed. Unfortunately, I'm stuck. Leave now, and I will prove these little lambs right—I'm a spineless opportunist who appropriates my own people for a fat check. If I stay, maybe I can salvage what's left of my professional reputation.

And my indentured morals.

"Your movies glorify slaves, drug dealers, and romanticize abuse. Care to explain how that's indicative of the Black experience, because it's not mine?"

Indicative? I couldn't spell that word when I was their age, much less use it correctly in a sentence.

The gorgeous girl flaunting her advanced vocabulary from the front row scowls at me like she's mincing my soul into teeny bits with a cleaver. Every blink feels like she's jamming tiny needles under my nails. I hadn't been tapping the heel of my pumps on the marble tile a good five minutes when this child leaned over and whispered something to the kid next to her, then smirked at me. I won't lie—my feelings were kind of pinched. Out of everybody in this room, she's the one I expected would click with me the most. Two massive Afro puffs on the sides of her head that make her look like a Black Supergirl, shadowy skin that's almost as deep as mine, long, athletic legs that barely fit beneath her desk, and the deepest dimples I've ever seen creasing her plump cheeks. A mini version of me. Perfect match . . . right? Except, she hates me.

"Hello? Why so quiet? That mouth of yours ain't never had no problem putting some extra pressure on the accelerator when you're denying that your movies amount to nothing more than modern-day minstrel shows. Well?"

I rubberneck around to clarify that this girl is talking to me. *Lil' Chucky.*

"That's Myzi," Luke pointed her out the other night at the rink. "Everyone jokes that she's my twin. Don't tell anyone, but that six-foot firecracker's my favorite student—not just because she's my niece."

I studied her, the vibrant center of attention, showing off her skills to the cheers of the crowd who were chanting her name. Her flexibility and technique are actually quite impressive. But I'm giving her hospitality a flat zero.

"She's a great kid," Luke gushed. "Crazy talented, positive attitude. You ever met that one person who has every reason to hate the world but goes out of their way to make others smile? That's Myzi."

Lies. All lies. Because if this girl is joyful today, I must be severely depressed.

"What's her story?"

"Last year, we found out that my sister, Elaine—Myzi's mother— needed a double mastectomy, so I moved them down here to the ranch house with me and Pops to keep them from having to go through it alone. Our little family's always been close, so it was a no-brainer. And it was a great move for Myzi because she fits in here. That kid takes great care of her mother too. Give her a mountain, and she'll find a way to blast through it so she doesn't have to climb."

Myzi's careless smile contrasted with Luke's account of her sordid history. "And her father?"

Luke shrugged. "Not around. Elaine never told us who he is, and I don't ask."

"I see." I cocked my head. Luke's right. There is something special about his niece that I'm drawn to as well. "You say she formed the skate club?"

Luke beamed with pride. "She sure did. Got the kids together who want to escape the world through fun. That's where the idea for No More Trauma came from. These kids aren't traumatized; they're on the come-up." He clapped his hands together, a sly grin on his face. "I'm just glad to witness my blood starting the movement."

"You really love her, don't you?"

He nodded his head. "I'd do anything for her." Luke's eyes lit up as if he were discussing his own offspring. "I even picked up some extra hours after school working car-shares to help Elaine buy Myzi a car for her sixteenth birthday. 4.6 GPA…she deserves it."

"That's a huge sacrifice." It was getting easier for me to stare Luke in the eyes. He was slowly converting me into someone who trusted him.

"When it comes to the people I love, sacrifice is the only word I know, JC."

I swear my ovaries flipped when Luke said that. Mainly because Hudson can barely spell paternal, much less embody responsibility past shooting the sperm. The other night, he cussed me out for his assistant's failure to competently get his Starbucks order right.

"She doesn't know a venti from a grande," Hudson whined. *"I haven't had a decent cup of coffee since you left."*

"I miss you too," I said.

"Don't be obnoxious, JC. Just get back here. And bring some coffee back with you."

Then there was the time one of the local Boys and Girls Clubs back home scheduled Hudson and me for a quick youth talk about following your dreams, you can make it, don't let anything get in your way…yada, yada, yada. Guess who went solo to convince the little tykes they could walk on water because her number one guy couldn't be bothered to suspend the zombie apocalypse game he was playing for an hour? While I told the kids, *"Everyone's capable of something great, your job's to be even better,"* Hudson was beating his own high score.

"Good job, babe," he said when I got to his apartment with the cookie basket and giant *Thank You* card the kids sent in appreciation for his absence. *"Did you hand out my autographed pictures?"*

Sigh.

Luke is Hudson's polar opposite. Good with kids. Check. Concerned about others. Check. Good with me? Triple check. I'm concerned about his honesty, though. Because the princess he passed off as his niece keeps daring me to knock the chip off her shoulder.

Myzi folds her hands and raps them on her desk. Punctuates her fundamental antipathy for my general existence by rolling the wheels of her skates on the floor, courtesy of H.E.C.'s progressive dress code. "My mother's never once hit me, and the only drugs she takes are medicines—" she quickly scans the faces of her peers, "for when she's . . . sick."

"All of you are tripping if you think Miss Priss knows anything about real problems," a tiny redhead with a loud mouth sitting next to Myzi waves a hand at me. "Look at how clear her skin is. That's a sign of no stress and light periods."

All right, how bad would it look for my image if I fought a kid?

Luke's no help, either. Leaning against his desk with his hand clamped over his mouth instead of, oh, I don't know—checking these little monsters. For a second, my eyes toggle around the large room, hunting for anything to block the remnants of hellfire being shot at me. But none of the television monitors, computers, video cameras, tripods, lights, or other equipment offer any form of assistance.

"Mr. Favors, may I be excused?" A husky, caramel boy with plump curls toppling into his eyes squeaks in a high voice, prompting Luke to rejoin the conversation.

"You good, Kam?" he asks. "What's up?"

"Yes, sir, I'm good." Kam drums his fists on the desk. "It's just that when you said you had a surprise for us, we thought it'd be something a little more exciting." He frowns at me like I left his daddy. "You could've at least got Bryce Houston or somebody."

Bryce Houston. The bum who plagiarizes every good thing Hollywood spits out and passes it off as *inspired by*. He called his rip-off of *Flogged*, *Whipped*. I should have a stake in his budding fortune.

"So, your takeaway from Ms. Burke giving up her time is that you can only learn how to become successful in film from a man?" Luke folds his arms and shakes his head. "An award-winning screenwriter who happens to be a woman can't teach you? Is *that* what you're suggesting?"

"It's not that," Kam keeps his eyes plastered on me. "You've seen her movies. I bet she thinks *Die Hard* is a Christmas film too."

"Hey, don't disrespect a yuletide holiday classic like that!" I yelp.

"See? Point made."

Before my mind has the chance to grasp a more mature rebuttal than, *Yo mama . . .* the classroom door swings open. The familiar sonance of taupe kitten heels scraping across the floor like the melody of a sad country song pricks my ears the same way it held me hostage during my four years at H.E.C. I don't even have to scrape my face off the ground to see the frail bird's legs, fecal-brown A-line skirt, ivory lace shirt suffocating beneath a plaid, tweed blazer in the middle of summer, and seventies hair flip with sprinkles of silver belong to Miss Kitty Wilkes—my former media tech instructor, now H.E.C.'s principal.

"Miss Kitty," I squeal and drag her teeny frame into my arms when she reaches me. "So good to see you. You look *fantastic*."

Kitty flashes a glassy-eyed smirk, squeezes me, then backs away. Years of smoking have definitely caught up with her rubbery skin. "And you are absolutely scrumptious, my dear." She issues a curtsey, every bit the Southern belle I remember. "I was so excited when Mr. Favors told me our most prestigious alumni was coming to give a lecture today."

"Nothing but the best for the Wildcats, right?" Luke says.

"Right." Kitty blows him off and keeps her attention on me. "Don't mind me. I'll be right here in the back enjoying this treat. Carry on."

I hark a nervous laugh. *You little crumb snatchers better not embarrass me.* "So, ah—where were we?"

"We were just discussing how you know nothing about the streets unless they're paved with gold. Isn't that what your mother sings about? Walking in heaven?" Myzi winks.

Everyone laughs except Luke. "All right, guys, we're done throwing rocks. I mean it. Remember, art is subjective. Opinions are okay, and we don't have to agree with them, but you must respect each other and JC. Got me?"

The girl sitting next to Myzi, who sucks her teeth every time I open my mouth, frantically waves her hands in the air. "Respectfully, both of my parents graduated magna cum laude from ivy league schools. The only crackhead I've ever seen is in your movies."

"I know, right? She keeps talking about the Black experience but grew up on the north side of Parable." Kam slams me with an eye roll hard enough to hear.

"*She* has a name. And I'd appreciate it if you use it when you give your opinions, okay? Be constructive, guys. You're sensitive about your art. I'm sure JC is too."

That's all you got, Luke? I need you to go Crazy Joe Clark on these children! Cuss 'em, swing a bat—do something. You modern teachers have gone completely soft.

"All right, *Miss Burke*," Myzi spits my name like a swear word. "I want to know why every woman in your movies is a single mother, broke, on drugs, forced to give up on her dreams, or abused by a man?" She turns in her seat, addressing the class. "Why are we always victims? Successful, Black businesswomen don't exist?"

"And by the way, I know who my daddy is, and he's never been to jail. Who hurt you?" This from a linebacker with striking gray eyes and enough stubble on his face to pass for my uncle.

"All right, kids. You all must stop this," Miss Wilkes interjects. "This is a discussion—not a lynching."

"Like the social and economic lynchings she writes in her scripts? *Respectfully.*" Now I don't see the face that goes with the mousy voice who had the gall to drop that little ditty from the back of the room, but . . . *ouch.*

"So what you all are saying is Mario Van Peebles was trash for exploring the start of the drug epidemic and introducing the Nino Browns of the world to audiences in *New Jack City*, the late John Singleton should be ashamed and discredited for being the first Black director to be nominated for an Academy Award for *Boys N the Hood*, and Whoopi Goldberg could've kept her Oscar-winning turn in *The Color Purple* because all of them showed Blacks in a bad light?"

"Excuse me, but Steven Spielberg is responsible for *The Color Purple*," Kam interrupts me. "We'd expect that from them."

"Exactly! It's always your own." Plot twist from the rusty-blond girl next to Myzi, who keeps glaring at me like I'm pinching puppies.

"Hey, hey, hey! I'm not asking you guys to respect JC anymore. I'm demanding it." Luke comes to my rescue, prompting the girl to sheepishly drop her head, pale skin turning the brightest shade of crimson. "Remember, we don't portray respect here. We *give* it."

"Shouldn't she have to earn it like the rest of us?" Myzi's puffs bounce as her head bobs back and forth, her squared jawline challenging me.

"So if you were me, Myzi," I start to ask.

"That's My-zee. Two long syllables. And I'm *not* you." Her arched brows furrow with disapproval.

"My mistake, My-zee." I annunciate the way she did. The heels of my pumps clank against the floor as I inch closer to Myzi's desk. Her eyes cement to me without blinking. "Let's say you're at Parable Park," I continue, "and over by the jungle gym and slides, a doting mother is playing with her children."

"Twin boy and girl, King and Kayla." Glasses Girl rocks her desk forward, with just enough control not to fall out of it as she names the imaginary characters.

"What's your name, sweetie?"

"Clarabelle," she chirps. "But you can call me Belle."

"All right, Belle. So, Mom is playing with—"

"King and Kayla," Luke reminds me.

"Right. King and Kayla." I cross over to the students seated closer to the exit in case this last attempt to win my audience over doesn't work and I have to make a run for it. I didn't have this much trouble presenting at the SAG Awards. "All right, on the other side of the park, a group of teens break out into a fight. A crowd gathers around them, and between the folks filming the scuffle and the others jumping in it, the situation's spiraling out of control really fast."

From the seat where she's perched, Kitty adds, "Meanwhile, Kayla has an asthma attack, which causes her to pass out. One of the teens who's involved in the fight notices the twins' mother screaming for help—"

". . . races over to her and gives her CPR," Myzi chirps. As soon as I toss an approving nod her way, she slaps her arms across her desk and buries her face in them. Stubborn thing won't ruin my high, though. Look who's undeterred.

"Kayla comes to, her twin is cheering, and her mother celebrates the kid who just saved her child with a huge hug," Luke smiles at me.

"But no one notices the hero because they're too focused on the fight." Myzi's next contribution to our story is almost inaudible with a mouthful of *The Golden Girls* long-sleeved graphic tee she's wearing, but my heart races a few beats faster knowing she's in this. Sort of.

"That's good, Myzi. Really good." At least with her head down, I can stop being scared she will pull a machete out of her pocket and plant it between my eyes. I walk over to her, squat in front of her desk, and tap on it. Surprisingly, she lifts her head. Annoyed, but at least I can see her face. "You're behind the camera, Myzi. Which narrative do you film?"

Myzi sucks in a deep breath, picks up her pencil, and brings the butt of it to her lips. Thinking in silence, she maintains eye contact without breaking it. "I choose to film the scene that makes us look better. I choose the hero."

"That's crazy," one of the boys who hasn't uttered a single word so far, calls out from the middle row. "Why wouldn't you capture the content that will get more views and be more popular?"

Myzi's eyes stay glued to me. "Because in this new world, we're just avatars and handles, defined by algorithms. The people who come across our social imprint either agree with our opinions or cancel us instead of choosing to get to know or understand us. No matter how reckless, opinionated, or wrong either side is."

"Because it's easier to cancel accountability than to correct what's unacceptable." I finish the shockingly astute sentiment for her.

Luke strolls over to the whiteboard at the front of the room, grabs a marker, and scribbles a series of words in neat capital block letters: **CANCEL CULTURE. RACE. HISTORY. CRITICAL RACE THEORY. BLACK LIVES MATTER. BLACK.** "What do all of these have in common?" he asks with his back turned to us.

"Fear," Kam calls out.

"Why fear?" I'm curious to know.

Kam scoots back from his desk and pops up. Hyper excited, he quickly paces the small space around him, out of breath, arms flailing overhead. "Because America's a pressure cooker, full of buzz words and trending topics instead of having open conversations where we can be ourselves. Everybody's on the porch because the kitchen's too hot, but not everybody's invited to the cookout."

"Or the picnic. Depends on who's hosting." Myzi spits an unamused chuckle. At this point, Luke's beaming like a father who believes all the football tossing he did with his son in the backyard is part of the reason the boy made it to the Super Bowl when he grew up. I feel the same.

"I don't think I've ever had the pleasure of being in the company of so many woke teens," I observe out loud.

Myzi's frown is louder than the smack of her lips popping. "Don't call us woke just because our intellect reaches past Google searches."

"Duly noted." Myzi's burn drops my arms to my side to hide the sweat spots forming under my armpits. My chest thumps a few beats, buying time for me to calmly gather my thoughts before laying out the rest of my defense before the prosecution.

"Look, guys, when I turned 21, I was catapulted from film school student to household name. It was unexpected and freaking exhilarating. I won't lie—the attention turned me on. Still does."

Kitty thrusts her index finger in the air. *Whoops.* Forgot these precocious lumps are under 18. I clear my throat and try again. "Anyhow, I stick with the formula that makes money: ruin an underdog's life, and when it seems like things can't get worse, rip their hearts out and forget to put them back in. It puts butts in seats and makes folks feel better about their own lives."

"So, violence, addiction, and general toxicity are acceptable forms of entertainment?" *Just asking for the sake of discussion*, Luke's shrugged shoulders explain.

I press my lips together, picturing myself killing the hopscotch board when I was eight. My big feet helped me keep my balance and move swiftly across the board with little effort. In my mind, I transform the classroom floor into squares, strategizing where to jump.

"Bruce Willis owes his superstardom to every single one of the tropes you named, Luke. Cleverly disguised as Christmas flicks, by the way." The kids are so quiet I almost forget they're in the room. Watching their widened eyes waiting for me to fall on my sword, I tuck the naughty words punching at my teeth under my tongue. "Some of the highest-grossing flicks of all time were created by white men and are full of blood and dismantled body parts. Why are the little bullet wounds I show held to a different standard? And for far less money, I might add."

"You're not being held to anything. We just want to know why you don't use your influence to set new standards." Myzi's nostrils flare as she interrogates me.

"Life's tough. I'm just showing the struggle," I defend myself.

"The real struggle's sitting through two hours of what you call entertainment."

"Myzi!" Luke warns in a stern voice.

"I'm sorry, Unc—I mean, Mr. Favors, but she—"

Luke plasters on his dad face, stopping Myzi's plea in its tracks.

"Listen, you guys don't know what it's like having your first movie suddenly making you the keeper of the culture." My hand involuntarily flies to my temple. "I didn't ask to be responsible for the magic and sure as heck don't appreciate having the finger pointed at me when it sucks. My decisions are based on either making money or losing money. That's all the industry execs care about in the first place—how much it's helping or costing them. Might sound wrong, but on paper, I'm right."

"Nobody's accusing you of being wrong," Myzi quips. "It's about choosing to film the fight over the hero."

SIX

DURING MY *LIMELIGHT* *Magazine* cover story interview, the blogger asked me to list three things I'd love to change about my appearance if I could.

My off-center nose.

My lips could use some bolstering.

Hyperpigmentation from occasional period breakouts.

Any of these imperfections was worth pointing out, but my mind got stuck on the lovely elementary school moniker my peers at the Adamson School for Girls christened me with: *Dark Meat.*

Never mind that my test scores were higher than those bullies, my folks had more money than their parents who wished they were as well off as us—not to mention their community influence and public notoriety, and . . . my clothes were better. So teasing me by claiming there's no way my nearly white mama could've given birth to such a "darkie" was all they had to come at me with. It stung a little . . . until I copped a modeling contract and realized that *I'm* the prime cut.

My adolescent paychecks took the edge off their sticks and stones.

My response to the blogger? *"You'd be surprised how often I'm asked what I hate about myself instead of focusing on what I love."*

I scan the article for the hundredth time. There's not a single mention of the hair products I use or which toner prevents my breakouts. The sister didn't hail me as a beauty standard; her prose turned me into a movement, not a brand. An acronym for the Black woman's experience. It was liberating . . . until Temper's congratulatory text hit my cell after my beheading at H.E.C. earlier today:

Temper: Finally saw the cover. You look beautiful, darling.

Me: What about what I said?

Temper: You know I don't get into all that industry jargon.

Me: Really, Mom? That's your takeaway?

Temper: What else should I glean, doll?

Me: Ummm, they said I'm taking over entertainment . . .

Temper: And if you keep exfoliating, you'll look marvelous while you do it, dear.

Sigh.

I didn't waste my keystrokes replying to help Temper differentiate between social acceptance and being crowned by merit. Deductive reasoning didn't stand a chance of making it past Monday's wig, anyway.

Tati finishes pouring over the magazine and tosses it across the table on my side of the booth we share in Phenom's Café. I slide it aside, opting to reach for the ice water instead of the shot glass of tequila standing guard over the untouched platter of street tacos in front of me. "You know what you need, kitten?"

"What's that?"

"A new man."

I stop swaying to the acoustic guitarist banging out a solo in the neo-soul band playing on the small stage at the front of the café to gulp my water, checking Tati with my pursed lips.

"There's nothing wrong with the man I have."

"Except the one you have is akin to requesting soy sauce at McDonald's. They don't have what you want." Tati dips her head, brings the glass of tequila to her lips, and takes it to the head. "*Ahhh.*" She closes her eyes, squeezes two fingers together, and taps them against her throat to help ease the sting. "Sorry, not sorry, kiddo. It's just that you and him have never made sense. Not together."

I choose violence with a sip of tequila of my own. Instantly, my throat feels like I'm swallowing razors. The sharp sting makes it feel like my bun's being snatched from my scalp. "Give Hudson a break, girl. He's been nothing but nice to you." I take another sip, sending more flames down my throat.

"Hudson only treats me like he has some sense because he knows I'll beat his—"

"Tati!" I cut her off. *Jesus.* Tati hops out of her seat, freestyling a song she's making up on the fly. "Prick," to the melody of Aretha Franklin's "Respect," shaking her nonexistent behind as she spells out Hudson's name in the chorus. Of course, the parties at the tables and booths in our proximity cheer this foolishness on.

I'm going to need another shot if I can make it through this one.

"All right, that's enough." I stand up and reach over the booth, snatching Tati back down in her seat by the pocket of the low-rise jeans she's paired with a flouncy white floral midriff. A sharp pain surges through the lower left side of my back, making me plop back down faster than I got up.

"You all right?" Tati's smug face flips to concern.

"I'm fine. Messing with you pinched my back, that's all." I'm trying not to grimace, but the pain is growing sharper pretty quick. "I'll be better if you stop making a spectacle."

"Because *Jonica* never causes a scene unless she writes it in a script." Tati gulps the rest of her truth serum, then relaxes in the maroon leather seat and sets her wide gaze on me. "Do I need to get you out of here and take you to see a doctor?"

"I said I'm fine. Probably a little constipation." I fling the lie like I'm swatting a fly with my hand to deflect from the intensifying pain. My face is tightening, chest caving. The same cramp snuck up on me last night, punching me in the gut at level ten. Right now, I'm at a solid seven.

"Constipation doesn't make that ugly face." Tati raises a dissatisfied brow and points at me. "Stop leveraging, Jonica. You know how you love putting off stuff regarding your health." She eases a thumbnail in her mouth and pops it between her teeth. "I'll be a thousand miles away when you go home, and we all know your man's not going to take care of you, so you have to take care of yourself. Got me?"

"Why does everyone hate Hudson so much?"

"Because even when this is supposed to be about you, somehow, you manage to make it about him." Tati crosses her eyes and blows out a hard sigh. Her eyes fall to the spot where I'm massaging my back. "You've never been that chick who gives a dude complete autonomy over every aspect of you, yet, here we are." She plasters on the same *I told you so* face she had after she tried warning me that my first major crush in junior high—Parker Williams—was smooching with another girl during study hall.

"*I knew he wasn't no good,*" Tati informed me after she caught Parker and busted him in the eye. This was before metabolism caught up to her chunky cheeks, she graduated from training bras to a solid "C" way before me, and slathered her hair with Luster's Pink Lotion secured in two thick braids that reached down to her butt. She shoved her hands on her hips and rolled her neck. "*I don't know what you see in that boy, anyway. His head's too big for his body, he's ashy, and has horrible taste in girls.*"

"*Ummm, hello?*" I raised a meek hand. "*Girlfriend here.*"

Tati pulled me into her body by both of my shoulders and flashed the grin that generally had the teachers eating out of her hands whenever she was acting up. *"Oh, not you, kitten. I'm talking about his mistresses."*

"Who taught you that word? Besides, we're not married."

"Okay, his side pieces. Whatever." She let me go and flipped her braids over her shoulders.

I sniffed back the tears, trying to hide how hurt I was. *"It's fine, really. I should've kissed him when he asked."*

"And have Pastor Daddy ground you for life if he finds out? Naw, I'll never see you again." Tati's eyes narrowed like she was gearing up to slug Parker again. *"We need to make a pact right now that we'll never let a boy change who we are or how we move. Got me?"* She held up a fist for me to pound, which I reluctantly tapped with my own.

"Now I don't have a boyfriend," I sniffled.

"Once he let that pimple-faced girl near his lips, he proved he wasn't your boyfriend in the first place." Tati's expression eased, but her face was still calling me stupid. When she noticed how sad I was, she said, *"My point is, since that boy can't appreciate you, I took care of that fool. Now, find a boy who doesn't make you eat crap."*

Tati's been trying to help me change my romantic diet my entire life.

After an eon passes, my pain level dips to a two, allowing me to settle back in my seat. Tati's pensive glare shifts to contentment.

"Guess what?" she blurts.

"The last time you asked me that question, I had to bust you out of a cult."

She laughs, but I'm serious.

"Hey, it seemed like a good idea at that time. And my forever boo came to rescue me like she always does." She blows smooches across the table, tossing her arms in the air like she just completed a victory lap. "As awesome as another round of *Operation Rescue Tati*

would be right now, my current situation isn't quite as dramatic."
She musses her fluffy hair, snags a cigarette from her purse, lights
it, and takes a long drag. "I'm opening a tattoo shop."

"Why didn't you lead with this when we got here? We should
be celebrating together!" I raise my shot glass, nod for her to do
the same, and we clink them together.

"When did this happen? Where's it going to be? Do you have
a building?" The questions fly from my mouth rapid-fire.

"Wait, baby! Mama can only take one question at a time."
Tati mocks me before she takes another drag off her cancer stick.
Two more puffs, and she kills it—Tati's version of quitting cold
turkey.

"When are you going to quit killing yourself with that mess?"
I ask.

"When you stop trying to find out how much mess you
can take so the rest of us won't have to take the bullets for you."
Leave it alone, I frown. "Anyway, I found a cute little loft in an
office building in downtown Parable. The vibe is everything! It
has the perfect view of Parable Lake, only six tenants in the entire
building, it's right off Main Street, and, oh my god, it's a wide
open space where I can do *anything*—" she winks at me, "anything
at all that I want. Business or pleasure."

"Please, chile. Spare me the prologue. The epilogue too." I
rub the dragonfly hanging from my necklace between my fingers.
"When are you moving in?"

"This weekend, actually." Tati wriggles her pinky finger with
the opposite hand, looking suspicious. "I was hoping you'd help
me break the place in. Maybe lift a box or two?"

"And why would I do that?" Of course, I will help, but I
plaster on a stern face.

"Because you love me."

"You better be glad I do." We lean toward each other across the booth and quickly peck each other's lips. "Anything for you. I'll be there." *Hopefully, this nausea will subside by Friday.*

"Perfect! Thanks, angel." Tati gives me a shimmy.

"Now, there's a favor I need you to do for me." I wave the necklace so Tati can see it. "I want a sleeve of these little guys on my arm, and I want you to do it."

Tati releases an obnoxious cackle loud enough to drown out the band, drawing the ire of a group of hipsters at the table adjacent to us. *Sorry,* I mouth with a slight wave. "What's so hilarious about me wanting a sleeve? You're covered in tattoos."

"It's just that—" she points at me, "why would a fragile snowflake like you who weeps over puppies and hides from conflict want her first tattoo to be so painful? You don't even like needles."

"*Snowflake?* I'm not that sensitive."

Tati's shoulders quake, and she laughs again. Loud. "Sure, the girl who was on a first-name basis with the janitors, hustled her cafeteria worker friends into giving her extra tater tots on Wednesdays, and spent lunch hour hiding out in the bathroom to write. Socially awkward and uber sensitive." She squints at me. "At least those stories turned you into something."

"But now that I'm grown, I'm paying for crouching on the toilet seat so long every day." I reach behind me and rub the small of my back. "It's really done a number on me. I'm going to my chiropractor when I return to LA next week."

"Mmm-hmm." Tati points at my pendant. "Why dragonflies?"

"Like you don't know this already?" I scrunch my face in disappointment that she's forgotten. "Daddy always taught me that dragonflies are the light of God," I explain in a hushed tone. "They represent searching within and dancing. Everything about them fits me like the pair of perfect jeans: warrior, fighter, agility, power, speed. Rebirth, transformation, adaptation, and spiritual awakening." I pause to smile like I can see one in front of me. "When I forget who I am, my little army can remind me I belong."

"Sometimes, belonging means climbing out of your skin," Tati says. "You ready to surrender?"

"Maybe it's not about surrendering. Maybe I'm claiming who I really am."

Tati nods in approval. I pluck one of the cold, soggy tacos off my plate and drop it back down. "This stuff isn't fit for consumption."

"That's because you're supposed to eat it while it's hot, mami!" I look up to see Phenom's curvy owner, Florenza, standing over me with a fake scowl. Her straight, coal-colored mane bounces around her shoulders as she wags her finger like I'm in real trouble. "I prepared this myself, *Jonica*. You don't like my food no more?"

"Get your tiny self over here!" I yell and slide out of the booth. "I miss you, work mommy." Florenza fits perfectly in my arms when I bend to kiss her cheek and wrap them around her.

Florenza rolls her eyes at me and tosses her glare to Tati. "This girl claims to miss her work mommy, yet I have to hear from my baby girl that Jonica's gallivanting around H.E.C. instead of coming to the kitchen to greet me herself," she fusses in her swirly Peruvian accent. "Six-time employee of the month when she worked here, this girl, but she can't be bothered to come see me and doesn't eat my food. You need a new plate?"

"No, ma'am." I slide back into my seat. "I'm sure it's awesome as usual, but I'm having a hard time keeping anything but water down. I promise it's not the food."

"You're not pregnant, kitten?" Tati slaps a hand over her mouth and darts a finger at my belly. "Oh Lord, is my baby having a baby with that thing you call a man?"

I snatch a black cloth napkin from the table and smack her with it. "No, I'm *not* pregnant. But if I were, I'd appreciate you not referring to your godchild's father that way."

Tati thrusts a hand over her cleavage, mouth frozen in a perfect O. "Godmother? You can keep that, hun. God stopped conversing with me a long time ago."

"That's because you're wasting all those gifts He gave you on this reality television junk when your star potential's right up there on that stage." Florenza swats Tati's bare shoulder with the back of her hand and points to the band, packing up to take a break. "You got the goods for plenty more than what you got going on, girl. There's not a soul who shouldn't hear those chops before they die, my songbird. You're being stingy, *mija*."

Tati's thorny chuckle makes the tiny diamond piercing in her top lip dance. "I've decided that the album I just released is going to be the only one I do," she says. "No more songbird, mami. It's not fulfilling me like I thought it would."

"Such a shame to die full," Florenza says. "All that talent to waste. You hurt my feelings, girl. Scoot over." She gives Tati a second to make room, then scooches beside her.

Florenza's light brown eyes dart between Tati and me. I remember being so jealous of her thick lashes, colorful style, and spectacularly angular face when I worked the registers here junior and senior high school years. Not that I needed the money, but with Temper on the road most of the time and Daddy being caught up at church, my folks and Florenza decided my mind needed to be occupied by more than how my body had started banging and paying attention to the boys who were paying attention to me.

"*You gotta keep your mind on those books, mija,*" Florenza reminded me at least once every shift I worked. "*You're starting to smell yourself, and I don't want any little Jonicas running around here.*"

Basically, Florenza got me through my last two years of high school. I really should've been a better human to her than ghosting her like a fired nanny.

"So, spill it, JC," Florenza says. "You sure you're not back here because you're carrying a mini-me and thinking about having her at home?"

"Oh, dear God, no. This is nothing a good kale or fiber cleansing can't handle." I unravel my bun, snatch off the rubber band, and toss it aside, giving my braids a good shake as they tumble over my shoulders. "All right, can we take my uterus off the table before I vomit?" I dart my hands toward Florenza like I'm directing a choir. "Did you say your daughter saw me today in class? Which one was she?"

"Her name's Belle. She's bright and beautiful. Full of her mama's spice!"

Ah . . . Glasses Girl. Now that I think about it, she looks just like her mother. I can't believe I let it slip by me.

"My brainy little pale skin," Florenza goes on. "She takes everything after her papi. I just hope she doesn't have his same fear of commitment when she grows up." She scoots my plate from side to side, almost like she's dreaming.

"How long have you and Brian been together now?" Tati asks.

"Twenty years, this guy. He says he loves me but not enough to give me a ring. Who knows?" She raises her shoulders, questioning. "Anyway, Belle couldn't stop going on about how beautiful you are, how she loves your voice, and Lord, she wants to be just like you when she breaks into the industry." Florenza pauses for a breath. "You really made an impact on my baby."

"I don't know what to say," I stutter. "I kind of thought they hated me."

"Seriously, you have to stop bleeding out every time things don't go how you want them to, Jonica." Tati clenches her fists and blows in the air.

"She's always been like that, even when she worked here. Everything always doomsday with this girl," Florenza cosigns.

"Chill out, guys. I had a rough day, that's all," I defend. "Those children came for my neck. I don't know who's raising them, but they're not the same as we were coming up." I wave a hand between Tati and me. "These kids are on something completely different. Grown-folks stuff. Hell, they taught me a few lessons. My brain's still swimming out of the deep end they tossed me in." I feel a migraine coming on.

"Stop it, J." Tati snatches my hands and stares into my eyes. She's a master of centering, like how she's kneading the center of my hands with her fingers. Almost every hill I've tried to throw myself off, Tati talked me down with her hands. "You know what the crazy part is?" She lets my hands go. "Every time you assume the worst, it ends up being one of the best things that's ever happened to you. Do me a favor: stop with the imposter's syndrome and accept the good that's coming to you without feeling guilty about it for once in your life."

I should flip her off, but I go with, "You're right."

"I know I am. That's why Miss Wilkes offered you a residency teaching media tech at the school."

Florenza's head jets toward me. "Really?" The sound of her clapping hands is reminiscent of the pity applause granted to award show losers when the winners are announced. I nod, confirming in silence. "Oh, you don't know how happy this makes me! My daughter will be learning from the best! I couldn't ask for more."

Since meeting with Miss Wilkes (who had to convince me the offer wasn't a joke after the way I bombed right in front of her), I've been thinking about the residency all day. You know how people list the pros and cons before they make life-changing decisions? I just imagine the worst that can happen, run with it, and still say yes.

Yes to the kids. Yes to the student project. Yes to helping my alma mater take home the prize.

. . . and yes to a potential new friendship with Luke.

But *Crack Dreams* is standing in the way. I have to get back on set soon, and I'm already overwhelmed. With me taking care of everybody else, my to-do list will never die. But that's me. Mama to all, second to myself. So, despite all the worst that could happen . . . I said yes.

And right now, I tell Florenza without a stitch of doubt, "It's only for a short time, but we'll see how it goes."

SEVEN

I ONLY THREW up on the plane twice.

Gas station sushi a few hours before takeoff has me repenting at the toilet at 3:00 a.m., less than an hour before Temper's daily call to get me right with the Lord before I die. The one day I actually welcomed her intruding on my rest for a little prayer, Mom overslept in St. Louis. The city with the best Chinese food, White Castle, and thousands of *Pearls* waiting for one night only with Temper.

I bet Jesus wouldn't leave you hanging when you're in the middle of blowing chunks.

Without the magic of divine intervention, I had to figure out how to appease my surly stomach on its own. Crackers and Canada Dry—Black folks' remedy.

For a minute, it seemed like it worked. The second my belly stopped percolating, I managed to make myself resemble a human and hop a ride share to the airport. But five minutes after the plane broke the clouds, I was facedown in a barf bag, breathing my own toxic breath, purging the remnants of cucumber and seaweed out of my belly. I pushed out what I could, apologized to the neighbors on my row, and headed straight to Sequestered Studios to meet with Hudson and Skye.

I'm going to throw up again.

". . . all I'm saying is, Quita doesn't need to kill Ammo, JC. She needs to forgive him and work it out. You know, retention."

"You mean redemption," I correct Skye's typical assault on the English language in her fraudulent, hood-boogie-valley-hood again monotone. I totally get crafting your voice for this business, but Skye's fake accent is just plain weird. Even worse when it's bouncing off the paltry acoustics in the small office space we're meeting in.

"That too."

Skye's unfortunate inability to grasp basic syntax pales compared to being subjected to her counterfeit boobs for the last hour. I hope she didn't pay over-market price for those lopsided melons.

The next time Skye opens her mouth to latch whatever nonsense on the tail end of the impending *HELL NO!* I'm about to issue, all I hear is *blah, blah, blah,* which makes way more sense than her antiquated dribble. Maybe it's that fact that her boobs need realigning. Or possibly the psychedelic spandex, barely bigger than a string bikini she has on. *Is it a string bikini?*

Could be that I've been sick all morning, stuck between these plain, ivory walls with no sense of color or escape that has me feeling like a, well . . . you know. I try to refrain from labeling myself or any other women that word that starts with "B" and ends with something needing to be scratched, but I won't deny that right now, it sort of fits my foul mood.

I can't quite put my foot on where miserable me is emerging from. Oh, wait, *yes, I can.* This particular thorn is Hudson propped next to Skye on the sofa across from the love seat I'm in, ogling her like he's figuring out how to cash in on her assets. That's why he's opening his mouth to defend her instead of protecting my artistic integrity.

"You have to give it to Skye, babe," Hudson chimes in on the wrong side of the discrepancy, "it won't hurt to revisit the ending. Think of it as growth." This he says to Skye's breasts.

"That's exactly what I mean, Huddy." Skye playfully pushes my man's shoulder, infused with the kind of affection that should be reserved for her own man.

Huddy? Let me annunciate the way Skye does.

Huddd ddddy.

By the time it's finished dripping from Skye's lips, Hudson's moniker emulates a long drag off a joint. One laced with something extra. The witchy vibrato tainting her squeaky voice makes me want to crawl inside my skin and stretch my face inside out to keep what I'm thinking from showing up on my face. One—how could I let Hudson talk me into ever thinking this girl was fit for a role as important as the lead in *Crack Dreams*, and two, why is Hudson tossing Skye the hush face like a gang sign?

My phone vibrates with a notification. A text from Luke:

Tati says you're not feeling well. Consolation—excited we get to work together. Feel better. See you when you get back.

Me too, I text back. See you next week.

I pull my feet from my flip-flops and plant them on the cold leather chair. Knees pressed together, chin resting on top of them and twisting a small patch of coils around my index finger that escaped from my braids. Everything I'm thinking is pummeling my brain instead of pouring out my mouth. I'm exhausted. Too drained to fight or reclaim my role in my own movie. These days, people feel entitled to so much that doesn't belong to them: others' time, emotions, and the movies they make. Demanding we feel the way they want us to.

The scene in particular that we're haggling over?

Standoff in the warehouse—Quita, Ammo, and six officers who were tipped off that a foiled drug deal was going down. Quita has a .45 pointed at Ammo's head; police have arms on her.

Policeman #1: Don't do it, Quita!

Policeman #2: Please, you have everything to live for!

Ammo (quivering, trying to still appear in control of her): You don't have the balls to make it happen. (Spits on the ground and wipes his mouth with the back of his hand.) You know I ain't no punk. When you put that gun down and I get out of jail, I'm going to show you what a real man is . . . just like I showed your baby girl.

Without a word, Quita shoots Ammo once in the heart. Police fire at her 20 times, killing her.

"Awww, come on. Not the sour face, babe." Hudson prods his way into my thoughts. Looking guilty without being placed at the scene of the crime. "Neither one of them has to die. It can be a real Bonnie and Clyde."

"Bonnie was shot 26 times, and Clyde 17," I advise him.

"What's your point?"

"They died. Flesh ripped off their bodies in a blaze of glory, *Huddy*." I make sure to pronounce it just like his friend who's over there grinning at me. "Bonnie and Clyde aren't couples' goals or one of the great American romances of our time. They were stupid and got themselves dead. Where is the love in that, homie?"

Hudson relaxes in his seat with a deep chuckle. "My point is there's nothing wrong with entertaining a happy ending occasionally."

I need some hot pork rinds and a Pepsi.

"One of my first amateur film treatments was a reimagining of *Living Single* with Kyle Barker as a homicidal maniac who offed Overton and Regine for having sex behind Synclaire's back in his bed." I slice my hand across my neck to be dramatic. "There are no fairy tales in Jonicaland." My next comment is directed to

Skye, but my gaze threaded to Hudson. "Only a woman who's never birthed a child or is completely dimwitted would struggle to understand why Quita literally detonated under the pressure of losing the child she did everything to protect but felt like she failed. The system failed her. People abused her. Her entire existence was a fight."

I peel my attention away from Hudson and focus on Skye. "Quita made the ultimate sacrifice. In essence, she found the joy she was looking for. Her birth into pain and escape through misery is the perfect ending. Outside of blind justice, nothing else would suffice for her."

"Well, you're wrong about one thing, JC." Skye pats her belly, a smug grin cracking through her caked-on foundation. "My tiny bundle and I would have to strongly disagree. Pain doesn't always have a promise. Sometimes, it just hurts."

"Baby? You're having a *baby*?"

Skye's silent nod makes me want to curl up in the past before I agreed to give her this role. I tuck my bottom lip safely under my front teeth so it won't do that quivering thing it does when I'm this close to falling apart. Because I already know.

Sis is coming at me like the revelation is more of a brag than a maternally ever-after. Popping her fingers, smacking her lips, practically pole dancing in her seat, talking about all the designer outfits she's already bought the baby, who isn't even close to giving Skye her first stretch mark if she doesn't already own a few.

Does Hudson know if she has any? I don't want the answer to that. I don't.

The only thing keeping me from climbing over the coffee table to choke the dog piss out of Skye is what I spot behind the cock-strong arrogance supporting the pile of lashes lazily glued to her eyes. Skye's tired too. Slut shamed. Abused. Subjected to rarely met conditions. Myself included. She's somebody's daughter, about to become somebody's mother. Even more mortifying. For a second—no more than a flicker—I want to eat every negative word I've projected onto her. Until I look at Hudson.

I slide my feet to the floor, my jaw bouncing off the end of my bare feet. Hudson looks guilty, but not of a crime I can convict him of unless he confesses or volunteers some clues.

Pregnant.

In the back of my mind, I know it's my man who planted the seed. This is what I get. I avoid direct confrontation, like dodging a necessary trip to the doctor out of fear of what I'll get diagnosed with. Just let the symptoms kill me. The family can figure out the cause of death after the autopsy.

In the stupidest, most naïve way, I don't want to prove that Hudson isn't the father. Pinning the child on him is my escape plan. The easiest out I can ask for because I've spent more time fooling myself into thinking this thing—we. can. work. As opposed to our relationship actually working. This is what I've been meaning to pray for, right? A guilt-free way to set myself free. So, I will keep my thoughts on this to myself—for now. Unborn babies don't have a dog in grown folks' fights.

"Congratulations, Skye." My voice cracks. "I'm sure you'll make a fabulous mother."

The sound of urine breaking water wakes me up.

I slept with Hudson. Despite what my mind says and what my heart knows, I surrendered. Maybe one day, I'll be angry enough to stop giving in. I don't hate myself for doing this, but my mouth tastes like steel. As if maybe I'm stroking out or something.

"Stop being neurotic, JC. You're not sick. You don't have time to be," Hudson told me when I made him stop because the back pain started kicking my tail again. "It's probably IBS or something. Get some Metamucil and take a good dump."

For once, I wish he would just cuddle me, offer me some soup and a good book, and let me lie on his chest while I recover, regardless of whether I'm really sick, instead of assuming I just need some fiber in my life.

"Why do you love me? What is it that I do for you?" I asked with him lying behind me, my back to his chest, still gasping for air as if the two minutes of effort he poured into our little romp exhausted him within an inch of his life.

"You know I hate when you ask me stuff like that. Stop fishing." He scooted away from me and rolled on his side, breathing harder, but not because of our workout. Pure aggravation air.

"Does every one of our conversations have to make me feel like I'm setting myself up for an apology? God, Hud. I'm only asking because you never just come out and tell me how you feel. And if you have to do all that for some air, get an inhaler." I breathed hard too. Purposely. Just to prove I can do it better than him. "If you don't like me, just say that." I pulled his black comforter over my naked skin all the way to my shoulders, creating a barrier between the cool air, me, and him.

Every once and again, the nuances in Hudson's voice—speaking like his tongue's a cocked trigger, sums up how easily he denies me the critical glue that holds relationships like ours together: bringing home pizza over the Pad Thai I requested for dinner and giving me flowers when he knows how much I despise them. Abhor is probably a better description of how I feel when he shoves them in my face. Listening to respond, deflect, or not at all. All those meteors crashing right into us. They're also reminders

of how, at any moment, he's ready to put me in my place if I dip a
toe over *his* boundaries.

"Can you please dead the negative attitude? I thought we
were having a good time." He flipped over with his back to me.
"What I love about you is your deep, dark skin. It reminds me of
midnight. The witching hour."

Did you just call me a witch?

Every compliment that followed was geared toward my skin. I
winced until my chest felt like it caved in. The more Hudson spoke,
the more I heard his grandfather—the first of three generations
equally named Hudson Pyke, openly admit to me that he denied
Black people mortgage loans before because *"their kind's known
not to pay it back"* in the middle of our first brunch. Dementia or
not, that was some sick stuff.

When Hudson stopped raving over how in love he is over
my skin and slipped out of bed to shower, I grabbed my cell and
texted Tati.

You were right about him.

I quickly deleted the draft.

No need to involve her in case my suspicions were wrong.
Once, when we vacationed with her and her ex, Tati threatened
to burn off Hudson's penis with a hot iron if he didn't stop
disrespecting me in front of her. I don't want to get into the details,
but he's been on cracked eggs with her ever since.

Why did I sleep with him?

I pondered why I gave myself over to a man who possibly has
another baby on the way while he rendered a shower concert of
dirty lust songs as a pat on the back for a job well done . . . in his
eyes.

The room grew stuffy while I listened to him carry his tunes.
He actually has a decent voice. Sort of a current Backstreet Boy

(take your pick of which one) during rehearsals, not in concert. When he hasn't pissed me off, I can listen to Hudson sing for a while.

I pushed the blanket away, propped on my side, and let my leg hang off the side of the bed. I cracked my bare toes, desperately needing a fresh pedi, and ran a hand through my braids. After I yawned a couple of times, I leaned over to grab the half-empty flute of Rémy from the nightstand with all intentions of finishing it.

That's when I noticed.

Our picture was gone. The one where we recreated Janet Jackson's controversial *Rolling Stone* magazine cover, her wearing nothing but low-rise jeans, Rene cupping her bare breasts with his hands. Tipsy me and Hudson's version came after a few drinks and a private session we'd just completed for *Limelight*, recognizing Hollywood power couples. Just being silly. But we decided the end result was too scrumptious not to display somewhere.

The picture was gone.

After that, I noticed dust-bunny coasters on the table instead of the Mann Made candles I bought Hudson two birthdays ago. He never bothered burning them, even after I explained they were for healing and centering.

Gone.

Did you have a garage sale I don't know about?

I stood, wrapped the comforter around myself, and stalked over to the dresser, headed for the drawer Hudson designated for me and my stuff. My acidic gut said don't check, but of course, I did.

Empty.

Stop it, JC. You don't have enough evidence for a trial or conviction.

By the time Hudson made it out of the shower, I had dressed, left, and sent him a text:

I need a break.

EIGHT

AT FIRST, TALKING Miss Wilkes into giving Media Tech a day to film some bonus footage for *No More Trauma* at Parable Park instead of being stuck in class all day seemed like a good idea. But after hauling equipment around in the treacherous August heat, directing take after take because the kids can't remember the synchronized skate routine they just learned last night, with sweat halfway blinding me and my guts stinging like backwash is about to shoot up my throat, I feel like cussing myself out.

For now, sitting on the bench under a tree with the last bit of shade Luke's sister, Elaine, and I can find will do.

"Can I show you something?" Elaine whispers with an indelible grin marking her face since bear-hugging me after Luke introduced us.

I raise an arm and press my nose to the pit, exposed in a sleeveless royal blue *That's My Mama* vintage television show tee. "The way I'm out here sweating? Girl, you can probably smell my answer, but go ahead—shoot."

Elaine straightens the silk fuchsia headscarf cradling her head and nervously pulls out her phone, darting her tight eyes to me, then back to the screen. "Okay, confession. I've been keeping a look book on you since your very first appearance on the red carpet, when you wore the *Alice and Olivia* embroidered jeans and see-through seafoam top that drove all the fashion mags bonkers.

Seriously, I can't get enough of your style. You aren't afraid to cross lines and look fly doing it." She scrolls through her phone until she sees a picture and turns the screen to me.

"Hey, my Golden Globes look from last year. That was so much fun!" I muse.

"Rose-gold Fendi sequin catsuit, hand-beaded, short-sleeved tulle overlay drenched in crystals." Elaine wiggles her fingers like she's drizzling diamonds over my head and describes me better than the gossip show commentators did. "Diamond drop earrings and strappy stilettos to match too? You were dripping opulence, honey. I wanted to steal that outfit for myself, but you filled it out way better than I ever could."

The memory brings a smile to my face. "Now, that was a good day," I tell her. "I hit every best-dressed list. *People, Vibe, E! Online.*"

"*. . . Vogue, Vanity Fair, Marie Claire, InStyle,*" Elaine interjects. She covers her mouth when she realizes she's gushing but goes on. "Sorry, I just love fashion."

"Oh, please, don't apologize for having good taste, ma." I cup my hands over my eyes to block the sun as we share a laugh. "It just feels good to be appreciated by someone who doesn't follow '*How are you?*' up with, '*Hey, listen . . .*' without bothering to wait for me to tell them how I'm actually doing. Clothes don't ask for anything, and they never let me down."

"I love that," Elaine squeals. She does that a lot when she's excited. And she chatters as if we're on a video conference call instead of sitting together. Her words are rushed like she's paying back borrowed time. Her pleasant, oval face is reminiscent of Luke's; her sparse eyebrows wrinkle when she smiles. She does a lot of that too. It's kind of infectious.

"You just look like luxury. You can rock a plastic bag and make it look high-end. Just *major*, honey." She wrings her hands together and lays them on her lap. "If I tried pulling off those ripped jeans you're wearing, I'd look a fool."

"Don't you know how beautiful you are?" I cup her hands with one of mine and squeeze them, then turn my back to the picnic table and lean against it. "I'm serious. Those high cheekbones and buttery skin? And that killer body? You could be a serious contender for a model."

As soon as I say it, Elaine's brown eyes gloss over, and her face turns solemn. She presses her hands to the chartreuse, airy fabric loosely covering her chest, stopping where her left breast used to be. "That was so stupid. I'm sorry."

Elaine shakes her head and waves me off. "It's fine. It's just that outside of my baby girl and my brother, I'm falling short on compliments lately. I'll take all I can get." She flashes a contented smile. "Anyway, model—no. I'm a behind-the-scenes woman. Been hoping for years to dress my own personal fashion icon—" she points to me, "and now, here we are. I still can't believe it."

"You're a designer?"

"And a stylist."

My face contorts a thousand ways. "We've been out here all this time, so why am I just now hearing this, girl?"

Elaine cuts her gaze to Luke, directing the kids in a straight line, spinning and dropping into the splits, then popping right back up in saucy poses. I'm not complaining, especially since these rubbery legs of mine would snap if I tried to coax my out-of-shape body into a lunge. A good 30 more minutes of basting on this bench while the kids try to get on the same timing, and I'm done.

"Fashion is just a dream for me," she mutters. "What are the chances of becoming a style icon all the way from good ol' Parable, anyway?"

"Ask me how I know." I wink at her.

"Good point." Elaine darts her index finger at me with one eye closed like I've solved a crime. "Don't get me wrong, I'm consumed with textiles and colors and how to make a woman feel sexy and give her the happy ending she deserves. Fashion's a blast, but my everything is *her*." She points to Myzi with a contented sigh, resting her head on her hand. "Turns out putting together the perfect outfit is the only thing I've ever been good at. But Myzi's the best thing I've ever done."

That last little diamond she drops is heading straight into a script if I can remember it. Definitely not *Crack Dreams*, though. I lean over to the side, wincing. The pain's back stronger.

"You all right?" Elaine's face suddenly floods with concern.

"I'm fine, just lost in thought."

"You sure? You've been making that face a lot today. Are you in pain?"

I'm flaring up again but don't want to make a fuss. "It's just a little hot out here; nothing a sip of water won't cure." I grab my bottle from the table and take a drink. "You were saying about your daughter?"

Elaine's smile snaps right back. I covet that superpower. The bounce back. "I loaned her my womb, but my baby gives me shelter." She leans over, snags a cucumber from the snack tray on the table, and pops it into her mouth. The sun catches flecks of green in her deep brown eyes that I hadn't noticed until she angles close enough for me to catch a glimpse. A flock of birds glides overhead, matching the kids' rhythm, only with better timing.

I stretch out my legs, resisting the urge to sit with them intertwined like I would typically do. That's why I'm constantly in pants because I can't sit right. Forever avoiding the lady Temper raised me to be. I nod toward Myzi, who's growing impatient as she demonstrates a spin combination to her peers. "You two are pretty close, huh?"

"Listen, Myzi hovers over me like *she's* the mama. Always fussing, making sure I'm straight." Elaine pauses to cup a hand over her mouth like she's exposing a secret. "Honestly, I kind of like the attention. But I just don't want Myzi to be so consumed with me that she misses a whole world that's out there waiting on her."

"Seems like she's pretty tough."

"Who are you telling?" Elaine harks a weak chuckle and clamps a hand on the back of her neck. "My baby's stuck with me like the grime around toilet bases nobody wants to scrub. I really adore her, though. She's young, but she knows how to take care of business. She cares for people and loves hard. She's lost a lot of friends because of me."

"Why is that?"

Elaine swings her legs away from the bench and rests her elbows on the table. "Myzi's never had a problem making friends, but the skipped parties, texts left unread, being accused of not checking on them when they could've been checking on her. I guess it all got to be too much for her *friends*." Hurt stilts Elaine's forlorn assertion. "My illness was never a secret, but no one ever bothered asking Myzi if *she* was okay." Elaine's eyes darken. "Truth is, anytime she went missing, Myzi was helping me. Every mother needs a daughter who'll hold her hair back when the time comes." She opens her mouth, pretending to jam her fingers inside like she's gagging.

"I know that feeling." I swing my legs up on the bench and twist them into a pretzel. Now, I'm comfortable. "How do you do it, Elaine?"

"Do what?"

The question tugs my shoulders up. "How do you become *her*? The woman who cares for her father, is there for her brother, and raises a unicorn daughter, all with a smile and so much grace.

My entire world gets out of whack when there's too much cream in my latte."

"Simple," Elaine notes. "I've learned to look past tomorrow because I don't want to use up all the time I have left today." A bucket list of *what-if's* adorns her sweet eyes. "You know what, Jonica? Having your breasts chopped off, the father of your child taking off because he wasn't ready for parenthood, and your mother stepping out on your father because '*Black men don't have mental illness*' kind of teaches you to accept what you can't change." Her wide grin wraps around me. "Nope, there's nothing special about me. I've just learned how to accept and navigate the hard parts."

Elaine's sentiments float in the air around us, flooding me with optimism I don't feel entitled to. Not with all this unfinished drama with Hudson making me want to blitz myself into constant inebriation. Turns out this Texas situation is just the diversion I need.

"Hey, have you ever considered telling Myzi's story for the documentary?" I ask. "It would really be the chef's kiss."

Elaine's head shakes vehemently. "No, ma'am. I teach my daughter that trauma's not a rite of passage. I won't subject her to it, and we're not going to exploit our misfortunes. We've been through it, but we're not bitter about what we've been through."

My cell buzzes on my hip like a Taser. I pull it out to check the caller ID. Hudson. At least he's stopped calling back-to-back. *I don't want to talk.* I stuff the phone back into my pocket, agitated and light-headed. The blue sky keeps randomly fading to white. I do my best to shake it off, but everything turns a blurry fog. Tiny breaths congeal into a massive gasp for air. My oxygen getting cut off mars what my brain's trying to tell me: *Get help.*

Seems like I'm reaching out to Elaine, but she's talking like nothing's wrong. I hear music. *It's a good day to be, a good day for me, a good day to see my favorite colors . . . my sisters and my brothers.*

Where's the music coming from?

One deep breath, and I see Myzi speeding at us on her skates in striped retro '80s gym shorts, Care Bears tee, and rainbow fanny pack. The music's coming from her phone, tucked in the front pocket. Her double Afro puffs bounce when she skids to a stop. "Mom, it's Kam!" her high-pitch screech can excise a hangover.

"What's wrong, baby?" Elaine hops up and grabs Myzi by the arms. She puts a finger to Myzi's lips when the girl utters something intelligible. "I can't understand you, baby. Calm down and tell me what's going on."

Myzi gulps, then sighs. Closes her eyes and presses her lips together. When her eyes pop open, they're bloodshot. "It's Kam's dad, Mayor Miller. He just got into some kind of accident or something down at The Square. He's at the hospital, Kam's over there going crazy with Uncle Luke, and I don't know what to do, Mom! Kam's father might be dead!"

I don't know what comes next.

Because I finally give in and stop begging my body for air.

NINE

WHEN I OPEN my eyes, Myzi's standing by the side of the rustic day bed, staring at me.

"I like your braids," her compliment sounds like she's mumbling through a mouth full of rocks.

"Thanks."

My response is as dry as I feel. My throat feels like I've swallowed the rocks Myzi spit out. I'm wearing the same clothes I've had on all day; Myzi isn't. I schlepp up onto my elbows and scan the dark room's décor, a cross between a bachelor pad and Gilmore Girls. A dimly lit lamp projects a blurry oval around Myzi's cherubic face, which shockingly doesn't scare me for the first time.

"Where are we? What's going on?"

"You passed out at the park, we took you to the emergency room, and Uncle Luke brought you back here to his ranch house when you got discharged. You've been snoring for hours." Myzi points to the pillow beside me. "And you're drooling on my pillow." The forced pleasantries undercutting her tone put me back on guard.

"Sorry about that."

"It's fine. If you don't mind, I'm going to finish reading my book."

Myzi strolls to the rocking chair in the corner of the cozy room, across from the 65-inch television muted on the news. She snatches the book and gray throw blanket strewn across the red plaid cushion and plops down with her legs folded. Looking at her all curled up with a book is like looking at myself. The way she cracks her toes doused in hot pink polish, her straight posture, how she bites a thumbnail when the story's getting good to her; our similarities intensify the awkwardness between us, but I like this girl.

"*Find a common ground, and you've got a best friend in Myzi for life,*" Elaine told me.

Before I passed out.

Gotta find something.

Breaking news scrolling across the bottom of the television screen catches my eye:

Black woman slung to concrete by police after being falsely accused of theft, city erupts in protest.

Can we have *one* day where this is not a thing?

Bonding through injustice isn't an option, so I flip my attention back to Myzi, already deeply immersed in whatever she's reading.

"Where's your mom and uncle?"

"Unc says you like Pad Thai and sushi, so they went to get you some, even though I wanted pizza." Her lips curl into a snarl.

"What you reading?"

The grudge caught in Myzi's voice tumbles out like a frog in her throat. "*Ugly Love*, Colleen Hoover."

"Hmmm."

"What?"

I take a white throw pillow, prop it against the wall behind me, and press my back into it. "I'm surprised you'd be reading Colleen." A huge yawn gushes out before I can catch it. "I mean, she's all trauma and triggers. Thought you had an aversion to dark stuff like that?"

"My *aversion* to senseless shoot-'em-ups and cracked-out hoes for no reason at all doesn't mean I don't have an affinity for a well written, genuine tearjerker about real-life troubles. Despite what you think about us, I *am* in touch with my emotions, you know." She closes the book and jams it on her lap. Her scowl fires at least 28 rounds into my chest. I should've shut up and let her finish the chapter.

"You do realize you're the source material that creeps into politics, schools, and everything that affects how *they* see us and how we're treated because you're a credible source, *Jonica*." See, that little snarky way she put air quotes on Jonica instead of *credible* where they belonged is exactly why Temper told me never to let kids address me by my first name.

"I like Colleen because she's real," Myzi detours back to my earlier question. "People are always talking about taking care of mental health, then telling us to shut up when we say how we feel. Like my granny did Pops." She sucks in a long drag of air like a cigarette and lets it go. "Colleen allows young people like me to vent without ever having to say a word or be shut down by anybody. Folks always judging." She cradles the paperback with the gentleness of a newborn. "Her books press all the right buttons. I don't have to go through what she writes to feel what she's saying."

Now we're talking. "What's she written that you've never been through?"

"I've never been in love."

For a second, I'm stunned at how easily she confesses to me. Until now, Myzi's made me feel like a stranger off the street, but her tone lilts in a more welcoming direction. My therapist's face that makes people open up to me must be kicking in. "You've never been in love?"

She shrugs, lowers the novel, and flips through the pages with a sigh. "Outside of Kam, I haven't met a boy I liked. Besides, Mama needs me. Between taking care of her, school, and skating, there's not much time left for me." *Never enough time to look after ourselves.* "Your braids really are pretty, though," she mutters through the straight line of her tense lips. It's the second time she's complimented them.

Find a common ground.

A woman's hair is her glory; a Black woman's air is her lifeline.

"When I was at Cox, all the Black girls stayed in Hyde Hall. And every one of them came to me to hook up their braids. All those hours were hard on my hands, but it paid for extra chicken and guac on my Chipotle burrito bowls all the way through graduation." Myzi rewards my flex with a giggle. "I can braid your hair . . . if you're up to it." Her eyes latch onto the flock of sky-blue dragonflies Tati inked on my forearm the other day.

"Butterflies. Cool."

"Dragonflies," I correct her.

Her brows form an arch. "Why dragonflies?"

Myzi's question reminds me of what happened in the emergency room a few hours ago. *"You're dehydrated,"* the doctor nonchalantly rattled off without glancing up from the chart she gripped. *"Drink plenty of fluids and get some rest."* Sounded more like a guess than a diagnosis.

"With all due respect, ma'am, look at her," Luke's disapproval thundered from my bedside. *"She needs more than bed rest and water. Shouldn't you be running tests or something?"*

The doctor's pug nose flared, and bloodshot eyes twitched. Had probably been on her feet for hours, tending to abrasions, exposed to bodily fluids, and being stretched beyond her bandwidth. Or she was one of those backwoods hillbillies Temper taught me not to fool around with when I was a kid unless I wanted to come up missing. The type who couldn't be bothered to save a Black woman's life if she was burning right in front of her.

"Don't get loud with me. I know my job, sir." She flipped her long, scraggly braid over the shoulder of her dingy blue scrubs and tossed the clipboard on the table. *"Look, I have patients here who are near death and don't have time to waste on a diva without the common sense to drink enough water if she's going to be outside in Texas in the middle of August. Grow up and give up your bed to someone who actually needs it."*

Luke was boiling. I was too, but I didn't want this woman touching me again. I mentally sketched her face along with every trifling characteristic and trait to kill her off in a movie later—my revenge.

I eased a hand on Luke's shoulder. *"Get me out of here, please."*

"If there's nothing else?" The doctor dismissed us with her rhetorical question, then walked out without so much as a "screw you."

Myzi's question about my fleet of dragonflies reminds me that no matter how much success I ever attain, in some way, I'll always be *Dark Meat.*

"Dragonflies are small, beautiful, and some of the most underestimated creatures on earth. Seems like they're doing nothing, but they're making the world a better place just by being there." I lazily trace over the artwork on my arm with my ring finger. "No matter how anyone looks at them, dragonflies say a lot without having to say anything at all. For that, they're some of the most powerful creatures in the universe."

Myzi's eyes gloss over. Her faint smile as she stares dreamily at my flock surprises me a little. "Must be nice to have the entire universe listen to you."

"I'll listen to you," I tell her. "If you ever need to talk, I'll listen. No judgment."

Myzi drops her head. A few moments drift between us, allowing the younger version of me ample time to tussle with the woman I'm becoming. And if the universe cares an inkling about my sanity, one day, I'll be just as strong as Myzi.

My cell rings. The first time I realize it hasn't been attached to me like a feeding tube. So disappointing to see Hudson's name on the screen when I pick it up. I send him straight to voicemail.

"Hey, I know we've had a bit of a rough start, but I'd like to be your friend, Myzi."

She frowns. "You don't even know me. Why would you want to be my friend?"

"Because the world needs more people like you," I say, "the ones who'd film the hero."

Baby, Myzi's grin can provoke me to fall out a thousand more times at the park just to see the joy immersed in her face again.

"How much do you charge?" she asks.

"Charge?"

"To braid my hair?" She clutches *Ugly Love* to her chest with one hand and plucks at one of her puffs with the other. "I know you're big time, but how much is it to hook up hardworking little sisters without a lot of cash like me?"

I wring my hands together like I'm weighing the options, then toss her a wink. "Well, my kitchen beautician days are far behind me, but I'll come out of retirement for you. It's on me, no charge." Score another smile. *I freaking win.* "Hey, what song were you playing when you came up to your mother and me at the park?"

"Oh, that was 'Colors,' by Black Pumas. Why?"

I don't get to tell her I think it belongs in the documentary's soundtrack before Luke and Elaine stroll through the door carrying an armful of bags.

"Hey, you're up?" Luke says.

I stretch my arms overhead, my torso left to right, and bust a yawn. "Just chatting it up with Myzi here."

Elaine nods an *I told you so* my way. "You two must be starving."

"Yes, we are, Mom. Did you bring pho and sushi? You know how much I love it." Myzi purposely avoids looking at me.

"I thought you wanted pizza," I say.

Her mouth stretches into a grin. She shrugs and rushes over to the large writing desk where Luke and Elaine unload food and toiletries from the bags.

"Extra spicy for mama's baby." Elaine wraps her arms around Myzi and kisses her forehead. They cling to each other for more than a few beats. Makes me mom-sick for Temper. How she hugged me whenever she came off tour, loaded down with gifts from wherever she'd been. With everything going on, I want to turn back the clock to 10 years old and curl up in bed with my mother like I used to.

"How are you feeling?" Luke grabs the desk chair, walks over, sets it next to the bed, and plops down.

"Slightly woozy, but way better than at that hospital."

"Good," he says. "I'm calling tomorrow to lodge a complaint on that doctor. I felt like she was playing with you. I don't like that."

"I wish I'd been in that room with you guys and heard her talking to you like that," Elaine says. "*Miss Doctor* would still be trying to GPS her teeth back into her mouth." She unpacks the last bag and hands a square black container to Myzi. "Give that to JC for me, baby."

"Sure, Mom." Myzi skips over and hands me what I've been craving all day: Sushi. Because God loves me, after all. I wrestle to pop the lid off as Myzi stands next to Luke, bends, and rests her chin on his shoulder. "Have you heard anything about Mayor Miller, Unc? Kam hasn't been answering his phone all day. Is everything okay?"

Luke and Elaine exchange somber glances before he reaches back and dips a hand into one of Myzi's puffs. Nervously, I cram a California roll packed with avocado into my mouth because I don't know what else to do. The rice, cucumber, nori, and sesame squishing between my teeth is pretty loud until Luke tells us, "He didn't make it."

Myzi jets up and backs away. Lip quivers. Ferociously digs her palms into her eyes, forcing the tears back inside as her lean frame wilts. Veins rise and scale through her arms like cracks slowly demarking delicate china plates. She rocks back on her heels, hands glued to her eyes, mouth widens as if she's wailing, but there's no sound. Luke turns away. I do, too. All I can do is sit here, chew, and witness a 15-year-old's deconstruction.

Elaine rushes to Myzi and snatches her in her arms, purging the reality of the news of the mayor's death across the front of her pale gray shirt. When Elaine pulls away, random blotches of mucus and tears soiling the blouse aren't hard to spot. Like she lost a game of paintball with clear acrylic. I bite off a piece of dry skin on my lip and try to spit it out without Luke seeing.

Is it possible to cataclysmically disappear off the scene to keep from saying anything stupid? I can't handle grief. Makes me uncomfortable. Don't know what to say to somebody going through it; can't figure out a way to rummage through my emotions when it dusts its shoes off on my front porch. In my family, we were taught not to cry. The Lord is good, but doesn't want to see your tears, even in death.

I'm sweating now. Of all days to fall out and end up at Luke's house. I want to disappear.

"I didn't get to say goodbye to him, Mama. He was our friend." Myzi's even-keeled sentiment echoes in my ears. I've tasted those words before. *I didn't get to say goodbye.*

"He was just skating with us yesterday, and now you're telling me he's gone?" Myzi wails. "I don't understand!" Her confusion wilts under a fresh batch of tears. "He was *always* there for us no matter what. I don't believe this! Why him?"

"Death isn't reserved for bad folk, sweetie," Elaine says. "We have to accept the grave when it comes calling for the good ones too." She gives Myzi another squeeze. "I'm sorry, baby. We all loved him." Elaine cradles Myzi in her arms again, rocking as the girl cries softly.

"Mayor Miller, he's close to all the kids?" I whisper to Luke.

"Was." Luke swipes his hands over his face. Sucks in a gulp of air and exhales. "Man, I don't believe this."

I feel the raw tug. A toxic cocktail of rage, despair, and empathy mars Luke's face. A small scar to the left of his brow catches my eye. Funny the things you notice when there's nowhere else to look. He clamps a hand over his mouth, murmuring through open fingers.

"You ever seen a man spat on, ostracized, and called *nigger* on his own lawn in front of his wife and children?" he asks. I shake my head.

"That was Guy's inaugural celebration as Parable's first elected Black mayor last year," Luke explains. "What a welcome, right?" The vibrato accenting Luke's strained recount of the harrowing inaugural night mingles with Myzi's soft whimpers. "I remember having to help Guy clean human feces from his yard because some idiot took a squat in it. Left a note on top of the crap too: *Since Parable's being run by a nigger, the town's going to . . . well, you know.*"

I'm trembling. I set aside the food container, unfold my legs, and scoot to the edge of the bed, letting my feet dangle off the side, wondering why this story didn't make headlines as I crack my toes. It's my first time hearing any of this.

"That blows me, Luke. Who does that?" I say. "What did you all do?"

Luke massages the back of his neck and peers over his shoulder at Myzi and Elaine, weeping silently. "We rolled up our sleeves, and helped Guy get to work doing exactly what he always did. He cleaned up the mess, then took care of the city he loved. Always gave the first and last out of his own pocket, just to make sure low-income families have more than one meal to eat a day. Opened up his home to folks who didn't have one and built the Adonia Center for Black Arts in the urban sector of town." He chokes back his permission to cry. "For a man who did so much for everybody, the brother didn't even make 50 years old."

"So, Guy never called the police on the people who did that?"

Luke shakes his head. "The crazy thing is, the fools he caught on camera dumping in his yard were the same ones he helped not lose their homes. They have no idea the hands that fed them knew what they'd done behind his back."

I want to cuss. Guy Miller was a movie in the making. Maybe one I should be filming. I hang onto everything Luke tells me about him until Myzi screams, "It's not fair!" and races from the room. Elaine trails behind her; Luke caves in his seat, helpless. A fresh pang surges through my body, convincing me I'm about to stroke out. I do my best to suck it up, but Luke doesn't miss it. His attentiveness is so in tune with me. Even though we barely know each other, Luke's playing chords on me that haven't been touched in years. I don't have to struggle to be heard by him.

"Hey, with all that's going on, I'm going to get out of your hair, okay?"

"No, ma'am, you're staying here tonight," he informs me without asking. "I won't hear *no*, either. Not after the jacked-up examination that ER doctor gave you. They're lucky I don't go back up there and—"

"I don't want to put you out," I interrupt. "I'll just go back to Temper's house."

"All your people are out of town, right?" My nod is more of an acknowledgment that he remembers me telling him, than me being alone. "Then you're staying here with me. You're not putting me out, and I could use the company with everything that's happening."

A soft knock on the door grabs our attention. Big Luke shuffles inside, the spitting image of his namesake. I try not to gawk at the long-sleeved, plaid pajamas barely hanging onto his frail body. "What's going on, son? Your sister's out there crying. Something happen to Harriet?"

Luke shoots me a look. His mother's been out of their lives since he was 10. "Mom's fine, Pop. Don't worry. Here, let me help you." Luke hops up from his seat and wraps an arm around his father, helping him the rest of the way inside. "Where's your walker, man? You know the doctor said not to walk around without it."

"He's a quack," Big Luke snaps. "Tell him to use that thing himself or shove it up his—"

"Pop!" Luke tries not to laugh, but I lose that fight. I howl from the lowest pit of my belly, drawing the elder's attention to me, his face a cross between bewilderment and excitement.

"Harriet, you're looking good, girl," Big Luke muses with a massive grin. "It's so good to see you smile. You haven't smiled this much the whole time we've been married, girl. I forgot how pretty that smile is. Sexy too." He wipes the saliva trickling from the side of his mouth to his scruffy chin with the back of his palm and winks. "The way baby girl's out there crying, I thought something happened to you. When did you get back from the store?" He shuffles toward me, arms outstretched. I stand up and accept his hug, peering at Luke over his shoulder. I've heard when elders suffer from memory loss, sometimes it's best to meet them where they are. Luke nods his approval, so I roll with it.

"I got back an hour ago," I lie. "Sorry I didn't come tell you."

"That's all right, sugar. Did you get my Cap'n Crunch?" he asks. Luke signals behind his father's back that he'll take it from here.

"Got a fresh box, Pop," Luke tells him. "How about we go to the kitchen and fix you a bowl?"

"That sho' sounds good, son. Let's go." Big Luke turns to me. "Can I get you anything, Harriet?"

"No, thank you. I have everything I need." I flash a smile, and Luke mouths, *thank you*. He takes his father by the elbow and eases him toward the door. As soon as Big Luke steps out, Luke lets him go and tips back inside.

"I appreciate you," he says. "Pop never got over Mom leaving. Some days, it's back to this." He points at the desk by the door. "We picked up some toiletries for you from the store, and Elaine might have something you can wear to bed if that's all right with you. Get some rest, and I'll see you in the morning, okay?"

I love a man who takes control. "Sure. Thank you, Luke."

He nods, walks out, and closes the door. Hopefully, I can take his suggestion and sleep tonight.

TEN

SO, THE SCATTERBRAINED solution the doctor casually rattled off to *fix me* after my examination's been holding me hostage in my car in H.E.C.'s parking lot for the last hour ... *"I know this isn't the news you want to hear; however, I recommend you have a hysterectomy to resolve this issue."*

Chocolate cysts. A by-product of endometriosis. The reason why I've been in a constant state of feeling like my intestines are about to extract themselves from my body, wrap around my neck, and squeeze the life out of me. It's draining and makes me not want to take more than a few steps anywhere because I get so exhausted. It explains the mood swings and why I've been sweating so much. The brain fog and lack of motivation. I thought I was evolving and being strong. Because that's what Black women do, right? Take the punches, slap a steak on the bruise, and keep it moving. As it turns out, I'm actually sick.

Dealing with all this makes me think death is better than hearing I need to choose between perennial pain or giving life.

I wondered if the middle-aged doctor could see past the crow's feet stretching her swamp-green eyes back to tell what I was thinking. Her flat, bland face was utterly devoid of any concern or compassion that would make me comfortable enough for her to put a scalpel anywhere near my body. Sis had the nerve to sit behind her desk, peering at me like she'd just prescribed me some vitamins or something.

I don't have an iron deficiency. I have a defective womb!

"But I want children," I sputtered like a dying transmission.

Did she just *sigh* at me?

A hand flew to her mouth, revealing five fingers of chipped burgundy polish that had been discontinued with Bonnie Bell cosmetics. Trying to convince me that my ovaries aren't necessary, with trifling grooming.

Is her house nasty too?

She snatched off her glasses and laid them on the desk, right next to a picture of her cute little three-piece: two auburn-haired girls and one rusty little boy with sandy hair and a huge, gap-toothed smile.

"Jonica, you're passing out, experiencing level-10 pain, bleeding profusely during menstruation, and watching your quality of life dissipate due to this issue. A hysterectomy is a normal procedure and the only option I can recommend for you to retain your womanhood."

I think I went temporarily blind for a minute . . . or maybe blacked out. The doctor's springy chocolate curls with heather highlights, straight, dry lips, and barren eyes disappeared. Everything in the small room turned black except that picture of her children. Happy. Free. *Living.*

Her mouth kept moving. Some mess about this being the best thing for me and how I shouldn't think of it as not having children but being able to live. To me, every justification for keeping me from reproducing translated to: *Black population control*. I've heard a lot about Black women being swindled into having our reproductive parts cut out, but I never expected it to hit my hungry womb. I refuse to go out like that. One day, I want a family. My part of the *American Dream* deserves the sperm to meet the egg too.

"I'm not even 30," I argued.

She folded her hands and laid them on the desk. Head tilted to the side, just enough for the diplomas and such hanging on the wall behind her head to bless me out in certification.

"I understand how overwhelming this must be for you—"

Do you, though? At this point, I had already scooped my purse in one hand and car keys in the other.

Twenty, nineteen, eighteen, seventeen, sixteen.

Nope . . . I wouldn't make it to zero before I impaled one of that chick's eyes on the end of Temper's house key so she could see how stupid her advice was with the one good eye I left intact.

"I appreciate your time," I lied, "but I will seek other options that won't threaten my fertility. Thanks."

The wooden chair scraped the floor with attitude as I jumped up and bolted toward the door.

"Ms. Burke," the doctor called behind me. My braids flew in my face when I swung around, demanding to know what she wanted. "I've been doing this for years. Please understand this isn't a race thing. It's about taking care of you. Seeing an African American doctor won't change the outcome."

. . . doing this for years.

Years.

How many Black children had she snuffed out with this same advice?

I sucked my teeth, then issued this woman a curt "Thank you for the advice" and bumped my hips right on out the door.

So, I've been sitting here in the H.E.C. parking lot ever since, trying to process what I heard without driving back over to the medical complex and storming into Dr. Reva McShane's office to air my grievances on the end of a baseball bat. I did that once . . . but I promised myself the dirty details would never see the light of day.

My cell rings, snapping me out of my trance. Hudson's picture pops up on the screensaver. The *Golden Girls* theme song I've set as my ringtone sings and thanks me for being a friend repeatedly while I stare at the plain sterling rings stacked on every finger of my left hand. I hover over the answer button for a few, then deciding to go ahead and answer just before the voicemail picks up.

"Yes," I answer dryly.

"You haven't been answering my calls," Hudson grumbles.

"Haven't had much to talk about." The imaginary elephant holding the DNA test I want Hudson to take shakes its rump in my face. I shake it off and check the time floating in the corner of the phone screen. **12:10.** "Kind of early to blast your booty music, isn't it?"

"Where are you?" he overrides my question with his own over the loud music.

"Just got back from a doctor's appointment. Getting ready to go into the school." I wave at one of the janitors rolling a large trash can to the dumpster a few feet from where I'm parked. He waves back with a huge smile and trots the rest of the way to the bin. "What's all that noise?"

"Packing a few things," he says. "That's not important right now. I need to understand why you're wasting time playing around with those kids when we've got a script to revise and a movie to start filming. When are you coming back to LA?"

"Yes, Hudson. I appreciate you asking what happened after I had to be rushed to the ER after nearly dying."

Hudson stops wrestling with whatever and huffs. "Why do the most insignificant inconveniences always end in death with you?" It sounds like he drops a box. "I bet it's not half as serious as you claim. A waste of insurance."

"Chocolate cysts." The diagnosis stubbornly tumbles from my trembling lips.

"What? Why are you joking about food when I'm being dead serious?"

"Do cysts sound like something you eat?" I wave at the janitor on his way back to the building. This time, he jumps in the air and clicks his heels before going on his way. My entertainment for the day.

My eyes latch onto a small patch of skin hanging off my middle finger. I pick at it, waiting. For concern. Shock. Empathy. Some sort of acknowledgment that the man claiming to love me on occasion heard me say I'm near death. Of course, I'm not about to die, but he doesn't know that yet. Because he hasn't bothered asking.

"Help me out here, babe." The exasperation in Hudson's voice burns my ears. "What's the emergency this time?"

I clamp my eyes shut, then pop them open. Everything's the same. All I need is a good 24 hours straight to find the bandwidth not to fall back. A small cluster of clouds that look like they've formed into a dragonfly floats over the car; my stress level deflates, but not enough. I feel so small.

"The other day, I passed out at the park and had to be rushed to the emergency room. I haven't been feeling well lately." *Oh no, are you okay?* He doesn't ask. But I do hear the faint sound of a female voice whispering something I can't make out.

"You said I have IBS. Nothing more than a stomachache," I say. "You also called me irresponsible for soiling your silk sheets when I tried telling you my period was flowing so hard that I was waking up to a bloodbath every morning. Didn't stop yelling at me about it for a full week."

The clouds break, taking my peace with them. A little itch like the one that comes right before your allergies start acting up comes in the back of my nose. I press my nostrils closed, hoping to press it away.

"I have endometriosis, Hudson. I may never have kids."

In a moment I could only have scripted as a plot twist in one of my movies, Hudson doesn't get the chance to react to the diagnosis that could snatch away the future we planned for ourselves. Three kids, four cars, and a two-story mansion in Calabasas disappear with the feminine voice that comes through loud and clear.

"Good. I don't want my baby's father having a pair of ghetto twins."

Skye.

Maybe I didn't hear her correctly over the bell sounding through the outside speakers.

"Hudson?"

"I told you I'd tell her when I'm ready!" My man never learned how to whisper. I clamp my hands behind my head and squeeze my arms against my ears.

"Hudson?"

"Did you hear me, JC?" he asks. "When are you coming back so we can get to work?" I hit video chat, so he can switch over and lie to my face. He declines the call.

"Hold up. I told you me and this baby ain't waiting on nothing, pooh. Your girl needs to know our party of two is about to become three."

Pooh drizzling off Skye's colicky tongue makes me heave. I fumble with the car door, trying to get out without realizing it's locked. My hand curls into a fist, and I beat the window. I don't believe you, Hudson! Finally, the door swings open, and I stumble out. Bend over, heaving, but nothing comes up.

Please, God. Don't let this be real.

"Don't do this, Hudson," I beg.

"Do what?"

"Disrespect me in such an inhumane way," I hark. "Don't turn me into some weeping, pathetic anomaly confined to raising your outside child because I can't have my own!"

I didn't realize my feet had carried me away from the school to an abandoned parking lot nearby. And now, I'm yelling.

"I love you, Hudson. I always have. Please don't return the favor by making me out to be one of these miserable chicks who eats crumbs instead of demanding the entire meal we deserve. I changed for you, Hudson. I changed. So, don't. Just don't. Don't, don't, don't—"

"I never asked you to change."

In the distance, I hear a tussle, like the two of them wrestling, before Skye barks, "Hello?"

"No, I'm not doing this." I trace further out into the field. "I'm not letting you rub this in my face. I'm not fighting over a man."

"Ain't nobody fighting, Jonica. Conflict isn't good for my little queen. Or king." *Breathe, JC. Breathe. One, two, ten. I can't.* "Besides, I've already won."

"How does Hudson know the baby's his?"

Skye erases all traces of the fake Valley girl accent; Oak Cliff—the hood where she's from, appears in its place. "Despite what you think about me, I'm nobody's ho. *That's* how you know."

"Give me the phone, Skye." Hudson tries to get it, but Skye's not having it.

"Shut up!" I hear her smack him. "I'm sorry, I really am. But this isn't about you, Jonica. Your man's made promises that me and this little seed plan on making him keep. So we need to do this little movie together like the professionals we are before I start showing and call it a wrap, m'kay?"

. . . end scene.

Without a word, I press END and disconnect the call. Finally, I wrench forward and throw up. Smelling it makes me want to do it again. I have to get out of here. I grab my stomach, race back to the car, and lean on it with my arms draped over the hood. Then I slide down to the concrete, crying like there aren't cameras all around.

ELEVEN

"GIRL, IF YOU don't stop all that crying, book a flight back to LA, and beat the ancestry off those pieces of slime for disrespecting you, I promise I'm going to jail in your place." Tati kills what's left of her third shot of a blue mystery drink that reeks like turpentine, then belches. The pungent stench floats across the table faster than her rage. "I'm not playing. Fix your face! Because if you don't stop crying, I *will* handle them. And I have the money to bail myself out."

"You're drunk." I point at the empty glass. "That stuff smells like Febreze, and it's got your mind out of whack. Anyway, I don't have to use my fists, I use my words. You know that."

"Good. Then you can use your words to keep my lawyer on standby when I handle it."

I drag my eyes from my full glass of cranberry juice and past Tati's scowl to focus on the FOR SALE sign hanging over Phenom's bar. Florenza's had enough; she told me she's leaving her man and moving back home.

"Temper says don't get mad at the woman. Blame the devil for using both of them," I mumble.

"All right, then tell Temper the devil made me do it . . . and put a few tithes in the collection plate for me when Sunday comes." The more she sips on that drink, the heavier Tati's thick, country-Korean accent grows. Her light, pink-coated lips match her sprouting curls. Her eyes are glazed over in anger.

"You're not hearing me," I argue. "I don't *want* to get drunk, I don't *want* to fight, and I *don't* want revenge. I want . . ."

"What do you want, JC? Huh?"

"I thought I found the one to share bills and the bathroom sink."

"But you ended up with a punk and possibly needing an STD test."

"Don't make me laugh," I protest, giggling in spite of myself. "I don't want to laugh right now. I want to be angry. And I want to throw things. I want to be angry and throw things and verbally assault that wench."

"I told you, you don't have to hit Skye, but a good face mush ain't never hurt nobody. That's grown-women stuff right there."

"Grown women," I agree. "I should've ordered something to eat. Been vomiting all day, but now I want some food. Is that crazy?"

"It's grief. You don't want food, you want your man."

"I wish I had seen this coming."

"There was a whole lot more than this you should've noticed."

"No, before I left LA," I say. "When I first suspected and noticed my stuff missing from Hudson's condo. I should've said something then."

Tati reaches over the table, frown lines fading into a gentle smirk when she takes my hand. "That's classic Jonica Burke. Extending your heart, even to trash who don't deserve it. Don't beat yourself up for wanting to keep the peace, babes." She takes her hand away and claps. "Applaud yourself for being a woman of integrity. Unlike me, who would've already busted every window out of that piece of crap's house and car."

The vision of Tati vandalizing Hudson's things makes me cover my face and laugh uncontrollably in my hands. "You're crazy, you know that?"

"Nope. I'm just a sister with plenty of experience at being a woman scorned."

My cell buzzes. I'm not in the mood to talk until I see Luke's name. In all the drama, I stood him and the class up today—a growing habit with me.

"Hey," I try sounding more upbeat than I feel when I answer.

"Hey, you! I got your text—everything all right?"

Tati mouths, *Who's that?* I turn the phone so she can see Luke's name on the caller ID. She winks, scoots back from the table, gets up and trots off to the bathroom.

I run my free hand through my loose braids and exhale. "I'm sorry about today. I know it must seem like I'm such a flake right now because I keep missing class, but I'm really in this. Normally, I don't break promises or commitments, I swear."

"Don't worry about the documentary. I'm asking if you're all right."

I suck up the last of my tears with a sniffle. "I'm not sure how to answer that."

"What do you mean?"

"Suppose I tell you I need some money, my hair's falling out, or my leg fell off? What would you say?"

"I'd say how much you need, we'll get you a wig, and I'll find you a cane. Next."

Now I'm laughing. Hard. Luke sounds so serious; the perfect comeback.

"You must handle your women well."

"Seeing that I only handle one woman at a time, I do all right. Pops taught me well." The lightness of the conversation deflates as his voice trails off. "Now, can you stop deflecting and tell me what happened today?"

"Please don't ask me how I am. Because then I'll have to tell you the truth. And if I have to repeat everything that happened to me in the last few hours, I'll cry. And maybe throw up. I'm sick of doing both today. So please, I know you mean well, but don't ask, okay? Because I don't want to . . . I can't break in front of you."

"I understand. You don't have to talk, but I want you to know whatever's going on, it's nothing we can't work through together, all right?" *We? Together?* "Where are you right now?"

"I'm at Phenom's. Oh, wait, Myzi's coming in." When she spots me, my new friend rushes to my table. The restaurant's gold embroidered logo on the front of her maroon Polo shirt reminds me that she works here. As soon as she reaches my side, Myzi bends over and gives me a tight squeeze.

"Where were you today?" Myzi demands, face filled with concern.

"Something came up, but I'll be there tomorrow. Promise." I bring the phone back to my ear. "Hey, Luke, I'm going to chat with Myzi a sec. I'll call you back, okay?"

"Cool, but don't think we're finished. I really want to talk to you."

"Hey, Unc!" Myzi hollers into the receiver, waving like he can see her.

"Hug my girl for me, and we'll talk later?"

"Yes, we'll talk." I end the call, relieved to push my latest emotional wound from my mind. "How you holding up, sweetie?"

Myzi shrugs. "Kam won't talk to me. I wish he'd let us be there for him. But he's not answering anything. Calls, texts, DMs. I just don't understand, all I want to do is help."

"Maybe the best way to help your friend right now is to give him enough space to deal with the fact that his dad's gone. I know how that feels."

"I wouldn't know since mine's never been around." Myzi sits across from me and scans the café. "You know, sometimes, I wonder if maybe I served my dad dinner before." She nods toward a handsome, brown-skinned man hovering over a book in a corner booth near the stage. Looks to be mid-thirties; white button-down and royal blue tie a bit much for a date with a book.

Feeling our eyes probing him, the man glances up with a smile, then spears a broccoli head drenched in cheese and stuffs it in his mouth. "For all I know, that's him," Myzi muses dreamily. "He comes in here almost every day and orders three fried chicken legs and two wings, with a side of broccoli and cheese, fried cabbage with sausage, and red beans. Same country stuff I like eating." We study him as he returns to his book and quickly makes the food disappear from his plate while slowly turning the pages.

My head bobs from the stranger to Myzi. "I have to admit, you do kind of look like him. Move a little like him too."

"That's what I'm saying!" Myzi sighs, relieved to have a cosigner for her theory. "Look at his pretend dimples and check out his ears." She pushes one of her ears forward with a finger. "They're as big as mine." She settles back in her seat and crosses her arms over her chest. "I'm telling you, he could be Mr. Daddy. Or any of these people." She plucks the black cloth napkin in front of her from the table, unfolds, and twists it into different shapes.

"Do you want to find him, Myzi?"

"I don't know." She drags her bereaved glower to me through glossy eyes. "Sometimes, I do want to know what it's like to have a father in my life. To show him how good I am at volleyball and soccer. Teach him how to skate. Steal his snacks, make him fuss at me for playing in makeup, tell me my skirt's too short, or watch horror movies with me." She swings the napkin in the air, smirking. "The good thing about not having a dad is that Uncle Luke and Mayor Miller went out of their way to make me believe

I'm somebody, no matter who can't see it. But if my father ever comes around, I won't be mad. We'll be cool. But if he never lets me see his face, I'll still be all right."

"I know you will."

"Can I ask you a question, JC?"

"Yes, you may."

"Is it all right to smile when your heart's broken?" Myzi knows I don't have the answer. She refolds the napkin like it originally was, carefully replaces it on the table, and pops out of her seat. "Don't answer that. I have to go clock in. Will you be here when I get off?"

"Do I need to be?"

"I could use a ride home." She looks hopeful. Up front, Tati's taking the stage with the band. I didn't know she was singing tonight when I invited her up here.

"I got you, Myzi. Go handle your shift, and I'll enjoy the band." She leans over and hugs me again, then darts off to the kitchen, leaving me to scroll social media by myself. Studying my feed, there isn't much interesting going on to make me forget about my own drama. Not even my favorite cooking videos I'm constantly bingeing, even though I never plan on doing anything in the kitchen.

I shut off the phone, prop my elbows on the table, and listen to the band for a while. I don't want to go to Temper's house and sit up alone. Getting a hotel room will only depress me more. And if I go to Tati's, she'll probably have me up drunk-dialing Hudson all night, telling him what kind of scum he is in Korean. So, I'll stay here until closing time, I guess.

Every song Tati dreamily sings in every key akin to a rainbow resonates with my battered spirit. It's obvious the bluesy playlist is dedicated to me.

"Hands down, I gave you my soul, but the return on my investment was a heart grown cold. The best of you turned out to be the worst in me, but the settling stops here. It's not me; it's you, my tragic baby. I may not be able to turn off my love, but I know I can keep you from hurting me."

That one's called "Specifically." I planned on using it as the title track for *Crack Dreams*, but with all the new revelations popping up behind the scenes, all that's on hold.

Tati repeats the verse, then belts the chorus. The lyrics surge through my bones like a codeine-filled pain reliever, draining the betrayal from my veins. Don't know how I'm going to get over this, but I'll start by not placing blame on myself.

Myzi rushes past me, flashing a tight, apologetic smile. She stops at the table next to mine. "I'm sorry, our equipment's not cooperating today, so the lattes are taking a little longer than usual," she meekly explains to the trio of guests—one guy and two females—scowling like she hacked their bank accounts. She takes her time setting the drinks in front of their prospective buyers. Her manners are fine, but the guy seated in the middle, dressed in a white T-shirt, denim jacket, ripped jeans, and oversized beanie, is frothing worse than the steaming cups.

"It takes over thirty minutes to pour three coffees? Dang, you people must be real geniuses." Frothy Guy's condescending drawl oozes from his thin lips, patting Myzi on the head like a stray mutt as she bends in front of him, his hair long and stringy with brown highlights. Lanky frame, rubbery face. A living caricature. The type of slime to make fast-food workers' lives a living hell over cold fries, then brag about it on viral videos.

"Our order's free, right? There's no way I'm paying for this," the skinny chick to the right of Frothy Guy spits her privilege like she's always right. The houndstooth leggings and sleeveless cheetah print blouse topped with a green beanie prove otherwise, though.

One of Myzi's long legs bounces, but she stands in place, taking the insults they spit at her remarkably well. Jaws clenched, she cocks her head to the side and draws a deep breath.

"Like I said, the machine's acting funny. You may want to enjoy your drinks before they get cold."

Frothy Guy sniggers and leans back with his hands behind his head, exposing the Confederate flag on the front of his tee. "You don't have to get all aggressive."

Myzi's chest heaves, but she locks her hands behind her back and stiffens. "Is there anything else I can get for you guys?"

"How about a better attitude, gal." Frothy Guy's wide grin reveals a missing incisor that he should be saving up to get fixed instead of sinking all his cash into what's probably causing them to fall out. Watching the disgusting scene play out, I fold my arms and glance at Tati onstage. Her posture in front of the mic stiffens. At first, my friend was making love to the mic; now, she's got her hands wrapped around the stand like she's strangling somebody.

The blue-eyed brunette rounding out the trio of bullies snatches the lid from her cup and takes a quick sip. "This is disgusting." She spits the liquid back into the cup, then, with zero warning, tosses the drink on Myzi. "Fetch me another drink. This one's cold."

Myzi stumbles backward, and Tati jumps offstage, bolting toward us. I'm so stunned, the best I can do is offer Myzi a stack of napkins to dry off. She snatches the napkins from me, scrubs the coffee off her cheeks and the front of her shirt, then tosses the soiled paper to the floor, glaring at her attacker. Too little, too late, a guy I've never seen before sporting a Phenom Polo shirt rushes over to investigate.

"What's wrong with you people?" Myzi shrieks.

"That's what I want to know." Leaning over the scum who instigated the attack, Tati grabs her cup and snatches off the lid.

"You want to try that trick with a grown woman?" She shoves the cup in the girl's face. "Here, go ahead. You get one chance, so make it count."

The girl's face contorts into an adult sonogram. A tiny voice sounding nothing like she did when she was degrading Myzi eeks out. "Oh my God, you're Tati from Battle Exes," she sputters, not the least bit embarrassed at how badly they've mistreated Myzi. Turns out, racists are fans of Black celebrities too.

"Glad you can identify the chick who's about to bash your face in." Tati grabs her arm, yanking her from her chair, which falls to the floor along with the girl's fedora.

"Wait," the girl's voice quakes, "don't go all-angry-Black-girl on me. We were just having a little fun." The fear of God—or Tati—swims all through her nervous giggle. Tati scoots so close to her that their noses are one sneeze away from swapping fluids. Sis snorts when Tati clenches her arm; she's definitely tinkled her panties a bit.

"Drenching a child in hot liquid with your spit in it is fun, right?" The coffee-thrower's wedge heels barely graze the floor as Tati drags her by the arm over to Myzi. "Apologize."

"Excuse me?"

"You heard me. Apologize to my beautiful friend Myzi here, before I have some 'fun' myself."

"I thought she was one of the good ones," Frothy Guy whispers, but his slick comment amplifies in my ears.

"I *am one of the good ones*," Tati snarls. "In fact, I'm one of the best. Because I'm the one that will whoop your—"

"Oh no, miss. We don't condone violence here." The husky manager manages to pry the woman's dress from Tati's grasp. The girl stumbles backward and wastes no time scampering as far away from Tati as possible. All the hard work getting them apart sends a flood of sweat gushing down the manager's bald head. His attempt to appear he's in control of this mess seriously rivals the ill-fitting khaki pants, putting his *business* on display.

"Are you okay, ma'am?" he asks . . . *her.*

Tati's fists clench, prepared to knock his receding hairline to the back of his neck. Her tiny frame belies her true strength; her muscular biceps pop without effort, quietly joining in the confrontation. "Who are you?"

"I'm the new manager," he spits with his chest, which would be more effective if his voice had more bass to back it up.

"Well, *Manager*, the person you need to be checking on is this baby, *not* her attacker . . . *brother.*" As soon as the words fly from Tati's mouth, the drink thrower bursts into fake tears, forcing herself into hyperventilation.

Acquitted by manipulation.

"Attack? I've never attacked anyone in my life," Coffee-Thrower whimpers. Scanning the crowd gathered around us, sis sounds her lack of accountability to the empathetic hearts beating around her. "My cup slipped, and you people went off on me for no reason at all!" She nods to the crowd for backup. "You all saw what happened. Who attacked who?" Her choreographed ugly cry includes trembling, chest heaving, palpitations, and sniffling . . . only she forgets to insert at least one tear for authenticity.

I raise my voice above the confused chatter swelling around us. "Come on; she's faking! Don't you dare absolve this woman's disgusting behavior behind some counterfeit tears." By the time this runs across the social media feeds, Myzi will be named the aggressor.

Who's going to protect our little Black girls?

Sis knows her emotions are working. That the onlookers witness everything except the fact that she hasn't once apologized to Myzi for what she's done. Myzi's composure is eerily calm. *Don't give them a reason, even when you didn't start it.* I recognize that training from my own mother to deter me from getting mixed up in playground fights, even when I got hit first.

I'm trying to ignore this woman, who's doling out a fresh round of heavier, more tortured sobs. Not one crocodile tear streaks her caked-on foundation. The heavy coal rimming her guilty eyes hasn't even come close to smudging; her incessant wails divide the restaurant like a ripped sheet of paper. Which side will everyone take?

Sis's friends get more intentional about comforting her for show. Frothy Guy clutches her and runs circles on her back with his hand while the other girl pats her shoulder. No one notices the occasional smirk crossing her smug face but me. The manager (whose name I still don't know) also aligns with her. He rubs his coarse hair, then brings his pudgy hands together as if he's about to pray. *You haven't prayed hard enough, brother.* He slides left and folds his hands over his round belly as he rocks back and forth on the heels of his run-over loafers, pensive glare turning the three offenders into victims.

"Ma'am," he addresses Drink Thrower, "I'm Brian, the new manager here. Please accept my sincere apologies and assurance this will never happen again. You have my word." He sidesteps Tati again, who blocks him with her hands like a shield. "Today and next time you come, everything's on me."

"No! Everything's on her!" I point to Myzi.

"Thank you, Brian." Frothy waves a finger in front of us. "You people are way too sensitive. Learn to take a joke. There's no need to act like animals."

Tati shoves Brian out of her way, and the group huddles together like an entire army's coming for them. She darts a finger at Coffee-Thrower. "That one there behaves like a banshee, but *we're* animals?" She scans the crowd, more interested in spectating with raised phones than helping to diffuse the situation. Tati turns from them, bewildered faces convicting the wrong one. "This spoiled, ill-mannered girl behaved like a dog. Next time you call one of us an animal, be prepared to spit teeth!"

Tati lunges for the girl, but Brian blocks her. "Listen, this former employee has a history that keeps repeating itself. In the short time I've been in charge, she simply doesn't live up to the excellence we've come to expect here at Phenom's."

"*Former?*" Myzi and I chirp together.

Brian turns his clammy face to Myzi, looking her in the eyes the way he's failed to do with Tati. "You can expect your last check in a week. You're fired. Hopefully, these nice people won't press charges against you."

"And hopefully, one day, you'll remember your ancestors were once residents of the plantation too!" Tati yelps as Myzi brushes past us and races out the front door.

I'm disjointed, hurt, angry. Helpless. Every one of us is dumfounded . . . except the trio who are exchanging high fives and congratulating Brian for "*taking a stand for what's right,*" as I overhear the girl who threw the drink claiming.

For once, I want to fight. Dejected, I shake my head and race after Myzi.

TWELVE

"**WHAT YOU NEED** is a good smash. I do, too."

"Excuse me?" I don't know what about today's developments makes Luke think it's a good time to shoot a real shot with me. "We haven't even gone out on a date yet."

"Not that kind of smash, JC." Luke chuckles. "Here, follow me." He stands in the comfort of his air-conditioned living room and extends a hand to help me up from the sofa. "Trust me."

Reluctantly, I accept his hand and follow as he leads me to the shed behind the main house. Myzi passed out asleep a while ago after I got her home and cleaned up, but I want to be there when she wakes up. Elaine's not feeling well, today's been messed up, and I just want to help. I'm still shocked about what happened. I make a mental note to call Florenza about the incident later. I know she'd never condone Myzi being fired like this. Not that she wants to go back.

Luke holds my hand as we make our way through the dark house and doesn't let go until we step off the back porch. Except for the crickets, the path is quiet as we stroll across the backyard, stopping when we reach the cute red brick structure that could be a funky she-shed or man cave. The motion sensors flick the outside lights on as Luke unlocks the door and ushers me inside.

"What is this?" I stumble toward one of the metal shelves in the north corner of the mini-house, gob smacked by the porcelain china, old bottles, and thousands of breakables littering the shelves. "You rob an antique store? A hoarder?"

"Only on occasion," Luke laughs. "You like it?"

"It's actually much more organized than my apartment. Except for all that broken glass over there."

With Luke following on my heels, I rush over to what looks to be a graveyard of demolished bottles, plates, and other ceramics lying on a green tarp. My eyes sweep from the fragmented casualties on the floor to six graffiti bubble words painted smack center of the mural on the wall behind them: **Smash Or Pass**.

"All right, I'll admit, I'm a little weirded out by all this. So, before I run out of here, I have to know," I methodically explain, "is this a sacrifice to the ancient china-wear gods or something? I'm not going to come up missing and end up on *Dateline*, am I? Because if I come up missing, maimed, or unalive, Temper will hunt you down, and your body parts will end up in three different states."

"What would my episode be called—*The Cutlery Killer?*" Luke reaches over and strokes my cheek, careful not to mishandle me like one of the fragile items housed in a temporary shelter on the shelves. God, he smells like . . . a future.

"I'd never do anything to hurt you, beautiful." Luke's easy grin turns my trembling legs to jelly. "Don't tell me you've never smashed before? Better brace yourself." He grabs my hand and rushes over to a closet beside the entrance, where he takes out a couple of thick, black work jumpers, tan Timberlands, and work goggles.

"Here, put these on." We dress together in silence. I slide one leg in, then the other. Pull up the torso and push my hands through the sleeves. The dim lighting is a complete contrast to this unsexy ensemble, but since I absolutely trust this man I've known less than a trimester, I roll with it.

We finish securing everything that needs to be zipped or tied and saunter back over to the demolition corner, hand in hand.

From the moment I returned here with Myzi tonight, Luke hasn't let me walk alone. My hand molds perfectly to his.

"Well, here's my secret to relieving stress," Luke says. "The Smash House."

He goes to one of the metal shelving units, grabs an armload of clear plates that look like they came from the Dollar Store, strolls back, and hands me half the stack. I watch while he steps about 10 feet away from the wall, standing guard over the litter of shards on the floor. Without warning, Luke flings a plate against the cherrywood, and it crumbles into a million pieces. He throws another plate, then another, and keeps going until I get the point. He turns to me and nods that it's my turn.

"I'm not so sure about this." I try handing him the plates, but he backs away from me.

"No, ma'am, you won't keep locking this junk in your spirit. Let it out." Luke flashes a quick smile. "Stop playing it small. Especially how you feel." He rewards me with a wink and nods at the plate a second time. "Go ahead. You know you want to. Everyone can use a good smash now and then."

I draw in a deep breath and sail the plate through the air. It lands on the tarp, barely making a thud, much less break.

Luke scratches his head, snickering. "You want to try that again? This time, try actually throwing it instead of like you're setting the table for Thanksgiving."

"You're hilarious." I take another plate in my hands and close my eyes. When I open them, I see Hudson's face on the wall. "That's for you, you sick, triflin', son-of-a ..." The way the plate breaks across Hudson's imaginary face sends an adrenaline rush through my body that's better than any climax I've ever faked with him.

"Yeah, baby!" Luke hollers as the plates crash in four-letter words. I black out and keep going, racing between the four walls, breaking anything I can get my hands on. Luke's right—I've never made love like this.

Euphoric. Orgasmic. Ballistic. Over the last 45 minutes, I've run through the gamut of emotions and still have a million left to spend. I'm not sure when Luke backed off and let me have the floor by myself, but by the time I finish murdering the last of the porcelain baby cow family, he's lying on his side with an afterglow on his face. I've never felt so ecstatic. My toes are curled in these boots. I need another round, an inhaler, a cigarette—something to keep this high from coming down.

By the time I plop down on the floor in front of Luke in my plain gray sweats, his eyes are hooded like he's half-asleep in full-on after-sex glow.

"So, this is how a young, virile man like you makes it without a woman."

Luke's eyes pop open when he hears me, pretending he wasn't drifting off seconds ago. "A brother needs something to hold him over until you come to your senses. How you feeling?" he yawns.

"Better." Luke frowns at my ignoring his open invitation. "Seriously, I'm better than I was when I came in. Nothing like a little destruction to make you forget you're failing at life."

"You're not failing, JC. You just haven't taken the right flight to help you fly." Luke trickles his tongue across his lips. *Please don't do that.*

"You ever heard of the woman with the alabaster box?" I ask.

"You talking about the CeCe Winans song?"

"Not quite, but yeah." I flip over on my side, mirroring Luke's pose, face-to-face, with the attentive lines etched across his forehead and smooth lips. His beard's growing out. Too young for a *sugar daddy*, but old enough to make my legs tighten. "I'm talking about Mary Magdalene. All she had was a bad reputation, and an alabaster box filled with oil. Everybody looked down on her, but she broke the jar open and poured out everything she had on her Savior."

Luke scoots closer to me, and swipes something from the corner of my mouth with his pinky. Or maybe he pretends to. I don't care. He strokes the ponytail flopped over my arm, dropping his voice to pillow talk levels. "I've read about the alabaster box a thousand times."

I draw my lips in. "What we just did, that was my alabaster box. Everything I've been feeling, I got to crack it open. It's hard to love yourself in a world that doesn't love you back."

"You're wrong about that. The world adores you, JC; you're the only one who has difficulty seeing it." His deep-set eyes grow intense. Luke's eyes are searching me now as if his attention is exclusive to me. Part of me is uncomfortable and wants to push him away. But seeing myself in his eyes makes me want to stay right here.

"How did you start smashing?"

"Well, I was 16, and there was this girl, Lola—"

"Not that, silly." I playfully smack his shoulder. "What made you start doing *this*?"

Luke smiles at me. "When you spend most of your time alone like I do, you'd be surprised at the life hacks you find scrolling online." Using his fingers, he ticks off his achievements one by one, like an egghead counting his degrees. "I know how to amplify my speakerphone by putting it in a jar, serve food on smaller plates to make it seem like bigger portions, and use ice cream to stop a headache. I know it all."

"Ice cream for a headache?"

"Apparently, brain freeze stops your head from hurting. Go figure. I find Rocky Road to be especially effective." The way Luke pronounces *especially*—as if there's a "C" in place of the "S" is the most endearing thing ever. I want him to repeat it.

"So, you started breaking stuff because you saw someone do it online?"

Luke lifts his head and glances around the gorgeously chaotic room. "On my thirtieth birthday, Pops flipped out. His faculties had already been deteriorating for years. Forgetting things, seeing things that weren't there, wandering off where we couldn't find him for hours. Bringing up my mom, knowing she hadn't been around forever." A huge sigh gushes from the back of his throat. "Until that day, I thought I could handle seeing the giant I looked up to growing up shriveling before my eyes. But that day at my party, something inside Pops snapped. He was so calm one minute. The next, he was turning over tables, swinging his cane, and cussing folks out. Pops never cussed a day in his life until this disease rotted his brain." He swipes a hand over the beads of sweat trickling down his face. "I haven't celebrated a birthday since that day because that was the day my hero died."

"You know what's crazy? I haven't celebrated since my father died, either. Not once."

"It sucks when the king is dead, huh?"

"I have the broken crown to prove it." My body quivers under Luke's intense stare without budging. I try to escape the pain in his eyes, but he has a solid grip on me.

"My pops has become a living memory, like fate's playing in my face." Luke's speech slows down, almost slurred. "Do you know what it's like having to dress the man who changed your diapers? Sometimes feed him too? Elaine does what she can, but she only has so much physical strength, and I don't want Myzi taking on that kind of responsibility. It makes me so sad seeing how tiny he is now."

"Was Big Luke ever a big man?" I want to know.

Luke nods. "Seemed like he was eight feet tall. Looked like he was straight out of a Marvel comic. Not that you can tell with how he's all hunched over now."

"I still don't get how the breaking comes into the picture."

"After Pops wore himself out fighting me, and I finally got him in bed, I lay down and scrolled for a while until I came across a dude with a smash studio. Soon as I saw all that glass flying, I knew what I wanted to do with this empty house." His disgruntled voice disintegrates into a tunnel of regrets. "On any given day, I'm a barber, home healthcare nurse, teacher, counselor, stylist, assistant, accountant, technical support, customer service, conservator, power of attorney, friend, and even though it's the last thing I want to think about, one day, pallbearer will be added to the list. I'm exhausted, but I'm pushing the best I can."

"You should be knighted. Sainted. Whatever they do for people like you, who listen to people like me whining. The stuff you're dealing with is heavy, man. I'm a tool for dumping my crap on you."

"You're a woman," Luke counters with a hint of admiration. "A woman with loud, boisterous emotions that she's trying to contain in that itty-bitty body until it implodes because she won't let it out. You're too sexy to be this self-deprecating." A glint pops into his eyes that wasn't there moments ago. "You don't have to cover up with me. You're too good of a woman for that."

"How do you know that?"

"Take one old man who confuses you with his deadbeat wife, add a sister with questionable health, a rambunctious, artsy child who's so far from normal it's like she's raising herself, one broke schoolteacher, and you're still here. *That's* a woman."

I close my eyes for a second. If I linger in his eyes too long, *something's* going to happen. "Don't do that."

"Do what?"

"Pretend like I'm not stupid for getting myself into the mess I'm in. Like the blogs and social media didn't foreshadow my fate for hooking up with Hudson." Hundreds of posts bashing our relationship race through my brain. "Here, I thought people were just hating because I was dating a white boy."

Using his elbows as leverage, Luke scoots closer to me like a diamond thief trying not to get busted surfing below laser alarms. I inch toward him too.

"Some folks in our lives are meant to be cautionary tales, JC, not the rest of our story." His breathing grows labored. "Life's about learning the lesson before we turn the page. Don't blame yourself because that guy fell out of formation. I know you don't need saving, but you deserve the kind of love that will set you free."

He scoots closer again, leaving no wiggle room between us. We collaborate on quickened breaths, silent questions that can make or break us swirling around. I'm consumed with doubt; Luke is not. He leans in, cradles my head in his hands, and swallows my transgressions in a single, magnificent moment with his lips pressed to mine. And that's when I finally realize . . . I deserve this.

"Pickles," I blurt when his lips release mine.

"Huh?" Luke's amused and confused.

"Pickles," I stammer again. "They're the most perfect vegetable on earth, and they taste amazing. Nothing tastes better than pickles. Except this."

Luke caresses the back of my head a second time. "I'll take that, I guess," he chuckles. "And if you don't mind, I'll take this too." Before I know it, he steals another kiss. Slow, steady. Emptying me of the toxins I've allowed to infiltrate my body. Luke's affection is an ointment to the battle wounds I've earned over the past month. Life's going in a weird place that I'm unprepared for. But as I return every bit of the fire he's igniting inside me, I know without reasonable doubt I truly deserve this.

I deserve me.

"Stay here."

I open my eyes. "What?"

"Stay here at the house with us," Luke clarifies. "You don't have to waste money on a hotel or stay alone at Temper's by yourself. Elaine makes a mean meat loaf, and Myzi's been happier since you've been around. I have too. So, stay here. We—*I* would love to have you. And you can break anything you want. It's a 24-hour stress reliever at your disposal. You won't be here too much longer, so stay."

Luke says, "Please."

I say, "Yes."

THIRTEEN

SUPERWOMAN TOOK SOME time off.

. . . but even Superwoman needs a few shots of gin after a week off the job.

The close-ups of the kids' feet skating backward across the concrete at Parable Park skit across the screen as I rewind the footage Myzi and I have been reviewing for the last half hour. Between taking a week off from class to get myself together and an extended sidebar with Big Luke last night, I'm spent like the last four quarters at the Laundromat. Totally drained. But time's catching up to us, and if me and my media tech babies are going to wrap this thing up before I fly back to Cali and win the film festival, I've got to pull my head out of the crack of my problems and get stuff done now.

Never mind the off-red, size-small *Poetic Justice* T-shirt that's been part of my wardrobe since junior year, ripped jeans from freshman orientation, and the to-do list I packed in these bags under my eyes. I'm going to need a whole lot of prayer and a caffeine IV to make it through the rest of today—no rest for the weary and no lunch for the starving.

"All your little cohorts are out there smashing square pizzas and corn while you're hiding out in here with me, little girl. Why aren't you hanging with them instead of this old lady?"

Myzi flips the blue-streaked goddess locs I installed over her shoulder, staring ahead at the monitor with a grin. "Because the old lady's kinda dope," she points out. "Even if she is out of touch. Schools don't serve that junk anymore, JC. We hit up Mickey D's across the street."

"You kids are missing out. Back in the day, you couldn't tell us nothing on pizza day."

Myzi clicks her head my way. "Were you all churning butter too?"

I flick her nose with my thumb and middle finger. "Real funny."

"I get it from watching you."

Myzi cocks her head to the side in full editing mode. She works way too hard like I do. Part of me wants to push her out of the room, force her to be a kid. Skip a class every now and then. Hang out more often with the few friends she has. Worry about running for homecoming queen instead of grown-up stuff. But then, I'd be denying Myzi the one thing most Black girls her age lack when the womanly adjectives slapped on them stick: *Being herself.*

"I like hanging out with you," Myzi notes out of the blue. "Even though you disappointed me."

My brows shoot up. "Disappointed? How'd I disappoint you?"

A contented expression I haven't seen from Myzi before briefly crosses her face. "I wanted to hate you. Like, really bad." She stops clicking through the footage and pops her purple-glossed lips. "You're not as into yourself as I thought. You've done a lot for all of us. Makes it kind of hard to hate your guts."

I ignore the smirk creeping across her profile. "I haven't done much of anything."

"Yes, you have." The wireless mouse seems to squeal when Myzi drums it on the table. "There's so much going on around here, but you kind of do this thing where you talk us through the fire at the same time you're putting it out. You're like IHOP. Pancakes make everything better."

I wish pancakes would make my problems with Hudson and my body disappear. But, thanks.

"Let's just say you make it easy to go where the love is." Myzi bites her bottom lip; I bite back tears. "I saw you last night with Pops." She swivels her chair around and latches her eyes onto mine. Sends me back to last night's date with Big Luke.

Somewhere between bedtime and delirium, I was missing my mama something crazy. Couldn't sleep. Barely touched the honey-glazed salmon and broccoli with cheese Elaine cooked for dinner. Whatever Luke, Myzi, and Elaine talked about buzzed right past me. I'm not the roommate-from-hell type (miserable, refuses to replace the toilet paper, or talks through movies), so when everyone else went for seconds, I stopped sitting there with a stupid grin like I wasn't the fifth wheel on this family's minivan before excusing myself from the table.

"I need you, Mom," I whispered to myself when I got back to my room. "You're running around singing to everybody about the goodness of Jesus when I need you here with me. I'm craving eating your banana pudding straight from the pan with a wooden spoon and laying my head on your lap while you stroke my baby hairs and tell me my uterus isn't broken and try convincing me I'm not an idiot for hooking up with the same guy you warned me is a charitable sperm giver who shoots it like he's giving tithes," I spat in a single breath. "I need to hear your '*I told you so*,' Mom! Come home!"

Anyone who's never whisper-screamed at an Instagram picture of their mother lounging in a skimpy, striped, two-piece on a Bahamian beach like I was mine during the wee hours of the morning through a brain fog has never lived.

"You can post, but you can't return your child's texts?" Granted, I hadn't told Temper why I needed to speak to her, but that's the whole reason sis should've called me back by now. Especially since Hudson won't quit blowing me up to explain himself, and I'm close to hearing his excuses. I was perfectly fine scrolling . . . until one of the keyboard crusaders on Temper's page flexed her index fingers to type the wrong message.

She's too old to be trying to be sexy. Showing all her body like that . . . don't she sing gospel? #thatsjustnasty

Go easy on my mother, I shot back at *Keepinthefaith*. Somebody's salty because their thighs aren't bustin' like hers!

Normally, a person of my caliber and influence avoids cyber street fights. My agent advised me not to read the comments on my own page, so I just post and scroll. But come for my mother, and my bank account doesn't have enough to keep me quiet. I would've kept tussling with little Miss "Faith" if everybody else in the comments section hadn't started trying to chat.

Eventually, I shut off my phone, curled up on the cushy brown sectional in the den with a copy of Kennedy Ryan's *Before I Let Go*, and started reading until I could force myself to sleep. After 10 pages in, Big Luke wandered into the room with me.

"Harriet, what you doing in here?" Big Luke's voice inched above a whisper, like the riffs on an old Al Green song when the loving got good. His latter years claimed the armor of his younger days, enshrining him in wrinkles and excess skin. His frail frame quivered beneath the red plaid robe he wore to shield himself from the thermostat being set to snow cone. I wondered what life was like when he was completely coherent—before mental illness, time, and dementia took control of him.

"Hey, you. I was just reading." I closed the book and set it beside me, then swung my legs so my feet touched the floor. "You okay?"

The air shot up full blast, making the scraggly silver strands sprouting across Big Luke's thinning hairline wave like they were blowing kisses. "I'm always good when I see you, but that son of ours been up all night, crying in his room again."

"Luke? Why was he crying?" I wondered which version of Luke was in tears. The one I'm getting to know, or the little boy I've only heard about through bits and pieces.

Big Luke shuffled over to where I was perched. His posture hunched, and pale jaws sunken. His teeth weren't in. "A 10-year-old boy will never understand why his mama doesn't love him, Harry. Cries worse than that time he broke his pitching arm and his team lost the Little League playoffs. That boy misses you. I miss you too." He jammed a small fist onto his right hip and wagged his left index finger at me. "I never done you wrong, and neither have your children. I love you with every part of me that makes sense. More than your own family. That boy does too. Why is it so hard for you to love us back?"

Now, the wrong answer could've set Big Luke off. I can write an entire script before a competent pot of gumbo is fully cooked, but it takes forever for me to figure out how to talk to this man. I've never dealt with anyone who's gone through what Big Luke's experiencing, and it seems like any little thing can fire the bullet. Do I pretend this is normal? Do I try to correct him?

"I didn't mean to." I wrapped my arms around myself, waiting for Big Luke's reaction.

"It's all right, Harry. You were thirty-eight years old, raising a daughter who wasn't yours and a baby boy who unexpectedly came along." Big Luke seemed confused for a second. He mussed his hair while he sucked his gums. "I'm sorry taking care of us was so hard on you. Maybe if my mind was right, you wouldn't have lost yours."

My lips parted, but nothing came out.

"Can we dance?" Big Luke grinned, showing all his gums.

"You know I can't dance."

"Of course, you can't." He smiled bigger like the entire world was in on our secret. "I always promised if you let me lead, I'd take you anywhere you wanted to go."

I smiled back at him, stood, and walked over to him with open arms. "What are we dancing to?"

"Don't tell me you forgot our song?" he chuckled. "Nat King Cole. 'Unforgettable.'"

I nodded, then held up my index finger. "One second," I told him. I raced back to the sofa, grabbed my phone, and pulled up the song. Turned up the volume as loud as it would go, then set it back down and returned to Big Luke. I stepped in front of him, he took me in his arms, and we did our version of a fox trot. Simple, slow, and sweet. By the time I got to bed, I was smiling again.

"You shouldn't have been up so late," I tell Myzi.

"I wasn't really up. Sometimes, I go in and check on Mom to make sure she doesn't need anything or isn't in pain. Besides, I wouldn't have seen Pops trying to dip you if I was in bed."

"He is smooth," I laugh.

Myzi chuckles, then abruptly stops. "I haven't really slept much since, you know . . ."

"Yeah. Me too." We break our mutual glance and turn back to the monitors. "Hey, I think this scene's missing something. The rhythm's off. Can't put my finger on it." I lean closer to the monitor as if that will help me figure it out.

"Kam's missing," Myzi says to the screen. "We need him here because this part's all about him. The close-up of the skate's wheels means we're moving forward instead of backward, no matter what life throws at us." Myzi tosses her braids over her shoulder. The soft wisps of baby hairs crowning her hairline are lightly gelled like artwork. Smooth skin sans makeup maintains a natural glow; her long, fluttering lashes finish her polished look. "We can make it if we just keep on dancing. At least that's what Kam said."

"Is that what you're doing, Myzi? Dancing?"

"What do you mean?" Her brows form a perfect arch.

"All this stuff with Mayor Miller, the drink throwing, balancing school with home. I don't know how you make dealing with it all look so easy, girl. Knocking out straight-A's like none of it ever happened. I would've already snatched out half my hair by now." *Not that I haven't tried already.*

"Oh, ain't nobody playing with my education. I figure if I get the grades now, I can collect my coins later," she smirks. "And I don't let scraps get to me."

"Scraps?"

"The term *haters* is outdated," Myzi sniffs. "People like that are scraps to me. They pick at my plate, but they're not keeping me from eating. At night, I sleep pretty, and they still have to wake up ugly." Myzi's deadpan delivery makes me laugh. She's so serious too. I laugh again . . . until a new text from Hudson pings my cell.

Hudson: When are we going to talk about this?

Me: Maybe when the DNA test proves you ARE NOT the father.

I spare my ex (is he my ex yet?) the six seconds it takes me to tap my fingers across the screen, turn off notifications, and place the cell face down on the desk. "Hey, maybe we can replace the voice-over with instrumental music to kind of smooth out the rough edges and make it less tedious? You get what I'm saying? Let the skates speak for themselves."

Myzi leans forward and cocks her head, scrutinizing. "I don't mind trying anything to make it stronger. I just want to keep Kam's vision for this the same. He was the first one to join the skating club, and it's not right to cut him out because he's not here."

"Of course," I assure her with a hand on her shoulder. "He deserves time off to grieve his father. No disrespect intended." My heart pangs a bit, knowing I've never stopped grieving mine.

"Cool. Then let's do it."

"Go ahead; you already know how to use the editing software—get to splicing." I silently watch as Myzi falls into her comfort zone, confidently clicking on buttons, deleting, reassigning, reviewing, and everything I've taught her. "You're really getting to be an expert at this."

"Well, I learned from the best." Myzi stares ahead, smiling.

"You sure you don't want to go to lunch?"

"Until everything's perfect for Kam when he returns, I'm working."

I lean back in my chair, quietly watching Myzi work for a while. Luke should be back shortly; he had an emergency parent conference, so he skipped lunch with me and the kid.

After a few more minutes pass, I pick up my phone to see what's happening in the world outside of here. More messages from Hudson, without the decency of a courtesy beg to sway me to forgive him. Yawn. Take a second to scroll through the rest of my notifications and notice a missed call from Temper. I dial her, but she doesn't answer. The news I have to share doesn't deserve a text or voicemail, so I don't do either one. Thinking of my mother suddenly drops an idea on me.

"What if we do something special to honor Mayor Miller?" I slap Myzi's shoulder when the thought hits me. She answers with a confused question mark etched across her face. "I know the family held a private funeral to keep down the confusion, but I know you all want to say goodbye too. So why don't we do a memorial our way? You all said the man loved to party. Well, let's make this his last party on earth!"

Myzi sits back, eyes popping with intrigue. "That would be so dope! We can skate, have some spoken word and art, just the way he loved it. Oh my God, Parable's about to be lit!" Myzi's heart pounds in my eardrums. Her smile has never been so wide. "We're going to send our friend off with a skate tribute!"

"A skate tribute," I repeat.

We hug, then put our heads together until Luke and the rest of the kids return to class. This isn't just the chance for the kids to say goodbye to Mayor Miller; it's my chance to say goodbye too.

Even if Daddy isn't around to hear me say it.

FOURTEEN

"OH GOD, I think I broke my nose!"

I squeal into my hands clamped over my mouth, trying to squelch the sting surging through my entire face. I'm seeing stars and double everything. I'm scared to pull my hands away to see what damage the clumsy museum wall did when it smacked into my face. Obviously, it's not the wall's fault, but I need to blame something for my slamming into the darn thing on these skates.

Luke's face is a concoction of bewilderment and amusement. "Here, let me take a look." He slowly pulls my hands away from my butt-hurt face. "There's no blood. I think you're good. Do you want me to get you some ice?"

"No ice, but are you sure I'm okay?" Of course, now my eyes are running, which is the one time I actually decided to throw on some makeup to be cute for Mayor Miller's memorial! Now, I'm positive it's ruined.

"I'm not going to lie. I am concerned about that eye. It looks like it's swelling a bit," Luke breaks the bad news with a wounded sigh that sounds like I feel.

I cup my hand over my left eye, which is throbbing pretty hard now that he says it.

"What should I do?"

"Get out of those skates, then take a minute to be alone with your father. I don't want you breaking anything." Luke nods toward an oil painting on the wall.

Daddy.

I almost forgot. It was Luke's surprise for me that started all of this. When I saw the last self-portrait Dad painted before he died prominently displayed in the middle of the exhibit wall, I forgot I still don't know how to skate and snatched away from Luke. I proceeded to sail right across the floor like a runaway shopping cart on a parking lot . . . and plastered face-first into the wall. My face hurts like hell, and my entire body's telling me to go there.

But Daddy looks amazing.

"You could've at least given me a head's-up that you were going to let me go." Luke gently chastises me without raising his voice or laughing at me.

I point to Daddy's portrait. "And you could've let me know this was here."

"Then you wouldn't have been surprised, right?"

I fake-scowl, then extend my hand. "Here, can you roll me back over there?"

"Are you surprised?"

I nod.

"Are you happy?"

"I couldn't be happier."

"Then let's go see your father." Luke wraps an arm around my waist and escorts me over to the wall. If he wasn't helping me get around on these things, I probably would've broken my tail. I don't know what gave me the idea to have a skates-only memorial when I can't stand more than 30 seconds on them. It's a hit, though. The town loves it.

Luke positions me in front of the portrait and holds me steady. My knight in shining armor, the man who cradled me, defended me, and dared the world to go against me, stares back at his pride and joy with adoration. His massive grin makes it feel like he's here in the room, like he never left me.

I remember walking in on Daddy painting this painting before I left for Cox.

"Why do you paint so many self-portraits, Daddy?" I stood behind his chair and wrapped my arms around his shoulders.

"Because when I'm gone, I hope everyone will always remember my smile," he said.

I ease my fingers onto the brown hues enriching his cheek. Stand there for a minute, thinking about birthdays.

After all the guests who bombarded me for my ninth birthday party left the house, I was about to settle into bed when Daddy sat me down for our annual birthday talk. Life, wisdom, get good grades, boys are nasty, wish Temper was here . . . I could make a PowerPoint presentation based on what he would say before he said it. Still, I loved listening to my old man, always coming at me all awkward, from a place of love.

"Who's Daddy's favorite girl?" he asked.

"I am!" He flinched when I yelped in his ear.

"And what's Daddy's favorite girl going to be when she grows up?"

"A preacher."

Yeah, I know. That was never going to happen. But with Temper on the road so much, she missed all my milestones: losing my first tooth, my first and final dance recital (I think we all know why), my first crush. My first kiss. She wasn't even there to help when I picked out the purple-sequined dress I wore the first time I was crowned homecoming queen. Don't get me wrong, Temper loves me. There's no doubt about that. Whenever she was home, she was all in, like she was trying to win a prize for making up all the time she missed. But she had to be present to be engaged. So, no matter what it took, I did my best to keep Daddy at home.

He gave up a lot for me, even declining out-of-town preaching engagements to make sure I wasn't alone.

Nope, I didn't want to be a preacher. Not even sure where to find all the psalms (thank God for smartphones and Google). But if it meant at least one of my parents was going to be at home, then preaching the gospel was where it was at back then. The irony is, once I got close to the age of consent, Jesus took Daddy from me anyway.

Daddy's hazel eyes turned serious, boring straight through me. *"As good as that sounds, you don't have to preach or follow in my footsteps to make me love you, baby girl. Because I already do, and I always will."*

Daddy tugged the thick pigtail grazing my shoulder. I'll never forget how his smile made me feel like my happiness was the most important thing in the world to him. I've never felt like that again.

"You're a creative storyteller and pretty good with that camera we got you for Christmas," he said. *"Absolutely superb for a nine-year-old. Better than most professionals. Spike Lee better watch his back!"*

We high-fived; I grinned with my mouth closed because the front tooth I knocked out during soccer hadn't been fixed.

"If you want to make movies, then that's what you do. And don't you let me, your mother, the church, or any devil in hell stop you. You got that?"

"Yes, sir."

Daddy set my feet on the floor and took me by the shoulders. Pressing his index and middle finger together, he tapped me between my eyes, followed by his own, to make sure I was paying attention.

"Let's try this again. What's Daddy's favorite girl going to be when she grows up?"

"Everything!" I hollered.

"Not that you can't be, but you don't have to stress yourself out trying to be." Daddy's hearty laugh sent goose bumps up my arms. *"Listen, you don't have to kill yourself trying to be everything*

to everybody, baby. There's only one of you; once folks see they can't squeeze any more juice out of you, they move on to the next piece of fruit. Got me?"

"Yes, sir." I nodded for emphasis, then tugged the bottom of my Sailor Moon T-shirt.

"Why do you think Daddy shuts down his phone every day by 5:00 p.m. unless it's an emergency?" I answered by shoving my hands in the pockets of my pajama pants. "I set boundaries because these folks ain't gone kill me. I have a life, and I have your mother and you. Nothing means more to me than that." He flicked my nose with a smile and took a deep breath.

"There won't be anything about sacrificing myself for somebody else's happiness on my headstone when I die. You have a long way to go in life but don't let it be on yours, either. Cool?"

"Cool, Daddy!" I kissed him on the cheek.

"So, we're going to make movies or whatever makes Jonica happy, right?"

"Yes, sir," I chirped.

"Promise?"

"I promise, Daddy."

I don't realize I've answered aloud until Luke lifts my chin with his hand and wipes my tears. "I'm sorry, JC. I found this painting in the stack Guy was planning to hold for an exhibit for later this year. Your father was quite the artist. I guess I thought you'd be happy to see this. I must've misunderstood."

Luke dries the rest of my tears like he's been salvaging them for years.

"I'm overwhelmed, that's all. But I am grateful." I glance at Daddy, then back to Luke. "Thank you for this, Luke. For everything. I can't thank you enough."

"Your smile is thanks enough." Concern washes over his face. "I really think we need to get you checked out. Your eye's starting to turn colors and getting puffier."

"If you think I'm missing any part of this tribute, think again. I won't." I slip from Luke's grip and balance myself. "What I look like doesn't matter right now. We'll take care of it later, okay?"

The tiny hairs on my arms prickle beneath the thin fabric of my white peasant blouse when Luke gently grips them to keep me upright. Thank God my Aristocrat foundation (#900 Chocolate Mouse, thank you) didn't smudge his white Polo. Not that anyone would notice; his scruffy face is stealing all the feels.

"Alright, whatever you say. But as soon as the DJ plays the last song, we're going to get you fixed up, okay?" Luke's authoritative tone hits all the right places on my body. I squeeze my legs together to keep it from answering back, even though part of me wants to disagree with him, just to hear him take charge again.

"Fine," I concede. "Now, will you stop worrying about me so we can finish checking everything out? And Luke?"

"Yeah?"

"This really was nice of you. I didn't know how much I needed it until now."

"That's okay, JC. I did."

"Because the earth was too small to hold you,
We have to say goodbye
Living on concrete dreams, frozen in time, it seems
To the laughter you committed
And your heart that was fully submitted
Set heaven ablaze, do that thang
We'll hold you up down here
Your heart was more than Man's empty worth
We got you down here,

We're going to finish the work
And when it's time to meet again
You're going to see what you started
Was more than empty words
You didn't mean much to them,
But you're a hero in our eyes,
You did the work; now rest,
And in the end, we will all rise!"

Two spotlights revealing a couple of boys on skates come on either side of Reelz Tha Poet as the red light she's rhyming under fades to black. The skaters spin in place to the backdrop of a hip-hop violin instrumental, bending, squatting, stretching their arms completely around their bodies, and contorting themselves into shapes I'm almost certain God never intended for man. It's so enthralling. The standing-room-only crowd is totally mesmerized.

The music comes to a screeching halt; Reelz races through the boys on her white skates splattered with yellow, blue, pink, green, and purple paint.

"When it seemed like we weren't gon' make it,
You taught us to try,
We won't give up; we won't give in,
Fly, Mayor, fly!"

Reelz skates a slow circle (frontward and backward) around the center of the stage in the middle of the floor seven times. By the time she finishes, "Scream" by Michael and Janet Jackson blasts through the speakers. She rolls center and skids to a stop. This time, a boy and a girl slow roll in front of her, holding a life-sized canvas with Mayor Miller's likeness. They casually glide in place like the King of Pop would have, popping their heads left and right until another group of skaters roll up. Together, the 10 of them execute a fusion of popping, krump, and African choreography in perfect synchronization on wheels.

When the song is done, the group parts center, leaving five skaters assembled on each side like they're setting up for a line dance. Myzi bolts through the middle in a white, knee-length baby doll dress splattered with yellow, blue, and red. A crown of orchids frames her head; she turns and faces the painting of Mayor Miller. Her long braids free fall over her shoulder as she extends her left arm and slowly draws it back in.

"You were never sad, never angry," Myzi announces with her back to us. "You were grace when we didn't even know we needed mercy. You showed us who we are and proved who you claimed to be. They called you Mayor, we called you Wheels. Because that's where you lived life the best and taught us to do the same too. We love you, *Wheels*. And we'll never forget you!"

"Rise" by Katy Perry slowly engulfs us as the skaters exit, allowing Myzi to perform the most eloquent, poised, lyrical solo I've ever witnessed in front of a silent video of some of the mayor's best skating caught on film. A eulogy in motion. The gracefulness she's flowing in says everything the awestruck room wants to say and probably should've told the mayor while he was alive to hear. Grief comes in spurts—it doesn't stop just because someone's tired of hearing how we feel. Myzi's fluid movement tells us that. Folks can choose not to hear us, but we don't have the choice to pause the pain.

Myzi hits every nuance in the music, rising and falling with the crescendo of Katy's commanding vocals. Suddenly, the other skaters rush in, enclosing a circle around her, trailing behind Reelz.

"DJ, if you will!" Reelz hollers.

Suddenly, the song Myzi played at the park weeks ago— "Colors," takes over. The kids break out in a flurry of spins, dips, and tricks that would send me to the ER if I tried them. They skate throughout the room, mingling with the rest of us who can't really skate, but follow dress code: *Skates only, no shoes*.

Luke stands behind me, arms wrapped around my waist. Somehow, it just feels like that's where I should be. I settle my back into his chest, letting his steady breathing keep the tears from spilling while we watch the kids do their thing.

Just when we think the kids are done, they jet to the center, forming a cluster. "Echo who you are, echo who you are!" they chant in unison.

"What does that mean?" I whisper to Luke.

"That was Guy's mantra: Don't let anybody treat you like a color or low-hanging fruit. Let your life echo who you truly are."

"Right. Echo who you are," I repeat to myself.

The entire room connects with the chant. I wonder if Tati can flip it into a song for me, if I could only find her tail. I hate when she ghosts me like this. But I have to shake the feeling something's wrong with her and be present in this room.

The chant ends, and the skaters separate and kneel on the floor on one knee. We watch another video of the mayor dressed in a plain white T-shirt and jeans skating. Like he was preparing for this day. At the end of the video, he jumps into a toe-touch; the frame freezes there on his glorious smile. Myzi skates over to Kam, leading him to his friends, who get up and embrace him in a group hug. Confetti shoots from the ceiling like an explosion of paint.

Following the kids' lead, everyone cheers and wraps their arms around the person nearest them. I don't know why, but I guess the moment's got me in my feelings. Maybe that's why I face Luke and press my lips against his.

"Jonica?" I snatch away from Luke to face the male voice thundering from behind me.

Hudson's staring us down, bewildered.

See, this is exactly why I don't do funerals.

FIFTEEN

"I'M STILL NOT understanding why you're here, Hudson. Why are you tracking me through my phone?" I throw my hands on my hips, indignant. "And isn't that illegal, by the way?"

"Because you haven't been answering my calls, so I decided to see what's up with you face-to-face. And it's not against the law. It's called a welfare check," Hudson hisses between clenched teeth. "Good thing I showed up. I had no idea I'd find you all hugged up with this nig—"

"Hold up, man." Luke's voice dips so deep, I bet the bass in it grabs hold of Hudson's prostate. He's so bold, he checks Hudson with his arms still wrapped around me. "Listen, I don't know you, but you better show me and her some respect." He tightens his grip. Sequestered by his masculine energy, I have to remind myself that God is watching.

Hudson's ears and cheeks start resembling the lobsters he drops hundreds of dollars on almost daily. Torn between a street fight and running, my eyes dart to the fist thumping against his left thigh. "What happened to your eye? Did this nigg—"

"I already told you once to watch your mouth, and I don't repeat myself often," Luke snaps. "Remember what your teachers taught you in elementary school? If you can hear me, clap three times so I can make sure you understand."

140

Hudson claps slowly as his brass balls carry him to my shared space with Luke. He stops so close, I feel threatened. Not physically, but by his adulterous audacity.

"I don't know who you are," Hudson says, "but this is between me and Jonica. Why don't you mind business that's yours?"

"You made it my business when you took it upon yourself to show up at *my* event, in *my* town, around *my* kids. This isn't one of your red carpets, son—don't bring that Black-curious mess here." Luke lets me go and cracks his knuckles. "You're looking real miserable right now, stalking JC."

Hudson draws me in and kisses me. He always does that in the presence of men he's not familiar with. Marking his territory. "I'm not the one sniffing around another man's woman," he says when he draws his lips from mine. "So who's the one looking desperate, bro?" He pokes his small chest out and pops the collar of his long-sleeve plaid shirt.

"It's all grins and giggles over here, chief. But we can make some unsolicited noise if you want to . . . *bro*." Luke's ready to earn a mug shot in my honor, but I won't let it get that far. The testosterone's raging, but the men's hushed tones make the mingling guests utterly oblivious to what's happening over here, and I want to keep it that way.

"You sure you want to try something on those things, my man?" Hudson points to Luke's skates.

"It ain't the skates you need to be worried about." Luke's biceps flex as his fists clench.

"Let's not make a scene, Luke." The way my hand so easily flies to his chest feels like we've got more history than we do. "Please excuse us for a minute so I can get this sorted out."

Luke's eyes say he's not convinced that's a good idea. I can tell he'd do anything to protect me. Anything. "If you need me . . ." his instruction trails off. I know the rest.

Hudson's scowl pummels the back of Luke's head as he glides to the buffet table where Kam's desperately trying to hold it together. My heart shreds for that kid. His curls have gotten longer since the last time I saw him, tumbling over his eyes like pollen blowing in the wind. Luke stretches his arms, and Kam immediately falls into them.

"Come on, help me over there."

Hudson tears his scowl away from Luke, takes me by the arm, and helps me roll over to the mayor's photography exhibit in a secluded corner. I brake right in front of a group shot of the skaters posing in front of H.E.C., taken a week before Mayor Miller's death. Stare at it through my throbbing eye, then take a deep breath.

Let's get this over with.

Hudson's messy hair and the scraggly strands on his chin failing to form a competent beard are more annoying than his unmitigated gall to step up in here.

"So, what is this about?" I demand.

"This is me taking time out of my busy schedule to come all the way to this hick town to reason with you, only to find out you're down here practically holding that dude's balls in your hands!"

"Don't be crass, Hudson." I want to smack the hypocrisy out of his mouth, but this isn't the place. "And don't even dare try turning me into the adulterer here—that honor belongs to you." I jab my pinkie finger on the bridge of his narrow nose. "By the way, do I need to get tested? Your baby mama's squatted on way too many laps for me not to feel like I've been compromised."

An insipid gurgle crawls through Hudson's pressed lips. "Something funny?" I ask.

"Just how ridiculous you're being right now, Jonica."

"Stop calling me Jonica!"

"Why? It's your name, isn't it?"

"Right now, your calling me by my government name feels like a violation. So I need you to stop. Like, *now.*"

The tiny freckles on Hudson's cheeks dance around like tiny little goons, bullying me. I don't turn my head but feel Luke's eyes boring into the back of my neck. I squat, quickly unlace and snatch the skates off to rectify this situation flatfooted. I whip back up, staring into Hudson's colorless face. He jams his hands into the pockets of his navy Dockers with a sigh.

"Look, I didn't come here to start trouble. I just want to know what's going on between you and that guy."

"*That guy* is my friend." I leave the insinuation dangling between my brick-tinted gloss and Hudson's perked ears.

"All right, then why are you here with your *friend?*"

"Because you're the type of guy who tells me to make you a sandwich."

"I'm confused, JC. I thought we were talking about us."

I glance over my shoulder at Luke. "Maybe I need a man who asks what he can cook me for dinner after a long day instead of ignoring me and asking me to fix him a sandwich. Take the burden off me for a change. Better yet, sometimes, it just helps to surprise me." I drag my eyes from Luke to Hudson. "Maybe I need you to surprise me and prove that our relationship still has a pulse. But not like this. This isn't a surprise, it's an ambush."

I walk a half-moon around Hudson and back. Dangle the skates from one hand and use a nail from the other to pick a popcorn kernel I'd eaten before the memorial from my teeth.

"It's been a long day, there's a million people here, and considering the occasion, it's highly inappropriate." At least I can delay the inevitable, for now. "Let's not try to fix us here. We can talk later." Suddenly, I'm light-headed, and the pain in my belly comes firing back.

"Hey, are you okay?" Hudson takes my elbow, keeping me from using the concrete floor as an air mattress.

"I'm a little woozy, that's all. Must've hit my head harder than I thought." *Stop looking at me like that! You don't get to care.*

"Can I get you something, Jon—uh, JC?"

"A cup of raspberry lemonade sounds about peachy right now." I reach up and slide the band off secured around my hair, letting my braids tumble to my tailbone. Should relieve the migraine I feel coming on.

"Blue. Your hair looks good like that." Hudson points to the sky's reflection weaved throughout my locs to match my tattoos.

"Thanks." I press my lips together, so Hudson won't expect us to start devising the cure for the cancer devouring our relationship before fetching my drink.

I cock my head to the side. A silent, *yeah, buddy—I hope you've learned how to beg since I've been gone.*

Hudson excuses himself with a nod and crosses the room over to the buffet area. Stops less than an inch from bumping Luke's shoulder. Glances up at that six-foot-plus frame and maneuvers around Luke like they're rivals. He takes several steps, stops, and glances over his shoulder. Hands travel to the brown leather belt securing his slacks like he's ready to drop his pants and whip out his manhood.

Luke returns Hudson's favor with furrowed brows scribbling a question: *What?* Sends Hudson on to the punch bowl, deflated. I watch him fill a cup with red juice and stroll back over to me without looking Luke's way.

"Appreciate it," I tell Hudson after he hands me the cup, then gulp the cool liquid until it's half gone. He's watching me the way he does after we make love. Drenched, musty, disheveled, and wanting to spoon forever.

Hudson takes off his glasses and cleans them on the bottom of his shirt. "Are you ready to explain what's going on?"

"I'm sure my eye looks much worse than it feels," I murmur. "Can't get my balance on these stupid things." I hold the skates in front of his face. "Face planted into the wall, no big deal."

I don't flinch when he reaches for my chin and lifts it for a better look. "*No big deal* is a nasty shade of purple and red."

"Like you can tell on my black self," I laugh. Hudson doesn't. "Why do you do that to yourself, JC?"

"The same reason you do." I finish the punch and stare at him. "Your lips are cracked."

"You know I bite my lips when I'm stressed."

"Or, when you're stressing me. Skye know you're here?"

Hudson jerks his head back and blows in the air like I'm getting on his nerves. "This isn't about Skye. I flew out here to work things out between us."

"Right, because Skye means nothing to you, this was all a big mistake, it will never happen again, you love me, and you're sorry." I drop the skates to the floor and applaud in his face. "Did I miss anything?"

"Don't do me like that, babe."

I lean forward, scanning the room as if I'm searching for the person Hudson's referring to. Sure as hell can't be me. "Don't do you like what, Hudson?"

"Don't talk at me like I'm—"

"Stupid, ridiculous, unredeemable?"

"I was going for something a bit less hurtful, but okay. You're right about all of it. The thing is, I'm here, right?" He slides his glasses back on, jams his hands into his pockets, and peers at Myzi, skating in our direction. "Let's talk this out without an audience. Please?"

Myzi slow rolls past us, holding a paper plate piled high with finger foods. She brakes lightly, pretending not to eavesdrop on Hudson and me as she bites into a jerk chicken wing. I make eye contact to let her know I'm all right, and she skates in the opposite direction.

"Why should I give you a chance to make another fool out of me, Hudson?"

"Because the best of you redeems the worst of me." Humility seeps through his pores in the form of tiny beads of sweat trickling down his face. His shoulders slump, eyes water—the closest I've ever seen him come to crying. "You're the most loving person I know, JC. Yours is the purest heart ever to consume mine, and I need that to keep going. Do you hear me? I need your resilience to help me make it." He takes my empty hand, leans forward, and nuzzles his face in my hair. "I'll die without you." His voice is thinner than a single strand of hair.

My spirit leaves my body, ready to push me off the ledge I've been teetering on for months. An excruciating burst of pain jutting against my belly is far too familiar. The cysts feel worse than they've ever been.

I bend down, pick up my skates, and hand them to Hudson.

"Here," I say as I give them to him.

"What's this?" He sucks in the tears from two seconds ago like a vacuum.

"Follow me so that we can clear the air."

SIXTEEN

*"**WHY ARE YOU** mad at me for being upset that I got dragged into a polygamous relationship that I never agreed to, Hudson?"*

"Skye manipulated me, baby. It will never happen again."

Yep, that's the hill my cheating boyfriend chose to die on, sitting stiff-straight on the mattress in his hotel suite after hauling me out of the memorial. *"Why are you sitting way over there on that chair?"*

"Because I'm creating enough space between us while I decide if jail's really worth it."

My stone-cold delivery broke Hudson's eye contact. He shifted his weight to his left hip and crossed his legs to keep me from getting any ideas about doing damage to what's between them. I glowered at him as hard as my face would get, watching him squirm while I shot down the litany of excuses he came up with to cover his dirty indiscretions.

When Hudson followed up with, *"You sort of drove me to it,"* without an ounce of humility, I could've slapped myself for following him here.

"Hudson, I keep waiting for you to conjure up an inkling of sincerity or something to motivate me to stay in this thing and fight for us, but you can't even defend yourself without plagiarizing me." I folded my arms across my chest with my lips pressed. *"You're just going to sit there looking dumb like you don't know what I'm talking about?"*

"I, uh . . ." Hudson babbled something, but all I heard was bull.

"Reciprocating Grace. *The women's fiction book I've been working on, remember? I've only been reading bits and pieces of the manuscript to you for over a year now. Every life raft you've thrown at me tonight is a direct quote from my book! You're using my own words against me!*"

Hudson's bushy brows formed a perfect arch. "*Oh, I thought it sounded familiar.*"

That's when I should've left.

Forty-eight hours later, I'm wallowing in the aftermath of Luke.

"You don't have to leave, JC. Seriously, I want you to stay." Luke delivers the news from the entryway of his guest room to my back as if I'm not already aware. "My sister's been feeding you so well, you can't just eat and run." There's a tinge of sadness in his joke.

"Maybe I've eaten enough."

As I quickly jam my things into my bags, I command my heart to expunge from my mind the visual of Luke in his plain white T-shirt and camouflage shorts that hug his perfect rear.

"Are you sure you won't stay here with us?" Luke's voice is jovial, but the hurt from my decision to leave with Hudson and work on us one last time abruptly rises, then falls. "Why won't you turn around and look at me? Can't you at least do that?"

"Because we're done editing the documentary, and I don't want you to see what *Boo-Boo the Fool* actually looks like in person."

"You're not a fool."

"Yeah, well, remind me of that in a few months when I'm wandering down Rodeo Drive with my future mother-in-law in search of what's left of my brain." I ignore the sound of Luke's feet dragging across the carpet, calling me crazy. Maybe I am. But I have to know if there's any chance left for Hudson and me. I have to. So, I ignore Luke and stuff the last of my clothes in my pink suitcase.

"So, that's it? You're just going to take off?"

"Looks that way." I'm being a turd, but if I give even the tiniest inkling that my feet feel like cement blocks and my heart's ripping in half, I'll never make it out that door.

"I appreciate you letting me stay here and everything you've done for me, but it's time to stop imposing upon you and your family." My pulse lodges in my throat behind the lame excuse. "Let me hurry up and get my stuff so you can enjoy the rest of your Sunday." I toss a pair of red and white Vans in the case and my collection of multicolored tanks on top of them, stuffing the bag like I'm on fast-forward.

"*Impose on me and my family?* Do you *know* how you sound right now, JC?" Luke fires at my back. "Listen, I get it. It's not like we're in a relationship or anything, but since *Black Curious* showed up in town, you act like we never happened, and I can't accept that. I won't."

He waits for me to interject. Any observation I can make about the outcome of this situation will make me look like the villain, so I respectfully decline the invite to jam my size 10 foot into my mouth. The deep breath Luke takes almost sucks me in like a vortex, which would be great if it'd spit me in an alternate universe where I meet him first.

"Remember when you were on the *Ellen DeGeneres Show*, and you told her that no matter how hot the weather is or how many you have, you're obsessed with buying blankets because being wrapped in them makes you feel loved?" Luke rubs his hands together, waiting. Either for me to get some sense or deciding whether he wants to give up on me. "For me, perfect love is the moon."

Luke's words freeze me. I glance toward the entryway to my right, with my head angled straight enough not to look directly at him; my stiff posture tells him it's safe to elaborate.

"Every day, the moon shows a different part of itself. Sometimes, we see half of it; other days, it's transparent, and sometimes, we get the fullness of it all." He pauses to swallow.

"No matter how much of it we see, the moon's always whole. Kind of like how I feel when I'm with you." He inches closer. "You see yourself in fragments, but I see you as a whole. And no matter how much you see, you'll always have all of me."

A shaky, noncommittal, halfhearted nod is all I have to offer.

"I'm a patient man, JC. Probably one of the most understanding you'll ever come across." Luke's voice grows thick like he's wading through mud. "But I'm also not a brother who's passive about what I want. I'm too old to play games and too young not to live."

He spins me around, arresting my eyes with his. His hands are clamped on my shoulders; my knees struggle to stay upright. "I'm not ready to go back to life without you. You've wrecked me in every possible good way, and I refuse to deprive myself of how I feel when I'm with you."

I try looking away but can't. Because once I do, I'm admitting that I don't want to deny myself of the possibilities standing in front of me, either.

"Luke, please. Don't say something—"

"—that you'll regret later?" he finishes for me. "Because I mean everything I've said from the moment you barged into my life. I hate how you keep promising old pain to new possibilities!" He sucks in a deep breath and brushes the braids over my shoulders like he's stealing every thought in my mind that doesn't end in his favor.

"I can't keep pretending that life exists outside of fairy tales, Luke."

"Who's a fairy tale?"

"You are!" I lay a hand on his chest; the fire I feel burning through his shirt's thin fabric makes me snatch it back. "How you're always coming to everyone's rescue, the way romance oozes from your pores without even trying, and that freaking altruistic attitude that makes you show love to everyone who doesn't deserve it, especially me! It's all a fairy tale! I don't deserve you!"

"Stop it!" Luke says. "I refuse to witness another Black woman's spirit die in my face because some fool doesn't recognize her worth or watches her devalue herself. If you think I'm going to let a grown woman who has an entire generation affirming and rooting for her go out like this, then I'm not the man you think I am."

"I can't do this, Luke."

"At some point, you must be accountable for yourself. Go to church, get some stuff and smash it, get some therapy. Do something other than just sitting here pretending you're okay when you're not. Just stop hiding behind trigger warnings to avoid accountability to yourself." Luke digs his hands into my braids and pulls my face closer. Every part of me wants to give in. To stay here in this world where I fit in with this piecemeal family who've inexplicably become my universe in less time than it takes to birth a child.

My left hand finds its way to Luke's back; my right arm falls lifelessly against my side. "Don't, Luke. Please." My husky voice doesn't sound like it belongs to me.

A slight gust of air escapes Luke's parted lips. "Why won't you let me love you?"

"Because you make too much sense. And when everything adds up, I know I'll never turn back."

"You can beg, but I'm never letting you go." Luke buries his face in my hair. Kisses the top of my head like he wishes his lips landed somewhere else on my playground. "I don't care how much you try walking out of my life like I don't belong in yours, but I'm staying right here. Do the fool if you want to, but I promise, I'm not going anywhere." He lifts his head and pulls me closer. "When you're ready for your *one day* to become your *day one* . . . I got you. Always."

And then, without fear, warning, or justification, Luke consumes my lips with his. He tightens his arms around my waist like mine is the first face he sees when he lands on American soil after being deployed for years. I inhale him like a savage, reveling in the masculinity oozing from his pores. Give in to myself so that, for once, I can carpe the hell out of diem and seize this moment for all it's worth.

Luke sways me without music. I follow his lead, immersing myself in the choreography without a soundtrack playing. He creates our song sans lyrics. Releases a slight moan as he allows his hands to wander the span of my chilled spine. I'm loosening under his touch. Direct his enticing lips to every spot that should make me feel guilty, but don't. There's a man across town who's been waiting for me for at least an hour. But the amazing human gently nibbling my ear right now has earned all this energy I'm giving back to him.

I'm finally learning to dance.

"Stay here," Luke whispers. "Every night when you close this door, I'm afraid it's the last time I'll hear it with you on the other side. Or hearing you snore, even though you're convinced you don't." He chuckles lightly. "If you leave now, you're taking the best part of me with you. Please. Stay, baby. Give me you."

I glance up at Luke, stand on my toes, and pour every excuse I can think of to abandon the promise of him out through a lingering kiss. I thread my arms around his neck and press into him, suspending all the *what-if's* that should be forcing me away. His scent, the way his arms feel like a mixture of angst and pride in a still room with nothing but the sounds of us exchanging deep breaths, is flawless.

. . . until the most excruciating pain I've ever felt in my life surges through my abdomen and knocks me clean out.

I used to be afraid of the dark.

Not because of the boogeyman, stuffing my face with pork rinds drenched in Tabasco sauce, and bread-n-butter pickles on the side right before bed like Temper's told me not to since I was 10, or bingeing Stephen King flicks, knowing how they scare me so bad, I have to run and pee. The entire day can be perfect, but sometimes, the minute I'm left with my own thoughts, the lights go off. And I get terrified I won't be able to turn them on again. The darkness shows me who I am . . . the chick who refuses to turn the lights back on.

"Tati?" I almost roll off the side of the bed when I open my eyes and see her. There's so many questions, but my throat burns like fire and brimstone.

"Don't sit up too fast. I got you." Before I blink, Tati's behind me, propping pillows behind my back and head, humming one of her songs.

"You smell like chocolate chip cookies." The words singe my scratchy throat.

"That would be because I've got the third batch in the oven. With pecans." Tati only bakes on two occasions: when there's something to celebrate or to lure me off the ledge. By the way my side's splitting like a gutted fish, I'm leaning toward the latter.

"Why am I in your bed?"

"Stop being hardheaded, hun. Take it slow." She leans over to the nightstand next to the bed, pours a glass of water, and sits beside me on the edge of the mattress. "Here, take a sip." She cups the back of my head, putting the glass against my lips so I can swallow. The room-temperature water chokes me. I cough, then sip some more.

"Why am I in your bed?" I ask again.

Tati sighs. "Because I'm crashing on the sofa since the bed's more comfortable for you. And because after what he did, there was no way I was sending you back to the hotel with Hudson after you got discharged from the hospital. Go with him, and you may as well be at home recovering alone."

I pin an eyebrow up. "Recover?"

Tati looks just as confused as me. "You don't remember any of this, do you?" My blank stare is her answer. "One of those cysts you have ruptured, JC." Here's the fun part where she stalls by biting her bottom lip instead of just telling me what I don't want to hear but obviously need to.

I prop up on both elbows, trying to read Tati before judging what time of day it is by the bit of sunlight fighting to trace in through the burgundy blackout curtains trying to shut it out. Tati's not like this. Says what needs to be said and moves on. Her silence terrifies me.

"Come on, give it to me."

Never once has my best friend denied me the truth when I look in her eyes. She drops her hesitant gaze momentarily, picks a tiny piece of skin off her thumb, and plucks it on the gray carpet before returning to me.

"The doctor . . ." Tati smoothes a hand over the low bun secured at the nape of her neck and clears the frog out of her throat. "The doctor had to remove one of your ovaries. I'm so sorry, hun."

My hand flies beneath my short-sleeved, royal blue silk pajama top. Without stretching to see my abdomen, I pull the shirt up and slide my hand around, groping at the pile of gauze I feel taped over the place where I've been cut. My mouth forms an "O," but the sound's trapped inside. I open it wider, hoping for a scream, a yell, a chortle. Something to verify the rage I feel—nothing.

I quickly shut my mouth, swishing my tongue around inside. I need more water. My eyes are damp, but the tears flooding my heart aren't falling. My burning skin feels like I'm a *plus-one* in hell, but I don't have enough strength to escape. I'm trapped in the body that betrayed me without remorse, unable to do anything about it. I need space . . . from myself.

"My . . . baby." I mourn the little guy—or girl—I haven't had the chance to conceive.

Tati sets the glass down and sits on the edge of the bed, stroking my edges with a half smile. "The doctor explained that even though it may be tough, you'll still be able to bear my gorgeous godbaby." Her smile gets bigger. "You're going to survive this, and one day, you'll name our little one after me, right?"

"I just, umm, you know."

"Yes, I do." She strokes my cheek with the back of her hand, then gently pecks it.

Why does it seem like Black women were only created to mourn?

I'm hurt. Angry. Confused. Two seconds ago, I was bold and bad enough to go for what I wanted. Now, I'm lying in bed, nursing my damaged body. I should be on top of the world right now, not having the world crash down on me.

All these thoughts hammer against my brain when it dawns on me. "Wait, where have you been?" I gently push Tati away. "And why have you been ignoring me?"

"We needed some time alone." She peers at me briefly, then drops her gaze to the red floral comforter I'm swaddled in.

"I didn't need time away from you, T. I was looking for you."

"I'm not talking about you, JC. I'm talking about . . . *us*."

Tati stands next to the bed. The hem of her pink palazzo pants falls around her ankles. She concentrates on her bare feet, which she's pointing off the floor in various ballet positions. Her go-to stall. There's something she doesn't want to tell me.

I haven't seen Tati this nervous since right before being announced as the *Battle Exes* champ. I crane my head to get a better view of the oversized T-shirt hanging off her frame, which I'm just now noticing is thicker than usual. She takes both hands and lifts her shirt, exposing her protruding belly.

"Tati, you're . . .?"

She nods.

The warm tears trickle onto the exposed dragonflies on my arm. "Why didn't you didn't tell me?"

"Because *now* is the worst time for *you*. Because sometimes, Black women have to protect one another. No one else does." Tati drops her shirt, and it falls back over her stomach. "I'll spare you the gory details, but after *Battle Exes*, one of the contestants—Adam Nation—and I sort of created our own Garden of Eden together."

"Oh Lord, Tati! Not Adam! *Really?*" It feels like I'm about to bust a stitch, but picturing those two together makes me laugh hard. I rest my hand on top of the bandages to keep them intact. "Adam's so—"

"I know, this tater tot probably won't be bigger than a beanie baby. She can't help her daddy's mini-genes." Tati caresses her belly, laughing with me. "Adam's awkward; he talks through his nose, and that stupid long beard he keeps dyed red and orange pisses me off to no end." She sighs with a contented smile. "But I love his bald head and his little dad bod, the way he opens doors for me, and how he fits in my arms. He's so adorable, JC.

"The way he says my name makes up for every bad thing that's ever happened to me and makes me want to live." Tati looks like she's drifting into the light. A good one. "No matter what it looks to anyone else, for me, Adam makes sense."

I can't argue with that, especially when Tati's describing what I want for myself too. "You're so lame for this, but I'm happy for you. I mean it. And I love you."

"I hate you too." She blows me a kiss. "Are you sure you're all right with everything? Considering . . .?"

"Considering that you have something I want most in this world that you never wanted?" Bad choice of words, but our friendship—our sisterhood—would lose its glue if I'm not honest. I'm jealous. And I can't help it.

"JC, I—"

"Have every reason to be happy," I cut her off. "Promise me you'll be the best mother ever, and we're square, okay?" I draw an invisible box in front of her for emphasis.

"Promise."

My phone buzzes with a notification on the nightstand. I hadn't noticed it was sitting there. Before I can reach for it, Tati scoops it up. Her frown identifies exactly who it is.

"What's Hudson saying?" I ask.

She tilts the phone so I can see it. Haven't heard from you. U ok? I shake my head so she can take it away.

"Guess he doesn't trust me since our little altercation at the hospital," Tati says.

"Altercation? Oh no, what happened?"

Tati shrugs, straining to appear innocent, but I see past it. "I mean, all I did was mention that if he tried taking you out of the hospital, I'd hack off his naughty bits, puree them in my Ninja Food Chop, smother and serve them to him on his appendix. I don't see why it upset him so badly."

"Well, that's not troublesome." I watch Tati scroll as if she's not invading my privacy. "Hey, there's some private intel on there."

"Actually, there's something you may find far more interesting on here." She pops her lips and hands the phone back to me. A selfie Luke texted, smiling into the camera. His black baseball cap has *NO FEAR* embroidered in yellow letters above the brim to match his canary shirt. The caption with it says, *What part of the moon do you see?*

"It's funny how close you were to death, and now you're smiling. Wonder why?" Tati drags out the end of the sentence with a purr. "Oh, that's right," she snaps her fingers, "Luke makes you happy, but you prefer *little cheating man*."

"Too soon, babe. I don't have the energy right now. In case you haven't noticed, my life's in a bit of an upending."

"Tati's right, *baby love*. Don't let your head steal what belongs to your heart." Temper slides into the room straight off the cover of a fashion magazine, complete with dark, oversized sunglasses and a giant floppy sunhat. "And Mommy's here to get it right."

SEVENTEEN

"MOMMY!" I JET straight up, ignoring the pain stabbing my side when Temper appears in the doorway. "Girl, why don't you answer the phone when your only child calls you?" I playfully chastise.

"Please, darling. I haven't had enough coffee to erase the last thirteen hours of connecting flights, turbulence, and strangers breathing all over me, all while enduring these unbearable hot flashes, trying to get to you. Give me a little grace and some caffeine, okay?" Temper leans against the doorway, pulls her short wig back, and fans her forehead with her hand.

"What are you doing here? What about the tour?"

"You think I'm going to keep slinging notes for cash when my baby needs me? Especially for folks pretending they love Jesus for a couple of hours?" Temper straightens her wig and pops her lips. "The tour can wait. I gave that promoter directions to the exact location where he can shove that contract he threatened to sue me over for breaching because I came home to check on you. Concert promoters are the worst, especially the *gospel* ones."

The open-toed slides matching Temper's strapless peach jumpsuit clank against the cream tile as she stomps over to the bed where I'm waiting with outstretched arms. Her white, rose-quartz-studded, floral Valentino Garavani shoulder bag lands on the mattress with a thud when she tosses it on the foot of the bed. That bag costs half my hospital stay, but when Temper embraces me, I realize one thing: no matter how rich she gets, my mama will never let her White Diamonds perfume go.

Being cuddled in Mom's arms takes me back to how, right before leaving on tour, she used to sit me down in the kitchen and press my hair with Blue Magic grease. The only thing that kept me still was grape or strawberry popsicles to distract me from the heat sizzling so close to my scalp. When she finished, she'd fry lamb chops because *"If I'm going to pay over $10 for some meat, I'm not wasting it on chicken."* A side of collards and dressing with fresh cranberry sauce, and there it was: Thanksgiving before the holiday. The best part was enjoying her homemade peach cobbler topped with Cool Whip over a game of Uno with Dad.

I always won.

Temper softly nudges me back, examining me. "Are you all right, baby love?"

"I am now that you're here, Mom." I cast my weight on her, right where it should be—my original burden carrier. I lift my head, peering at Tati. "Thanks for letting my songbird know that I need her."

"It wasn't me," Tati says.

"Oh. I'm shocked Hudson reached out to you." Tati shoots Temper a strange look.

"Actually, Luke contacted me on his way to the hospital," Temper clarifies. "That man loves him some Jonica. From that luscious skin to the kitchen in the back of her head. Doesn't he, Tati?"

"He's just a friend, Mom," I intercept before Tati agrees with Temper.

"Well, your *friend* is quite enamored of you. And from what I've heard, you seem quite smitten yourself." Temper crosses her legs, regarding me with the knowing smirk only mothers are privy to.

My phone chirps, alerting all of us to the incoming call. Temper and Tati's eyes stay glued to me as I check the Caller ID and send Hudson straight to voicemail.

"See what I'm talking about, Mama T?" Tati snitches. "This girl won't bother answering Hudson's calls, but she's insisting on going back to LA with him. Please tell me how that makes any sense at all."

Temper jerks her head to me. "Chile, a man whose calls you won't answer shouldn't have access to your cash and prizes." She darts a French manicured nail towards my pelvis. Which, by the way, hurts too.

"Don't be gross, Mom."

"I'm just saying." Temper raises her hands above her head like it's an altar call on Sunday morning. "I know how you young adults are these days. All free with your bodies and things."

If a cringe were worth a thousand words, Temper would be getting drowned in a swear word shower. I mean, if I were brave enough to talk to her like that—which I never will be—I'd still be holding my jaw from the *Dynasty* soap opera slap she'd give me.

Temper winks to prove she's not a prude and eases the aggravation out of her voice. "Good Lord, it's not like I'm condemning you to hell, baby. I was the first person you told that you lost your virginity, remember?"

Actually, Tati was the first person I told that I lost it on prom night, but Temper doesn't have to know that. Which is why Tati's inching toward the door now with her index finger pressed to her lips behind Mom's back so that we can take that secret to the grave.

"Guys, I'm going to finish getting brunch ready," Tati says. "JC must be starving."

"I don't care if you're cooking smothered squirrel tail with brown gravy, just make sure you give me a biscuit to sop it up with." At the moment, my belly's growling too bad to worry about my horrible relationship choices. "Oh, and can I have a Pepsi too?"

"She'll have a ginger ale," Temper interjects. Her stony expression pushes me back against the pillows without a fight. Good thing I didn't ask for a mimosa.

Tati sees herself out and closes the door to give us some privacy.

"So tell me, baby—what kind of hold does that man have over you?" Temper leans back on one hand with her head cocked to the side. Her thin lips are bare; wrinkles over time are subtly settling in. My mind wanders from the shock of seeing Tati's baby bump for the first time to wondering if I'll age as gracefully as Temper.

"Is it the money?" Temper presses. "Because I have more than enough savings to carry both of us if you've already blown through yours."

I sink back into the cushy pillows, chortling. "I'm nowhere near broke, Mom." I point at the box of tissue on the nightstand. "Do you mind?" Temper snatches a tissue out and hands it to me. She waits long enough for me to blow my nose, then starts right back in.

"Is he putting his hands on you?"

"No, Mom."

"Blackmail?"

"No."

"Cooks good?"

"Not enough seasoning."

"Grease your scalp, suck your toes?"

"Mo . . . therrrrrr!"

"Well then, what is it?" Temper claps her hands in front of her face. "Why do you insist on being stuck in this time warp of a relationship? Is the sex *that* good to make you tolerate this guy who keeps failing you, honey?"

"Let me guess: he's a failure because he's white, right?"

"No. I can't stand him because he's a jackass. Especially to you." For Temper, that's a hard cuss. She swipes her pinkie across her lips, reaches inside her purse, and grabs out a small container of Vaseline. First, she dabs a bit on her lips, then hits the ash on her elbows before she shoves it back into her bag. "If that man really loves you, he'd be right here by your side, no matter what anyone says. And in my humble opinion, you can do better than a fool whose lineage brags about *owning* your ancestors."

I press my forehead into my palm. "Most mothers ask when their nearly thirty-year-old daughter's getting married. Mine is encouraging me to stay alone."

"If you're lonely, get a dog, Jonica." Temper snaps her fingers. "Oh, that's right . . . you already have one."

"All right, Mom, let's dead this." I shield my rolling eyes with my hands. "I'm fresh out of the hospital, exhausted, in pain, and I'm trying to wrap my mind around the fact that my future doesn't look anything like it did before I went in. Can't you just be here for me?"

"That's why I'm here, darling."

"Then please be here without all the extra, okay?"

"Whatever you need." Temper's hurt. As if the quiver in her voice isn't enough, I see it in her face when I lower my hands. Everyone's always on me about doing what's best for me. Well, right now, my body can't take any more stress, so this is where I'm starting. Sort of. Because those puppy dog eyes she's putting on me are close to making me backtrack.

Temper softly breaks into a few bars of "Jesus Loves Me," then takes one of the braids piled on top of my head and rolls it between her fingers.

"You about ready to take these things out?"

"Actually, I am. You think you and Tati can spearhead Operation Takedown?"

"If it'll give me more time with you, I'll do whatever you need, baby."

Temper's smiling again. She always bounces back so fast. Like when Dad died. At first, Temper was so broken I thought I'd lose her too. Dropped 15 pounds of her slender frame in two weeks. Baby, that grief don't play, does it? Temper got so skinny, word on the street was "The Pearl of Gospel" was high off more than the Holy Ghost. Because, of course, unexpectedly losing her husband and having her entire world upended had zero effect on the drastic shift in her appearance. As upset as I was, taking care of my mama took precedence over defending her against the vicious lies folks told about her.

For weeks, I'd build a pallet on the floor outside my parents' bedroom, trying to rest while Temper screamed and cried over Dad. I never went inside. I hung around, just in case. "Why, God!" she'd scream. "Give him back to me! Please, God, give him back!" Anyone who's ever heard their mama cry knows it feels like a warm-up for death. I couldn't take it.

One day, just as fast as they came, the tears stopped. Temper was Temper again. And she rejoined life on her own timing.

"How did you do it, Mom?"

"Do what, baby?"

"Turn it off?"

"Turn off what, dear?"

"Depression. How did you turn it off and stop being sad?"

Temper stops fiddling in my hair and clamps her hand over mine. "Oh, honey, I've never stopped grieving; let's get that right. I just refused to let the sadness consume me." She raises our conjoined hands, kissing mine.

"Then tell me how you keep singing to a God who didn't take your suffering away, even though He knew how bad you were hurting?"

"Grief doesn't keep us from living, sweetie. And God doesn't cause grief. He keeps us through it." She lets out a long sigh. "Do you know what my favorite part of the tour's been?"

I shake my head.

"At night when I unplug. No responsibilities, no one asking me for anything. It's the only chance I get to be Temper. Not the platinum-selling artist or the teenager who was kicked out of church after having a miscarriage. According to the powers that be at the church, losing my baby was what I deserved for 'spreading my legs in unrighteousness.'" Her deep laugh is pelted with the stones those folks cast at her. "But at least I got my rainbow baby when I married your father. Which proved God is just as good in bad times as the good ones." She smiles at me. "Did I ever tell you about your father's and my first date?"

My mouth spreads into a grin matching hers. "Only enough for me to know it wasn't exactly the point of my conception, but it got the ball rolling."

Temper rears her head back, snatches off her wig, and swings it in the air. "Well, the library Charles's mother ran would've frowned on actually conceiving in there rather than reading up on it." She tosses the wig on top of her purse and digs into her natural cornrows that stop at the nape of her neck.

"Your father was a fabulous listener. He knew I was into books, and everything peach, so he put a large table in the middle of the library's romance section, covered it with a peach tablecloth, and put a bowl of peaches and six pack of peach Clearly Canadian water in the center. That was the drink back then, you know." She smacks her lips like she can taste all of it now. "He also got me a bag of barbecue Fritos and a box of Honey Buns and put them next to a stack of books by my favorite authors that he'd bought from the bookstore."

Temper's eyes turn dreamy. "Bebe Moore Campbell, E. Lynn Harris, Francis Ray. Charles paid so much attention to the littlest details, down to the white orchid I love wearing in my hair." Her hand absentmindedly flies to her braids as if she's wearing one now. "Out of all the wonderful things your father did that day, the best part was the handwritten note he left on top of the books."

"*It's easy to read the pages, but will you take a chance on reading my heart?*" I chime in with the line I've heard recited a thousand times. It slips off my tongue so easily, like Dad's saying them himself.

Temper nods with a reminiscent smile. "It was so sweet, even if your father's handwriting was so bad, I had to ask him to read the note for me." I scoot back, giving Temper enough space to stretch out in front of me. She lies close, careful not to press into my abdomen. Once she's comfortable, I stretch my arm over her, like we used to do when she made it back home off tour. I never wanted to let her go.

"Do you know why I'm telling that story again, baby love?"

"No, ma'am, I don't."

"Because that was the day I fell in love with your father. Years later, it didn't matter how many fights we may have had or how many times we threatened to leave each other. My mind never stopped returning to that moment." She sniffles, fighting back tears.

"Your father spent our brief lifetime together crafting moments that proved love is enough when you're loved good. We were meant to stay together, not just be together. That single date gave me exactly what I needed to believe in love for the rest of my life. Even after my love left me."

Temper taps on the mattress, then cups my arm with her hand. "Honey, I realize you're grown and have the right to live as you please, but may I ask you a question?"

"Sure."

"Has he given you any moments to last you forever?"

"Husdon?"

"Isn't he the one who's supposed to?"

Not once in all our years together have I even thought on that level regarding my relationship with Hudson. It never occurred to me. We've kind of been floating.

"You're surrounded by too much noise to live in the quiet moments, my dear. Connected to everything and everyone but *Jonica*, and it's draining you. That's how you ended up here."

"I ended up here because my body pooped out on me."

"Your body didn't poop out. It just got tired of you not listening to what it has to say." Temper stops talking when we hear a crash come from the kitchen.

"I'm okay!" Tati calls out before either of us makes a move to help her.

"You have to take a break from all this movie stuff, dear."

"But this *movie stuff* is what I do, Mom. I live to create."

"Then you need to create some common sense, chile," Temper chuckles.

"I'm serious. Making movies keeps me sane."

"But there's something else making you crazy. You may not want to admit it, but your health's telling off on you." Temper rolls over and searches my eyes. "Women who aren't happy stick with what's familiar, so we can't be disappointed because we already know what to expect. The familiar does what it does, and we pretend we're fine when everyone else can clearly see that we're not." She caresses my cheek with a faint smile. "There's no shame in depression, dear. We can get you some help."

"I'm not depressed." My weak defense would be more convincing without the vibrato in my voice.

"Well, these sad little braids that need refreshing say otherwise. And is that a black eye?"

Temper picks at my roots, then sits up and reaches for her purse. Digging around inside, she pulls out a paperback and hands it to me—*Every Black Girl Dances: A Near-Life Experience* by Dr. Izzy Prince. I flip the book over and eye the headshot. Dr. Prince is a gorgeous, racially ambiguous woman with a giant mop of chestnut and sandy-brown curls and saucer-sized gray eyes peering from behind the big, black-framed glasses I'm guessing are a fashion statement as opposed to using them to see, almost like a disguise.

"What's this?"

"Your first step to a near-life experience, my darling." Temper takes the book from me and taps a nail beside the title on the soft cover. "Dr. Prince's dance therapy sessions have helped me a lot. After what she's done for me, I'm guessing she can help you find your rhythm too."

EIGHTEEN

"SO, YOU'RE SAYING you can't dance because you're struggling in your relationship?"

"No, Dr. Prince. I can't dance because I suck at it."

"I told you, call me Izzy. This is just an informal session for us to get to know each other and see if we're a fit."

I don't bother answering Izzy because I'm desperately gasping for air. The small studio room looks like Christmas with a gazillion white LED lights lit all over the place instead of a good ol' lamp and a sofa like most normal therapists.

I know her electric bill must be high.

These mood lights make me want to go to sleep instead of dance. I have to squint just to see the clock mounted below the neon pink *Dance Therapy* sign: **11:25.**

I've only been here 25 minutes?

"Your clock's off-center," I cheerfully inform the good doctor from my seat on the hardwood floor. I stretch my legs in front of me and bury my glistening face in the bottom of my oversized gray T-shirt, stifling a laugh. Full-on mean girl for no reason.

Izzy sighs. Long and hard. "Why are you here, Jonica?" She wants to know with one of those threaded brows wagging my way.

I stop cleaning my face and frown at her. "That's what I'm trying to figure out." My silk-pressed hair's reverting at the roots. The bun I wore here is quickly morphing into a puffy cone. I sniff under my arms and get slapped by my own funk. "Let's see: I'm dripping wet, musty, locked up in here while you're rationing air smack in the middle of hot-butt September, and my pain threshold's dwindling really fast. I'm paying you to tell me why I'm here."

Izzy's thick, wavy ponytail swings over her face as she does lunges beside me. "I'm being serious, Jonica. You're a grown woman who can get up off that floor and prance right on out of here on those retro Fight Club Animal Instinct Jordans any time she wants to." She reverses her lunge, peering at me through the space between her legs. "Are you a size 8? You can leave those shoes with me on your way out. They match my outfit."

And with that, I'm dismissed. Except, I don't really want to go.

"Insurance," I mumble.

"Excuse me?" Izzy pops upright and jams her hands on her hips.

I dip my head with my eyes squeezed shut to avoid seeing my reflection in the mirrors behind the ballet barre. "It's just that I have insurance. Good insurance. And my mother says there's something terribly off about having something the average American wants—well, needs, but leaves it lying around like clothes we know we're never going to wear with the tags still on." I'm stalking so fast I have to catch my breath. When I lift my head, the arrogance I've been talking through is gone. "I'm here because I still have the tags on."

Izzy walks over to the barre where her gear's lying, retrieves her water bottle, and starts chugging without acknowledging a thing I've said. And now I'm watching her drink. On my dime . . . that by now's stretched to a dollar.

"Is that a camera?" I point to a device hanging by the entrance, pointing in our direction.

"Security purposes." Izzy swallows some more water, then sets the bottle on the floor and waves me to meet her by the mirrors. I get off the floor, bones cracking, and mosey on over, thinking how she's almost too beautiful to stare in the face. Not a blemish marking her olive skin, except a large keloid her solid black tank with a cheetah print running down the sides doesn't hide on her shoulder. She's a tiny little thing, except for those long legs that make her seem taller than she is. I step in front of her, studying the mocha mole strategically planted just above her heart-shaped lips.

"I understand your apprehension, but I need you to trust me, Jonica."

"I'm all for creativity and living outside the box, Doc. But what exactly made you start torturing your clients and calling it therapy?"

Izzy's brows furrow. "What made you want to traumatize people and call it entertainment?"

Ouch.

"You can call me JC. If that's cool with you."

"All right, JC. You ready to try this again?" Izzy's voice is husky and commanding. Much bigger than I expected for a woman her size.

I quickly scan the room, then rub my eyes. "Ready."

Izzy nods at the barre, my sign to put my hands on it and prepare for death. "Remember what I told you earlier. It's only been a week since your surgery, so don't overdo it. Respect your limits."

"If I knew my limits, I wouldn't be here." I slap my forehead. "Sorry, it's a reflex."

"I already know." I can tell Izzy wants to laugh but maintains a business exterior. "You're going to try the demi pliés again, but this time, I want you to stop looking at the floor and watch yourself in the mirror."

"Why?"

"Because the only way this will work is if you'll be honest with yourself. The mirror doesn't lie about what it sees. Even when it's ugly, at least the truth is real. Now, remember what to say?"

"Breathe in, dance out." I repeat the mantra Izzy taught me when I got here.

"Good. You're not trying to be Debbie Allen. You're JC Burke, telling herself the ugly truth. Dance is the only place where we can't tell a lie. It's not about the moves; it's how you feel when you're free." She slides over and rests a hand on my shoulder. "Why are you here, JC?"

"Because I'm surrounded by tons of people, but I'm alone. I'm my own person. I hate being *my person*."

"Stop dropping your head when you make your confessions," Izzy reminds me. "Look in the mirror. What do you see that triggers you, binds you, and keeps you from yourself? That's your choreography. Go ahead, plié as you say them out loud. And don't lie. Look in the mirror."

"Sometimes, I can't see my part in conflicts, and I hate that because it makes me think people close to me are hurting or doing me wrong." I grip the barre with both hands, bend my knees as I dip to the floor, and watch myself slowly rise. "My boyfriend's tone deaf to my needs, even when it means I can die." I dip faster this time and pop back up. "And I won't leave him because the pain he causes me helps me create." Another plié. Cleaner, smoother this time.

"This is so good, JC! Keep going. What else?" Izzy starts mimicking my movements.

"I barely rest, I give everyone a pass for walking all over me, I miss my daddy, I have imposter's syndrome, I offend everybody trying not to offend anybody, and it's impossible for me to recover from any of it because I try catching the bullets instead of dodging them!"

My emotions sear through my veins, tearing me away from the barre. Before I know it, I'm spinning around like I've seen some of the dancers on *So You Think You Can Dance* do. Not nearly on the same level or even an ounce of swag or balance real dancers have, but every ounce of what's been beating me down pours out from my head to my two left feet.

I've found my reason.

"Come on, JC! Dance! Who's covering you while you recover?" Izzy's shout pierces my skin. I usually pass psych tests because I have all the right answers. Too bad I don't have the right ones to fake this with Izzy.

"Face the mirror," Izzy commands. "Take your hands and brush away every burden on your shoulders." When I do as she asks, she encourages me some more. "You don't need rhythm to dance; you just have to surrender to the moves."

My chest feels like it's caving in. Lungs burning, legs shaking. I'm slinging tears and snot all over the floor and don't care. When you've lied about loving yourself as long as I have, you have to get messy to get to the good part. The part where you don't have to cheat or convince yourself that you're worthy of looking at yourself in that mirror. The part where you think you can't be happy unless your soul is suffering or you must be damaged to be valuable. Stress isn't love. Fear isn't love. It's all in the mirror. I'm finally facing it.

". . . and I'm jealous of my best friend." It feels astonishingly right to admit this out loud. But if I don't, I can't go on being Tati's friend. I just can't.

"I'm jealous that there's not a motherly bone in her body or anything close to a nurturing instinct, but she's lucky enough to have this tiny human growing inside her while my chance is being taken away!" My sobbing grows more profound as I release a wail that doesn't sound like it came out of me. "I hate that I'm jealous, I hate that she's first, and I hate myself because as hard as I'm trying to be happy for her, I can't help wondering why it isn't me!"

Izzy takes me by the hand, escorting me to the middle of the floor. I mimic every step she makes along the way. To the best of my limited abilities, at least. Every step has a name:

Capture.

Pour.

Release.

Testify.

Heal.

Forgive.

That last one, that's the one right there. It was today that I found out dancing is more than perfect posture or pointed toes. It's way more fulfilling than a twerk at the club or a line dance at a family reunion. It's the one thing that's for you, and only you. You can be in a group of a thousand, but when you're dancing, every step belongs to you. It's the one thing no one can take from you. It's a love language.

I'm learning how to speak.

It's taken my feet hitting the floor to understand my part in what's manifesting in my health. Mainly, unforgiveness. I haven't forgiven the unexpected moments in my life. Strangers who don't know any better; familiar folks who do. My expectations, letdowns. Death. Even Luke for coming into my life at the wrong time. Every moment in our lives—good or bad—is dictated by whether we choose to forgive and let go. Until I can figure it out, I'm going to dance. Just like I am right now. With no music.

I think I've fallen in love.

"Excuse me, *what*? Your boyfriend *shot* you?" I choke on my spit. Who just drops a huge bomb like this, all willy-nilly, like they forgot to tell you to pick up something from the grocery store? My new therapist, that's who. *I got shot, oh yeah—don't forget the almond milk.* At least the keloid on Izzy's shoulder makes sense now.

"Ex-boyfriend, and it was years ago." Izzy clamps a hand over the wound, hiding the parting gift from the bullet her boyfriend put in her arm.

"Where is he now?"

"In prison, about to come up for parole."

I let that fact about Izzy's assailant sink in while we lay on our backs, recovering. My sutures are still intact, and I'm not in pain like I thought I'd be. Actually, I'm surprisingly good. Better than good. Yet, instead of basking in the afterglow, I'm mentally storyboarding this moment into a movie instead of living in it.

I'm going to need another session.

1:05.

I shift my focus back from the clock and onto Izzy. "Nothing about you screams *shoot me*," I observe. "What happened?"

Izzy stays flat on her back, feet planted on the floor, knees in the air like tents, blocking my curious stare. "Before I became a pastor, I was a principal dancer for Intentions contemporary ballet company back in the day."

I shoot straight up, eyes darting at Izzy. "Whoa, *pastor*? Since when are you a pastor?"

"Since my near-life experience made me want to have a little talk with Jesus," Izzy jokes. "Brought in Dirty 30 on a Saturday night with a bunch of friends, tacos, and the strongest bottle of tequila we could find," she says with the remnants of the past dripping from her voice. "Got ordained Sunday morning, and here I am, five years later."

"Temper strikes again. Trying to bully me back to Jesus."

"I hardly doubt that," Izzy says. "Your mother's concerned about you, JC. She wants to help you get your balance back, that's all. I don't have a hell or a sanctuary to put you in."

"So, you're one of these new-age pastors without a church?"

"The church is anywhere I want it to be, JC." Izzy waves across the studio. "Including here."

I still feel like I've been set up for some kind of spiritual purge, but something's making me cleave onto Izzy. The only thing I really know is she's 35, a pastor, and can seriously dance. Oh, and she's a beast at what she does. Clearly, Izzy understands the assignment. I'll stay here to feel her out more and understand how she keeps her makeup so fresh after working out this hard. There's not a streak running through her olive-toned foundation.

"I don't know any women of God who get down like you do. Why don't you have a church if you call yourself a pastor?" All right, the nasally way *pastor* trickles off my tongue is a low blow because I'm irritated about being tricked. Still, hanging out a little more with Izzy will buy me some more time before I have to meet Luke at the hotel.

I mean, Hudson.

"Consider me more of a servant than an evangelist," Izzy clarifies. "See, folks keep trying to shove God in a box of tradition that He didn't create in the first place. He's not traditional or religious, so why are we? You've got to unlearn the *order of service*, girl." Izzy rolls her eyes. "I'm just here to help women get better. Which we have a hard time doing because we think vulnerability makes us soft. What's wrong with being soft? We don't have to be hard all the time. My booty's soft. My skin's soft. My hair's soft. And my heart's soft too."

"Being soft gets you hurt," I whisper.

"No, ma'am, being soft gets you healed." Izzy sits up and rubs her hands together, staring at me. "We cry, scar, and bruise. Our wounds roll deep from generations, but eventually, we heal." She points to the scar covering her shoulder. "This thing is ugly, but it's my history. I nearly lost the opportunity to get better by circumcising my vulnerability. Don't be so hard, or you can't heal, boo."

"You don't know me," I retort. "All you've seen is my two left feet and what I want you to know."

"Based on your films, I know you equate being traumatized with being tough. That doesn't make us stronger. It makes us afraid to take care of ourselves. Which is why you refuse to focus on the mirror." She harks a laugh. "Even though Michael Jackson told you that's where you should start."

Twenty steps to make it out the door. Give or take a few to scoop up my saddlebag along the way.

My cell chimes from my bag in the corner.

"No phones," Izzy reminds me.

"Sorry, forgot to turn it off." I nod at the scar on Izzy's shoulder, shaped like Louisiana. "What's the story, Pastor?"

"Izzy."

"Izzy," I give in.

"Back when I was dancing, I was a heavy drinker." Her smile doesn't seem to match the memory. "It was around the time I found out I was adopted, even though I should've guessed I didn't belong way sooner."

"How so?" I ask.

"Well, my parents were your . . ." her voice trails off as she bites her bottom lip.

"My color?" Never fails. I'm used to finishing that sentence.

Izzy nods. "Anyway, finding out my biological mother abandoned me at a fire station like some Hallmark movie hurt, but it explained a lot. I started acting out and stayed drunk. Didn't matter the time or day, cognac, vodka, champagne—any time was happy hour." She reaches behind her head and wraps her ponytail into a bun. Slurps and pops her lips like she still has a taste for all the above. "I was also a notoriously terrible flirt. Reckless and risky, served with a side of nasty."

I bolt up. "Not *you*, Pastor!" I tease.

"Girl, I was so fine, no one could tell me anything. Couldn't let all this body go to waste, could I?" She runs her hands down her curvy sides and over her thick thighs. "Well, there was this dancer who I was always partnered with—Vince—who had a major crush on me. I had one on him too, but it wasn't anything I was trying to pursue, even though Vince was built like Adonis and as strong as Thor. And his voice was so deep, it could drill holes through a chastity belt. Gurl . . . *gurl*."

Izzy fans herself with her hand, then remembers we're not gossip buddies and reigns herself back in. "I'm not ashamed to admit that back then, I woke up guzzling half a bottle of the red stuff and let the harder brown liquors tuck me in bed at night." She picks at her sporty nails, slathered with thick, black lacquer. "I was always so drunk, it was a miracle I never missed a show or fell off the stage, especially with Vince lifting me.

"This man wanted me so bad, but I had a live-in boyfriend, Darren. Darren was so jealous, he hated Vince's guts."

"So, he shot you because he was jealous?" I try rushing her to the end of the story.

She nods. "It was my fault."

"Your fault? Why?" The suspense is causing me to take out my frustration on the tip of the nail on my ring finger that I gnaw off.

"Darren did what he did because one day I got so drunk before a show, Vince and I practically had sex on that stage. I mean, we were raw. I'm talking costumes coming off, hands and mouths everywhere, parents snatching their kids out of the theater, and the dance company's artistic director straight cussing us out for ruining the show." Izzy buries her face in her hands, then peels them back and looks me in the eyes.

"Darren was so enraged, as soon as the curtain closed, he rushed backstage, took out a .45, and blasted Vince once in his left leg, then once in the right foot. Didn't try to kill him; just wanted to make sure he'd never dance again. Before security took him down, he got me in the shoulder. Mission accomplished."

Some people cry on cue; other people's pain crawls into my tear ducts and pushes out the wet stuff regardless of whether I want to cry. Like they're doing right now. I cry easier over other people than I do myself—my fantastic flaw.

I scoot over to Izzy and pull her into my arms. She whimpers softly and sinks into my chest. I don't even flinch when I feel her nails dig into my back. "This is terribly unprofessional of me," she weeps. "I promise I never unload on my patients like this. It's just that it's been so long since I've been able to speak to anyone about what happened. I apologize."

"It's all right. You're off the clock," I assure her. Until now, Izzy's been one-note to me—dissecting folks for money, like some preachers choose tithes over souls. Somehow, the tears complete her. Gives her dimensions that her credentials don't. Behind the ministerial collar and the medical degrees, Izzy's a messed-up human like me.

Turns out Temper knew exactly what she was doing, throwing Izzy and me together. To give the finger to the myth that strong Black women can't coexist with both Jesus and therapy. I'm not sure when Temper changed her mind about therapy, but I believe the level of self-intimacy I've experienced today is what amazing grace must feel like.

"Are you all right with Darren being granted parole?"

Izzy lifts her head and nods. "I pushed Darren into breaking. He accused me of cheating on him, and I literally dared him to do something about it. As long as he saw how bad other men wanted me, what's a boundary, right?" She tugs at her tank. "The crazy part is, Vince and I never slept together. Not even once. Because of me, all three of our lives were ruined that night. Consequences without actions."

My cell's ringing again. Only one person is obnoxious enough to dial me back to back when I don't answer, and it's not my mama.

Don't worry, Hudson, we'll make it to the airport on time.

"So, is this why you opened the studio?"

Izzy's voice is murky as coagulated milk. "After what happened, dance became too painful for me. But once I finished putting in the work to get back to myself, I decided to take my gift back."

Izzy wipes her eyes with her palm and forces a smile. "You have everything you need, JC. It's time to start working on *your* wants."

"And what if what I want is to disappear?" Admitting that out loud is about as refreshing as letting an aspirin sit on my tongue until it dissolves itself. "Maybe I don't want to be JC anymore. What if I want to be just a regular somebody, with a normal life where nobody notices me except the people who matter?"

"Sometimes you have to accept that you're dope, even when you don't understand why," Izzy says. "Do you realize how you stand with your left arm crossed over to your right shoulder?"

"I do that?"

Izzy nods her head. "Yes. Like you're hiding something. But all that pretty brown skin and well-kept edges can't be concealed, girl. We see you, even when you don't want us to." Izzy stands and helps me off the floor. The floor's immaculate, but we dust ourselves off, anyway. "If you don't absorb anything else from our session today, I want you to know you can still be great and do what you do, JC. The way you want to. But do it for yourself first."

"Babe, why aren't you answering your phone?" The door flies open, and Hudson drags his Flogged T-shirt, mid-knee, khaki shorts, and Timberland boots into the studio with Izzy's receptionist on his heels.

"I'm so sorry, Pastor Izz." The assistant hunches over, out of breath. "This gentleman insisted on seeing Miss Burke." *Sorry*, she mouths to both of us.

"I can't believe you haven't stopped tracking me, Hudson. This *has* to stop!" I rush to the wall next to the barre and scoop up my stuff. "Thank you for everything, Izzy," I call over my shoulder as I rush back to Hudson and grab him by the arm to get out of there. "I'm so embarrassed."

"You know what to do, JC," Izzy hollers as I drag Hudson out the door. "Near-life experience, girl."

NINETEEN

"EITHER GIVE ME my son, or I swear I'll blow your head off, Quita!"

"Please, Ammo! Just put the gun down, and I'll do anything you want. Anything! I love you too much to play with you, baby!"

I'm hidden behind a makeshift dumpster in the dank, smelly warehouse, watching the scene go down as we film. The stiff air is sucking up whatever life's left in my lungs, but I can't move. Not if I don't want to mess things up.

"You said you love me, Ammo!"

"You think them fake tears gon' do somethin' besides make me mad, trick? Shut yo' mouth before I make you eat this gun!"

I cringe when Ammo's arm swells like a balloon when he tightens it around Quita's throat, bending her limp body backward. From my hiding spot, I see the jumbo triangles coated with fake gold slam against her face as the hulk of a man applies more pressure. She's bent so far back it looks like her spine's about to snap in half.

Quita's swollen eyes turn bloodshot; the thick coating of jet-black mascara rimmed around her eyes streaks into her teeny blonde 'fro. Drool runs out of her mouth and down her cheeks. She's trying to say something but gasping too hard to speak coherently.

In either an act of mercy or defiance, Ammo lets go and shoves Quita onto the concrete. The tiny shorts and neon green bikini top amplify the sound of her bare skin smacking the ground. Ammo flings the blue cap he's wearing beside Quita, flips her on her back, and spits in her face before driving his knee into her abdomen.

"I'm gon' ask you one last time, Quita: Give me my son. I WANT MY SON!"

The first smack startles me. The two after that lodges what feels like vomit at the top of my throat. I want to charge Ammo and gouge his eyes out with my acrylics. I need a fill, anyway.

Quita disappears underneath her man's massive weight, like a shaggy rug.

"Stop, please! Arrrggghhh!" Quita gurgles.

"JC!"

I'm over here.

"JC?"

Can't you see me? I'm right here.

"Cut! I said, cut!" Hudson stomps over to me and yanks me from behind the cameraman, snapping his fingers in my face. "Christ, Jonica, what's wrong with you? Why am I doing your job? It's like you aren't even here!" He clamps a hand on the back of his neck and waves the other at the *Crack Dreams* crew. "Don't stand there gawking, people! Take five."

No one moves or makes a noise. I don't blame them. All the behind-the-scenes drama's been serving better tea than this played-out movie. I don't want to be here, and everyone knows it.

"I guess I zoned out. Sorry."

"You've been zoned out since you got back here three weeks ago," Hudson growls. My eyes drop to his hand, dangling less than an inch away from Skye's, who is standing next to him. "Are you trying to sabotage this thing or what?"

"Look, I said I'm sorry," I reiterate through gritted teeth.

"Sorry? Girl, you playing!" Skye pushes up on me in her six-inch stilettos, index finger leading the way. "This is *my* debut, and you will not ruin it for me!"

"You'll be fine, muffin." I don't extend her the courtesy of a glance when I blow her off.

"Muffin? Who do you think you're talking to?" Skye's screechy voice is hollow. You could sit a bottle of Coca-Cola straight up on her behind without it falling off, the way she's poking it out. Picturing a two-liter balancing on her backside without wobbling makes me giggle.

"What's so funny?" Skye demands.

"You." I dart a finger at her, sniggling again. I grab Corrine, Skye's stand-in for the role of *Quita* in the film. Poor thing's trembling. Big Bass—the Southern rapper playing Ammo, probably scared the child half to death. Either that or my manhandling has her shaken, the way she's holding her breath.

"You've got the emotional depth of a mosquito, Skye. At least Quita here—"

"Corrine," the girl corrects me.

"At least Corrine here bodies this role when she stands in for you. She makes the words on the pages more than what they are, and she has a range that, unfortunately, you can't fathom. If I had my way, Corrine would replace you. You're not the actress you think you are, LaDonna Sheridan. You're just a gutter princess trying to make everyone forget the pole she fell off of." Maybe calling on Skye's government name is low. But it's not beneath me.

Hudson plants himself between us before we can take this disagreement beyond words. "Not here, JC. Be professional."

"Right, just like how discreet you and Skye were when you decided to screw each other behind my back? Or how about when she outed you as her baby's daddy?" I crane my neck to get better aim as I insult Skye to her befuddled face.

"Uh, JC?"

"What, Corrine?"

"My wrist. It kind of hurts." Corrine points to my vice grip on her wrist with her free hand and scampers off as soon as I release her without an apology.

"I believe this is a private discussion." Hudson takes off the gray fedora with a white feather in the side that doesn't come close to being adjacent to the brown, pin-striped vest he threw on over a *Purple Rain* T-shirt. He's morphed into a hipster when I wasn't looking.

I study as he musses his hair and tosses the hat back on. Twenty-one days he's had to help me not look stupid for having his back instead of celebrating the fact that he won't need a baby registry after all, and he hasn't done a thing to make me feel okay with any of it. All he's done is squander every available minute between us by pandering to public opinion, leaving me to sort out the dirty details he's not man enough to.

"*Skye's not pregnant—we're good now*," Hudson reasoned a few nights ago. Didn't bother looking up from whatever game it was he was playing on his sofa. Not sure the name of it, but it was something where somebody's head gets blown off.

"*Why you chose a woman in such close proximity to me—to us—is mind-blowing, Hudson. I just don't get it. Now I look like the fool for standing by your side.*" I maintained my calm but sliced him with the sharp edge of the knife with my scowl. "*Do you know how many DMs I get from girls who are so young, they don't know how to put their Tampons in straight, but think I'm a hero for being a real rida for her man?*"

Heavy on the air quotes for "rida."

"*Apparently, I'm more of a woman for staying with you since we're relationship goals.*"

Even heavier on the air quotes.

"Stop being dramatic, babe. You don't look like a fool. Hey - are you burning the cheese?"

"Oh, crap!"

I hopped off the love seat and raced back to his kitchen, where I called myself mixing a batch of queso. Concession nachos for dinner. Apparently, I forgot to turn down the burner when I went to confront Hudson about Skye's fake pregnancy.

"Did you even look at the tweets I sent you?" I hollered from the kitchen.

"I told you, I don't read that junk. It's pointless."

Another animated explosion erupted from the television, dismissing me from my end of the conversation. Later, after I scrubbed the scorched pot and we had pizza delivered, Hudson reminded me that Skye's contract was iron-clad, and firing her meant she could sue both of us. And how if I'd been more emotionally available, he wouldn't have slipped and fallen into her vagina in the first place. That right there was the chin-check I needed to see that Hudson turned me into something I promised myself I'd never be: the woman who takes somebody like him back.

"Hey, would a stack of singles be enough motivation to get a better performance out of you, Skye?"

"That's enough, JC!" Hudson grabs me by the elbow.

I blow out a puff of air and force myself to recant my next argument. Two things I've never been into: public spectacles and slut shaming. Not even the woman sleeping with my man.

These two have reduced me to both offenses.

Without a word, I snatch away from Hudson and push through the cast and crew.

"Great job today, guys." Hudson heaps on the praise super thick as I shove the heavy warehouse doors open and bolt outside. "That's enough for today. Check your call sheets, and we'll get back to it next week."

Cali better get ready for Favor . . . wheels up!

Cali might be ready for you, Luke, but I'm not.

The selfie Luke just texted me of him, Myzi, Elaine, and Big Luke making crazy faces with that caption is the cutest. With his grown-out hair and fuller beard, Luke looks even more like his old man spit him out instead of his mother. I run my fingers across my cell's screen, wondering what that beard feels like. Would it make kissing him feel different?

Stop it! You almost died the last time this man kissed you.

I miss him.

Luke.

His voice. His scent. His optimism. The way he nails my main love language by sacrificing his time, no matter what stage of stress he's in, and without considering what he'd have to sacrifice. Luke doesn't make me feel like he's losing something by paying attention to me or that I'm taking him away from something he'd rather be doing. Pouring into me doesn't make him feel like he's missing out. That's what hits my sweet spot the most.

Now that I'm back home, time is a commodity I mostly spend alone. Like a dummy, I assumed Hudson and I would be actively salvaging what's left of what brought us together in the first place when I got back. I really thought he was going to fight for me.

For us.

Girl.

Hudson's giving me enough time away from him to climb all the way in my feelings and focus on another man.

I stare at the picture Luke sent. It might be the tiny wrinkles that creep in the corners of his eyes when he's excited or how his nostrils flare when he's hanging onto my every word as if he doesn't want a single one to fall to the ground. I miss that the most about him. It's like if he stops paying attention for even a second, whatever I'm saying will escape his ear. I also miss the way he looks at me. Like he'd go blind without me there.

My eyes fall to the jagged scar on Luke's left cheek, which he told me was courtesy of a fishing trip with Big Luke when he was five.

"*For a split second, his back was turned, and I tripped and fell into the lake trying to get the pole that fell in,*" Luke explained. Big Luke dashed into the water, slammed him face-first on the deck, and then flipped him over to give him CPR. That scar is his forever reminder of the day his daddy saved him.

"*I could've died,*" Luke told me. "*All it takes is a minute for life to end.*"

It's taken three weeks for my life with Luke to die.

I lean over the side of the bed and scoot the empty Taco Bell wrappers out of my way. Underneath the stack are three packs of fire sauce with inspirational messages printed on the front. I scoop a few of them in my hand and read:

Let's go on an adventure.

That moment when.

Yes to forever.

None of these vague sayings do anything to help my current situation, but maybe I can apply the packet wisdom to future relationships.

I snatch the wine cooler I've been nursing for an hour and a half while I wait for Hudson. This thing's past room temperature, and the peach flavor tastes fermented as it oozes down my throat. I get so tired of getting stuck by myself at Hudson's place or mine, meal-prepping takeout orders, stressing over the flurry of think pieces dissecting my films on social media, and my relationship failures suddenly popping up all over the internet.

Freedom of opinion is making creative targets for every keyboard hustler with a computer, smartphone, and avatar like it gives them the right to be nasty to each other. I hate it.

The other night, a particularly scathing dissertation about my Cox thesis film—*Bye, Church*—blew up on one of the vlog sites. The reviewer called me a mess of a visionary, trying to pass off my muddled messages into a cultural cry that folks should run from. What should've been my boyfriend consoling me with a hot fudge sundae and vodka shots turned into a full-blown war between us.

"Who's the one who showered you with sushi and your favorite beer when you had your meltdown over *The Black Masses* entertainment blog accusing you of being a—wait, how did they put it? Oh, they called you 'Black-curious hack who hustled your way into Hollywood, banking on your Black girlfriend's talents and your daddy's money,'" I screamed after Hudson accused me of being dramatic and codependent on what people think of me.

We were at his place since, according to him, my place is too inconvenient a commute.

Inconvenient.

Like dealing with me.

In protest of going to waste my time with people who wouldn't care if I was wiped off the face of the earth the next day, I was in the one pair of boxers Hudson didn't get around to throwing away with the pack I gave him for his birthday, and a man's old, white-ribbed tank with a hole ripped just above the right boob. All I wanted was an ugly night at home, loaded with calories and lots of booze. Hudson had other plans.

"It was me, that's who. *I* defended you! And I didn't force you to go hang out at some stupid industry party with watered-down gin and more side-boob than should be legal in a public setting."

I slammed the bowl of popcorn I was eating on his wooden coffee table, sailing kernels all over the table and floor. "Can you stop messing with that bow tie on your tux and look at me while I talk to you?"

"I don't want to be late." Hudson examined himself in the hall mirror, slicking his hair up to the sky. "So, that's where your boyfriend got that from?" He turned his head from side to side, performing a final hair check.

I jammed my hands on my hips so that I wouldn't put them on him. "I've told you a thousand times, there's nothing between Luke and me other than friendship. And he got what from where?"

Hudson popped his collar and finally turned to face me. "*Black curious.* Your not-boyfriend-boyfriend said that to me," he chuckled. "Should've known that guy couldn't be more original. That's why he's chasing after you; I already shaped you up."

"*Excuse* me? *What* are you implying?"

"When we met, you weren't anywhere near as polished as you are now," Hudson said.

"What are you talking about? My folks didn't have the same money as yours, but we were just as affluent." Hudson's inaccurate, raw-dog assessment of me had my skin boiling. "Stop acting like I was dropped off at Cox from the projects with a hooptie and a meal plan. And don't you dare call yourself putting me in my place."

"Your place is by my side at Sahara's party tonight." Hudson slid over to me, took my hands in his, and tried to peck me on the lips. I turned my head and rewarded him with a mouthful of my freshly flat-ironed, shoulder-length bob instead. He spit in the air and frowned.

"You slept with him, didn't you?"

"If you have to ask . . ." I cut myself off, shrugging to fill in the blank.

"Whatever."

Hudson returned to the mirror and brushed a hand through his thick hair. Twenty-fifth time in less than 30 minutes. How it looked right now wouldn't change, no matter how much he fussed, but okay.

"Hooking up with me elevated you, JC. Without me, you'd never be invited to something like this." My stunned gaze traced down the dapper black tux, white-collar shirt, and polka-dot bow tie, screeching at the brown loafers that were out of tune with the rest of the ensemble he had on.

You elevated *me*?

"Bye, Hudson," I grabbed my purse, purple Nikes, and keys and stormed past him.

"So, you're seriously not going with me tonight?" Hudson asked.

I waved a middle finger. *That would be a hard no.*

I swing my legs over the side of Hudson's king-sized bed, staring at Luke's text. Except for the stray orange cat I sneak and feed when Hudson's not around, there's zero activity on the security camera, and my phone's been dry too. Hudson hasn't even called to check on me.

Girl, down.

With my phone in my hand, I slide off the bed and pad over to the large oak bookcase between the matching black lacquer dresser and chest of drawers stuffed with Hudson's obsessive collection of plain white T-shirts, black-and-white crew socks, and tighty-whities. I reach the bookcase and lift my foot to pull up the white ankle sock that slid down along the way, brushing off the dirt, lint, and hair stuck to the bottom.

"If you're going to be lying up in my man's bed, the least you could do is sling a mop and learn how to dust around here." Apparently, Skye's a bed warmer, not a homemaker.

I pace in front of the shelf, spying literary gems by John Grisham, Stephen King, and Jodi Picoult. Hidden amongst the elite is the set of bloated business books Hudson's grandfather wrote. Specifically, the *You've Got to Do Much Better* series. Oh boy, if I could get in on the conversation regarding these pompous pieces of . . . never mind. Hopefully, Old Man Pyke hired a ghostwriter to make him sound like less ignorant than he usually does. But I'll never know because I'll use the pages for toilet paper before actually reading them.

I'm stalling.

Aside from answering his texts with one-word responses or safe emojis, avoiding Luke has become a full-time job. At night when Hudson's asleep, I stalk Luke's IG account, thinking about our undeniable vibe that almost held me hostage in Texas.

That moment when. The tingling sensation grows stronger between my thighs, the same way it lingers whenever Luke crosses my mind.

Let's go on an adventure. Either I can call Izzy to move up this week's online dance session, or I can cater to my craving. My fingers fly across the screen before I chicken out.

"I was hoping you'd call," Luke's deep voice greets me.

TWENTY

"**WHAT MADE YOU** think I'd be calling?"

"First of all, even though you hate talking on the phone, you're a terrible texter," Luke observes. "And second, I knew you wouldn't deprive yourself of hearing all this sexiness too much longer. How are you doing?"

Stuck on a slow fall to hell. Other than that, I'm gravy.

"Fine." I sail my lie in the air.

"That good, huh?"

"Even better." I'm pacing in front of the bookcase, scanning the titles Hudson hasn't bothered to crack open. How do I know? Because unless I spoon-feed him the words like he's cramming to pass a third-grade assessment test, Hudson's not trying to read anything other than a contract or a script.

"Are you taking care of yourself? Been staying up on your doctor's appointments and following their instructions?"

"Yes, boss," I laugh. "My doctor gave me a clean bill of health, I've adjusted my diet, and I've even been dancing."

Luke gulps so loud, I can hear it. "Dancing? You? As in, with your own feet?" he muses a little too hard.

"Yes, funny guy. Well, I'm not dance-dancing. It's therapy. Long story that I'll fill you in on later." If Luke could see my massive grin, there'd be no denying he has a hold on me. Even though I don't always respond, it's good to know my cyst ruptured, not his empathy. His weekly texts checking on me and my health keep me going. The way he cares with his heart reaches me on a level that his hands can't touch . . . watching over me from thousands of miles away.

"Why do you keep sending me messages that I barely answer?"

"I hear what you're saying before your mouth makes a sound," he says. "Every time you wake up, somebody wants something from you. You don't even have to tell me how that wears you out." He gives me a second to let that marinate. "All I want is to be the one who doesn't want anything from you. If you'll keep me in your corner."

"Everyone wants something, even if they never ask."

"Not me." Luke's tone stiffens. "As bad as I want to feel you in my arms again and as bad as I'd like more than that with you, you and I don't have to be intimate to connect. Don't even try pretending you can't see that." There's tapping like he's typing on his end. "All I'm asking is that you grant me a tiny corner in your world, until you decide you want something better."

I chuckle softly. "And I suppose *you're* something better?"

"I like it when you call me that—*Something Better*," Luke laughs. "I see you, JC. You know that, right?"

Yes, Luke, I do. Because I see you too.

"Just wanted to put that out there. Do you know how powerful you are?"

"Because I make movies, right?"

"No. Because your energy is so strong, I feel you even when you're not close. You don't need to be in front of me to feel you, JC. Keep running, but there will always be a fine brother in a tiny Texas town who's feeling you."

"Luke, I can't—"

"I'm not asking you to do anything. But when the time comes, be honest with yourself," he says. "You know you made a mistake when you got on that plane and flew back to California. But trust me—if you ever come back to Texas, I'll never let you make that mistake again."

I turn and slide over to the packets of hot sauce and plunk them and their messages in the small trash can next to the bed. I don't need to subject myself to any more false hope.

"Enough about me, Luke. How's my Texas crew?" I ask on my way back to the bookcase.

"We miss you, JC!"

"I miss you too, Myzi!" She squeals in the background when she hears my voice, bringing a much-needed smile to my hellish day. "What's up with you, girl?"

"The better question is, what's up with Unc," she giggles, her voice growing closer. "Now that you're gone, Miss Strammel's been pushing up on him. Going hard for her man."

"Oh, really? That woman's a mess. What's she got going on over there now?"

I lean against the color-coded books, shaking my head. Miss Strammel's a jealous biddy. You'd think by the time a woman reaches middle age, she'd stop being so petty and concentrate on finding a man since she's obviously hurting for one. She can't stand me, and Lord knows I can do without her.

"She keeps rolling up in Media Tech, begging to see the film, talking about, 'You all are going to bring national attention back to H.E.C.' Since when does the guidance counselor even care about all that?" Myzi barely takes a breath, she's talking so fast. "And then, do you know she tried to come on the Cali trip with us, even though Unc told her a million times we have enough chaperones? Acting like she really cares about us when what she really wants to do is stare at Unc's booty. Ain't nobody blind. I see her old butt drooling over him all the time."

"Whoa, whoa, whoa! Enough about her old bu—I mean, Miss Strammel," Luke interjects with a mortified laugh. I cover my mouth, stifling my own. "Can you chill, please?"

"Can *she*?" Myzi counters.

As the two of them go on arguing like I'm not on the phone, I walk in front of the case, lingering between the classics and the contemporaries. Every book's usually in its place, but something's off. I keep pacing until I stop in front of Shakespeare and C. S. Lewis, which aren't as neat on the shelf as the other books.

"When are you guys getting in?" I ask absentmindedly.

"Thursday," Luke and Myzi chime together.

"That's great." I notice a small piece of paper with a gray and black picture sticking out between Shakespeare's *Othello* and C. S. Lewis's *The Problem of Pain*. I tug it out slowly, fully aware of what it is before I lay eyes on it. Close my eyes. Take a deep breath and pop my eyes back open.

A sonogram.

Scribbled across the front, red marker, in Skye's fifth-grade penmanship:

Looking just like his daddy.

Hudson lied about the pregnancy.

I'm going to throw up.

"How is asking JC to take us to Disneyland begging, Unc? We're already going to be out there, so why not?" I hear Myzi say. "If we can't go there, can we go to the beach and make some skate videos? I bet they'll go viral! Can we go, JC? JC?"

"Huh? Oh, sure, Myzi. Anything for you."

The first tear drops on the picture of Hudson's child. I wipe away the others that follow when Hudson's security monitor buzzes. Watching him jump out of the car and race toward the house makes me realize the gaping hole in my heart isn't because I miss Luke.

I miss me.

"Hey, guys, it's been cool, but I have to go." The keys rattle in the front door's lock like a warning. "Can you send me your itinerary for the weekend?"

"Of course." Luke's voice turns serious. "Is everything all right?"

"No, but it will be."

TWENTY-ONE

"BABIES DON'T JUST disappear into thin air, Hudson! What happened to your child?" When he crosses the threshold, I ambush him with the sonogram and my stale taco breath.

"JC, I—"

"No! You will *not* stand here nurturing your lie like your mama trying to grow that raggedy garden of hers, all right? Somebody needs to teach her those tomatoes aren't ripe. They're rotten—just like what you're giving me." I shove the damning piece of truth against Hudson's cheek, pushing out my anger with my howling.

Hudson's eyes buck. "Will you just listen to me? It's not what you think."

"I know piss on the toilet seat when I smell it, my love. Stop pissing on me and tell me exactly what I already *know*." What little's left of the color in Hudson's face vanishes.

"Somewhere between you and Skye spreading seed on that bed, on the same nasty mattress you haven't had the decency to replace and lying to me about it," I dart a finger toward Hudson's bedroom, "your child got lost in translation. As crazy as it sounds, I would've eventually accepted, welcomed, and treated your kid as my own. You know how I feel about babies! No one would've been able to tell me that child wasn't mine."

The lame justifications well in Hudson's protruding Adam's apple, but he says nothing. He hangs his head, making that clucking sound with his tongue that I hate so much, while he pats a hand against his thigh.

"Listen, I'm bleeding profusely, and—"

"Spare me your clever metaphors for our hemorrhaging relationship," Hudson interrupts. "Either we're working this out, or we're not."

"Okay, I was referring to the actual blood spewing from my vagina because, in case you've forgotten, while you've been humping around, I'm dealing with *real* medical issues." I ball my hand into a fist. "Before anything else comes out of your mouth, please know that I'm frustrated, exhausted, and fragile. Tread those Adidas lightly."

"Your priorities are messed up," Hudson spits in a shaky voice. "Right now, we need to focus on how much money your tantrum on my set cost me today!"

"*Our* set, Hudson? Ours? Our set, our movie, our life!" The sonogram slips from my clammy fingers and sails to the floor, taking both my lungs with it. "I guess you're just going to keep glaring at me like I'm stupid. And I am—for fooling myself into believing any of this was ever real. I knew it wasn't...*everyone* knew!" I slap my hands over my face and take a deep breath.

"You know what I'm going to do, Hudson? I'm going to go pour myself a nice ol' glass of bourbon until you're ready to tell me what I already know."

"If you already know, then there's no need for me to say it, right?"

A cloud casts over Hudson's stubborn face. He's torn between the truth setting me free or him getting fired from our relationship—like I should've done long ago.

I shove Hudson against the wall and stomp to the mini-bar in his western-themed den.

"I don't know what it is that needs explaining, JC," Hudson steps over his baby's first photo and scurries behind me as I flee to the next room. "There's nothing to do here other than move forward." He gets in my face as I guzzle down the drink I poured myself.

I tip the empty glass to Hudson like a delayed toast. "You know what the difference between you and me is?"

He shakes his head.

"Talking and listening," I slur. "If you'd stop talking so much, you'd be able to hear that moving forward is a problem!"

I turn my back and pour a second round, liquid splashing until it hits the rim.

"Do you know how tired I am of being stuck with the consequences for crap I didn't cause?" I mutter between swigs. "Too black, too woman, too . . . me. *Get over it and move on, JC.* Do me dirty? *The Bible says forgive—forget about it, JC.*"

My spittle sprinkles Hudson's face as I mock him and everyone who's downgraded my feelings. "*You've got to learn to stop allowing things to hold you back, JC. Just move on. You'll never get anywhere if you keep rehearsing things in your mind, JC.*" This time, I take a huge gulp, ignoring my buzzing cell. "You know what? If you all would stop forcing me to push my misery aside, I wouldn't be as close as I am to quitting."

"Quitting what?"

"Me," I clarify. "Hiding behind happy walls is what got me here. But here's where sis gets off the ride before you people kill me."

Hudson takes the glass from my hands and sets it carefully on the bar. Smart move.

"Why do you always insist on being so dramatic?"

"Go to hell, Hudson. Respectfully."

My cell rings again. I hold up a hand in Hudson's face and snatch it out to see who's blowing me up. I see Temper's number; she can wait.

"Are you coming at me straight, or am I about to have to tear this place up?"

Hudson rubs his temples like I'm the one getting on his nerves. Counting backward has never once helped me, but I'm going to give this another try, just in case it'll save me some stress.

All right, here we go.

100, 99, 98, 97 . . .

. . . This isn't working.

I give up and wrap my arms around myself. "In the middle of an all-out war waging through my body, you make the one thing I want—a child, disappear like you took the trash out."

"So, you're upset that I didn't keep a baby that's not yours?"

"No. I'm crushed that you created one with a woman who's not yours!" I sink my fist into my mouth, take a deep breath, and swallow. "Women should be able to sue men like you for making us wake up every morning to eat your disrespect for breakfast. I can't take it anymore, Hudson. I can't."

I move to the door, but Hudson grabs me by the shoulders, swings me around, and shoves me against the nearest wall. Not hard, but enough to force a little wind out of my chest. He's never put his hands on me before, but the redness ravaging his eyes has me scared.

"You can't leave me, JC," he stutters. "I'm not losing you!"

"You already have." I try to push Hudson off me, but he pins me harder. I write this stuff, not live it. My legs quake beneath me; I don't want this to turn into something domestic.

"Calm down and get off me, Hudson." I sputter in the calmest, most even tone I can muster. He backs away with raised hands, putting enough space between us for me not to call the police.

"You can't leave like this." Hudson's voice quivers like he's on the verge of tears, but there's not one crocodile lurking in his ducts.

My cell rings again. *Not now, Temper.*

"I was going to forgive you. Again," I spill the beans on my thwarted plans. "With everything in me, I was ready to work through our problems. But you made the choice for me not to. I'm done."

"Please, JC. This is how I was raised. You know what I've been through. " He's a beat closer to crying on cue, but I haven't yelled "action."

"Until you experience you, Hudson, you haven't been through anything." Standing there with our entire history rolling through my brain like a vintage black-and-white, silent story reel, it dawns on me that my half of our story is the only one making any sounds.

Hudson jams his hands in his pockets and drops his gaze to the floor, sweeping our problems underneath the abstract Tuscany area rug with the rest of the dust. His shoe sliding back and forth sounds like the clock ticking our relationship to a close.

"You keep seeing me as the source of our breakdowns, but it's not my fault," he murmurs. No passion, no conviction. "I've told you over and over again how when I was coming up, there weren't hugs in our house, and *I love you's* came with price tags," he tells the floor before lifting his eyes to me. "You're so desperate to label me as a bad boyfriend that you don't even stop to think about how being raised the way I was affected me. It's not fair, JC. You want me to love you the way you want to be loved without me ever having a blueprint of what love is!"

"*I'm* your blueprint," I squeal. "Been that since you took me out on that first date. And it's so sad that after all these years I've wasted, you *still* haven't paid attention."

I shove his head back with the three fingers in the middle of my hand pressed together. "You know what? We can stop right here. There's nothing else to say that's not going to make me end up hating you."

I caress Hudson's cheek, letting my hand linger longer than it should. "Listen, I mean this in the best possible way—really, I do. The only way for me not to hate you is to remove myself. Because this right here? This is how people end up on the news talking about, '*She always seemed so nice. I never knew she had that in her.*'" I pat his cheek again. "It's in me, baby. And I need to get out of here before it comes out, okay?"

I gently peck his cheek and move to exit, but Hudson blocks the entryway. He raises his hands to prove he's not about to try anything stupid. "I'm sick," he claims with a straight face. "I suck at love, but I can do better. I *will* do better. Stay here, and let me prove it to you."

A cluster of hairs that escaped the rubber band securing my high ponytail in place grazes the back of my neck when I shake my head. "Hudson, I'm not about to coddle you until I reach menopause and break up at the age when most men think they're settling if they get with me. Nope. Can't do it. I won't." I shake my head. "Before my body changes any more than it has, before I have to accept someone who's not for me because my options are low, and before I get completely jaded that not only love does exist, I'm worthy of it, I have to do this. For me."

"Wait," Hudson cuts me off before I can say anything else. "You're doing that therapy stuff, so why can't we go together?"

"Together? I'm in therapy *because* of you," I spit a gravely chuckle in his face, waving my hands like he's crazy. "You need help, so go get it on your own. In the meantime, I'm finally going to get what I need—self-care and triple-chocolate cake."

Nothing could have prepared me for Hudson to drop at my feet and start weeping. The emotionless, careless bundle of nonchalance that has slept beside me all these years melts into a blubbery heap. It's not fair. Tears aren't fair.

Don't look, don't look, don't look. If you look, you'll never leave.
I look.

Using my legs to support his weight, Hudson pulls up onto his knees and wraps his arms around my waist, his face buried in my crotch. "You're supposed to love me through my mess," he squalls.

"Not if it means losing myself!"

Hudson baptizes me in tears I feel through the depths of my soul. I'm desperate to help him, but I can't handle the weight of his shortcomings anymore. Maybe it isn't fair for me to step away because of his imperfections, but this isn't about pet peeves. Blind loyalty is draining me. If I don't get out now, I'll be the shell I pity on other women like me.

I gently nudge Hudson away. "I have to get my stuff."

"No! It's not ending like this. I won't let it!"

I kneel in front of Hudson. Avoid his eyes so that I won't change my mind for the millionth time. Sometimes, tears are healing. But mostly, they're manipulative little things. They make wrong right and right wrong—skew common sense. Make us change our minds and pivot opposite of where we should be heading. Force us to sacrifice ourselves for the other person's wants over our needs. Tears are some of the greatest weapons known to man. They're one of our most finite, tiniest parts, but they carry the biggest consequences.

Sometimes, distance separates the villains from the victims in our stories. Watching Hudson drench the cold floor with his wounds makes me wonder which one I'll be 10 years from now.

I take Hudson's hands in mine. "Come see me to the door."

He slams his hands on the floor, snatches off his glasses, and screams at the top of his lungs. "You will never find a man to love you like I do! You're nothing without me—I *made* you!"

And there it is. His project, *not* his partner.

"Hudson, if God promises never to send me another man like you, I'll volunteer to get baptized in a pit of burning holy oil and plant my butt on the front pew every Sunday dressed in white to make sure it sticks." I stand and brush myself off. "I'm done making this easy on you." My cell rings again, and I snatch it out. "Yes, Mom!"

Hudson struggles to his feet and jabs a finger in my face. "Until the investors saw my face, nobody would give that ghetto mess you pass off as art a chance. You couldn't even get a meeting!"

"What? Hold on, I can't hear." I wave a hand to shut Hudson up. "Mom?" She sounds muffled, so I cover my ear to hear better over Hudson's ranting.

". . . and it was *me* who helped you when you wouldn't stop crying over your dead daddy!"

Hudson's teeth cut into my knuckles when I lower the phone from my ear and do my best to flip them backward with my fist. He stumbles back, holding the spot where I sideswiped his jaw.

"JC?" Mom's voice sounds like she's immersed in water when I return to the phone.

"Why did you hit me?" Hudson hollers.

I shake my stinging hand without responding to him. "Mom?"

"Hang up the phone and talk to me," Hudson demands.

"Back off. Something's wrong with my mother."

"I don't care if she's dying," he says. "Leave from that door, and you'll never hear from me again."

"Finally, I'll get what I've been begging for the last hour!" I roll my eyes and storm out of the room.

"Come back here, JC!"

"JC," the faint voice on the line mutters again.

"What, Mom? Why are you blowing up my phone?"

"It's Tati," the weary voice says.

"Tati? Why are you calling from my mother's phone?"

Tati sounds like she's holding her breath. "I'm with Temper at the hospital. She's had a heart attack."

TWENTY-TWO

EVEN IN THE face of death, my mother will forever and always remain her gloriously vain self.

When I was ten, I broke my arm, filming myself baking snickerdoodles in the kitchen. Don't ask. I still don't know what made me sadder: the immediate rise and fall of my baking career or Temper putting me on ice until she got her face together.

"I know you don't expect me to show up at the hospital a mess and risk one of my fans seeing me with an ashy face," Temper purred as she smudged her lip gloss on a tissue and tossed it aside like only Temper can do. Thank God my father rushed home from Bible study and drove me to the hospital himself while Mom threw on an extra coat of mascara from the passenger's side. That's what I'm thinking about now while I prance around her hospital room, documenting her miracle.

"JC, darling, get that camera out my face before I get out of this bed, girl."

"I dare you to," I laugh and round the bed, moving the camera in and out for the *Blair Witch Project* effect instead of zooming as I go. "The doctor says you don't have enough strength to squish an ant. Get up if you want to, and let's see if he's lying."

"Don't let that doctor get you whipped. I'll show both of you just how much strength this old gal has." She raises her hands and coughs in them. "Go on and cut that thing off, baby. You know I look a mess."

Actually, she doesn't. I don't think I've seen Temper's natural hair without wigs, braids, or dyed since I was 12. The cluster of silver forming a small pond on the right side of her dark brown crown is startling, but I see it as proof of a life that's been well lived. The woman smoothing the sterile white cover over her lean frame has survived things that would've caused others to die, including me. Motherhood, racism, gender inequality, religiousness, classism ... even though her status put her in a higher class than her harshest critics. As misguided as some of her steps have been, Temper's a fantastic mother. The only one I'll ever have.

"You look fine, Mother."

"What I look is my age," Temper snaps. "And where is Tati with the wig and lashes I asked her to bring back here last night? She knows that trifling EMT dropped my good hair on the ground and got it stuck in the gurney's wheel when he rolled over it. If that young man were here right now—"

"I'd give him a reward for saving my precious cargo." My lens catches the fine lines etched throughout Temper's face like delicate paint strokes when I zoom in. "You should keep the gray. It actually looks wonderful on you."

"That's how you cheer people up? Where have I failed you as a mother? The last thing I want is to run around looking like somebody's grandma." Temper swallows hard when I lower the camera, stone-faced. "I'm sorry, baby."

"It's all right, Mom. No eggshells, right?"

"No shells," she agrees.

I hit stop on the recording and set the camera on top of my duffel bag in the chair by the door. Then I let out a huge yawn. Knowing that Temper's okay will help me get some sleep later. I walk over to the side of her bed and settle in.

"If you wanted to get me back out here to pamper you, then just say that. Don't go having a heart attack next time, you hear me, girl?"

Temper's eyes survey my red joggers matching top with **I Hate It Here** stamped over the Supreme Court logo. "Trust, I certainly didn't plan on passing out during my rendition of "What You See Is a Miracle" with 5,000 people trying to get a shot of my wig halfway off my head. Good thing I was covered by the Blood of Jesus and good ol'-fashioned slip."

Temper's cracked lips form a faint smile. She cocks her head and picks at my hair. "You, on the other hand, might want to consider a bit of pampering yourself with these plaits all over your head, my dear."

"Cornrows, Mom." I rock my head away from her hand. "Sorry I didn't have a chance to get fancy before I hopped the red-eye to come check on my almost-departed mother." I lean in and kiss her forehead. "I'm glad you're still amongst the living."

"Me too, sweets." Temper's stable breathing beats the sound of her greatest hits. "Are you okay, baby?"

"I'm so good right now," I say. "You know that silver really does bring out the brown in your eyes." Temper chuckles and swats at me, but she's too weak to put any power behind it. Kind of like a halfhearted prayer. "Tell me again, Mom."

Temper rolls her eyes. "What is it about hospitals that make you want to revisit your birth story?"

I shrug. "I don't know. I just like hearing you tell it, I guess."

"Scoot back," Temper says. I nestle my backside to her abdomen—careful not to put any extra weight on her. "For eight months, you were the easiest pregnancy a mother could ask for." Her voice turns dreamy. That's why getting her to tell this story so much is a beautiful distraction.

"I didn't have any morning sickness," Temper goes on. "The bump your little feet stretched out was adorable, and my skin was never clearer." She gives me a light squeeze and buries her face in my back. "A month before your due date, you decided to give me 30 days' notice that you were moving out of my belly for a bigger place. Suddenly, my legs and feet swelled to the size of an elephant. I couldn't breathe and threw up everything I did and didn't eat. I was a mess, child."

"Daddy said he'd never seen you more beautiful."

"One thing you should remember about your father is he was quite the charmer. That's why I fell in love with him." Temper's probably winking behind my back. "He wasn't a liar, either. Despite you terrorizing my body, I still looked marvelous!"

I slide my hand over hers. "I gave you hell, huh?"

"If you deem the placenta rupturing and you swallowing the amniotic fluid, then yes. It was something out of a horror movie. You almost killed both of us, girl." Temper's arms slide from around me. "Hey, look at me." I turn sideways and stare into her eyes.

"I had an emergency C-section because you had stopped breathing. That and the following weeks with you in NICU was the scariest time in my life. It was like torture. All I wanted was to hold you in my arms. I had lost so much blood, I was too weak to hold you, but I didn't care. All I wanted was my little coffee bean to be healthy and safe, even if it meant giving up my own life."

"You did, Mom. You did."

"People change when they're loved well. You know that?"

I trace her thick brows with my pinkie. "I didn't before, but now I do."

There's a soft knock at the door before Tati bounces in the room, bogged down with at least four shopping bags and a ring light. "Finally," Temper says without giving her a chance to speak. "I do hope you brought Mona with you, honey."

"Who's Mona?" I hop off the bed and jam my hands on my hips.

"Mona is her red bob wig that resembles the Roaring Twenties." Tati drops the bags on the floor. "I couldn't find her in that apartment you call a closet, Mama T, but I did run into someone interesting in the waiting room."

"Who?" Temper and I chime together.

Tati strolls over to me with a massive grin and laces an arm through my arm. "Luke's here. You might want to tighten up those braids and pop a mint before you go in there, boo."

TWENTY-THREE

GIVEN THAT I can currently pass for "Cleo" Sims in *Set It Off*, that I keep plane hopping between Texas and California like it's a short commute, and that mere hours ago, my mother had a gaggle of tubes shoved down her throat, the last thing I'm expecting when I round the corner to the secluded second-floor room where Luke's waiting for me is a romantic picnic.

Somebody's lying to me.

The first thing I see in the space that's no bigger than an apartment bedroom stands an open-faced tent constructed with wood, a white lace canopy, and LED lights illuminating the faux vine tracing down the beams. Three yellow throw pillows are propped against the back of the tent, which sits on a beige and white crochet rug. The pillow on the left is checkered with silver squares; a giant sunflower spans most of the one on the right. It's the middle pillow that catches my eye, though—the one embroidered with LOVE in silver lettering.

"Follow me." Luke grabs my hand and escorts me inside, oblivious that I haven't muttered one word. Maybe he thinks I'm in awe. Or maybe he forgot how much I hate surprises.

There are less than 10 steps from the door leading to this sweet universe Luke created, to where my mother is recovering from a heart attack.

"Here, have a seat."

Luke helps me sit on the floor at the short wooden table in front of the tent. A yellow runner parts the middle of the table with a supersized, silver grazing platter bookended by two sunflower-accented place settings. I snatch a strawberry from the round tray packed with grapes, meats, cheeses, crackers, pretzels, rye, and wheat bread cut into compact squares. There's more hot, dill, and bread-n-butter pickles, black and green olives, nuts, and dips than I've consumed in the last five years. Two silver wine flutes are filled with clear sparkling water, and chocolate candies are peppered around the bases.

The foot of the table is flanked by two wicker baskets supporting it like an extra pair of legs. To Luke's right is an easel holding a blank, 16 x 20 white canvas, and a small wire basket stocked with paints and brushes. Scanning the elaborate table, my gaze parks on a pile of books with plain white candles stacked next to them, and a miniature white baby grand piano-shaped music box settled on top. A spattering of sunflowers is randomly sprinkled throughout the table, along with six gift-wrapped boxes in an assortment of shapes and sizes.

If I were in a position where love still matters, I'd be impressed. But all the turmoil grafting my heart makes me feel so out of place, so opposite of Luke's plans, I'm almost angry.

"What's this?" I take a sip of chilled water.

My lack of enthusiasm drops Luke's expectant face to the bottom of the white stripes running down his black joggers like arrows. His hurt gaze parks on top of his solid red tennis.

"I thought you'd . . ." his deflated voice trails off. Probably distracted by the way I nonchalantly snatch a piece of pastrami, plop it on a cracker, and pile a pickle chip and green olive on top.

"You're disappointed. I didn't mean to infringe, but I thought this would help relieve some of the stress with everything that's going on." Luke's voice is gruff, like I've criticized him for coloring outside the lines. He stretches one leg in front of himself on the floor, raises his other to rest his arm on his knee, and waits for me to explain myself.

"I'm thinking a get-well card would've sufficed." I finish the cracker and quickly build another snack tower. I start jamming the food into my mouth to hold off what's next.

"Have I done something to upset you?" Luke raises his hand. "Why are you mad? I mean, most women like you would be happy I went out of my way like this for them."

I unwrap a praline and pop it into my mouth. Smack real hard while I let that marinate like the melting chocolate on my tongue.

"Tell me, Luke. How would *most women like me* react when they've gone through as much as I have for the past few months? The past few days? And how would they react when they haven't had a bath, done their hair, brushed their teeth, or had a good, strong bowel movement because their mother's well-being means more than their next breath?"

I toss the empty candy wrapper to the floor and swipe my hands over my plaits. I mean, cornrows.

"I didn't mean it like that, JC."

"Then what is all this, Luke?"

"This is me trying to get you to see me as a prospect, not your peer." *Well, hold my beer.*

"So, you thought now would be an appropriate time to push up?"

"That's not what I meant. This is all coming out wrong, nothing like I intended. I'm not trying to get in your drawers, I'm just trying to be here for you." Luke massages his goatee, blowing frustration in the air. He leans over, reaches inside one of the baskets, pulls out a thin, hardcover book, and hands it to me. "Maybe this can explain."

On the book's cover is an animated version of Luke with exaggerated features, including a grin as wide as the cover. I pop it open, skeptical that whatever's inside will improve any of this.

Page one—Luke's miniature body and bobblehead hold a ginormous bundle of sunflowers like he's handing them off the page to the reader.

Luke says sunflowers bring positivity, strength, admiration, and loyalty. Good luck and forever happiness. It's going to get better.

Page two—Luke's seated at a piano like the music box sitting on top of the books.

Luke says Temper never travels without a white baby grand to bring hope to everyone who hears her angelic voice. May you always hear the sound of love and feel the joy of being cared for.

Page three—Luke's holding the camera, taking a selfie.

Luke says taking selfies is all right, but memories should be created together.

Page four—Luke's standing at the easel, painting red hearts across the canvas.

Luke says the heart becomes less heavy when it's out there for someone they trust to see.

I glance up briefly, tears stinging my eyes as I brace myself to continue reading.

Page five—There's a real Polaroid of Luke superimposed on the page. He looks about five or six years old, with both front teeth missing from his smile. I trace the empty spaces with my index finger and try not to laugh at the thick frames that cover half his face. Who could foresee the astonishing grown man this awkward kid would grow into? I don't know whether to smile or fling this thing at Luke's head.

This little guy understood love, even before he knew how love defines who he is. And before he learned how complicated, out of sorts, and sometimes messy it gets, he also knew love doesn't take forever to identify.

I don't want to turn the page. I really don't . . .

... but my fingers betray me on bated breath.

When I flip the page, there's a photo of Luke and me together, dressed in white, at Mayor Miller's memorial.

It may seem fast or out of nowhere to you, and it may not even make any sense.

On the opposite page, animated Luke and I face each other on skates, holding hands and smooching. Little JC has one foot kicked back.

Despite how crazy it seems, the love you brought to my life is right on time for me.

In the corner of my eye, I spot a tiny black box I hadn't noticed before.

I flip to the last page.

A sketch of us at the altar in wedding attire and fancy white skates peeks at me. There's a phrase I never expected to see this soon—or ever—painted in red graffiti above the skates:

Jonica Burke, marry me.

"How dare you think I'm going to neglect my mother for this ridiculous insta-love, happily-ever-after fantasy you have of us, Luke!" He ducks when I whizz the book past his head, missing hitting him by less than an inch.

"I got Temper's permission before I did any of this." Luke scrambles to his feet and rushes over to the easel, out of range.

"There's no way my mother granted you permission to be this stupid!" I stomp to the throw pillows and hurl them at him, one by one. "You're a great guy, Luke. A great guy, with the worst possible timing." I melt to the floor on my knees, out of ammo to fire from my hands. "I'm broken. And neither of us knows if I'll ever get put back together."

Luke shoves his jacket sleeves up his arms and takes a couple of steps toward me. I push my hands forward to stop him. "This isn't the love story you want it to be, no matter how hard you wish." I close my eyes and swallow the regret swelling in my throat. "You want the slipper to fit so badly, but Cinderella doesn't live here."

"We're adults, JC! Why are you always throwing fairy tales in my face?" He inches closer and squats close to the floor. "Everything I do is real. Real feelings, real life."

I mush the back of my hand against my nostrils to block the mucus from leaking onto my face. "In real life, I'm at the point where if one more thing goes wrong, I don't care how tiny it is, I'm going to make somebody's evening newscast. So when I say no more bad news, I mean it."

When I lift my head, Luke's eyes are sullen. "If you're sincere about marrying me, then I'm about to break your heart, and I don't want to do that. The suckiest part about love is when the person you fell in love with, the person you know, becomes the one you knew." A thousand butterflies explode in my chest. "I need to know you, Luke. Don't you get that? I need to *know* you."

"I know it's hard for you to believe, but I really do love you and want to spend the rest of my life with you."

"You don't even *know* me," I screech. A middle-aged man dressed in scrubs pops into the room, dragging a cleaning cart behind him, interrupting my tirade. "Oh, I'm sorry. I didn't know anyone was in here," he apologizes.

"No problem, man. I think we're almost finished." Luke holds his breath until the man disappears. "I *do* know you, Jonica. I know you keep gels on your fingers since you bite your natural nails off when you don't. I know you burn popcorn because you get distracted and leave it in the microwave too long." He flashes a wounded smile. "I know your life's full of extremes and excesses, but you crave quiet moments like those fancy chocolates you always eat. You hold everything inside because you're afraid of disruption. You laugh when you're nervous, cry when you're happy, and when your smile's genuine, it takes up your entire body. Tell me I'm wrong."

He waits for me to refute any of those things, but they're all facts.

"Don't sit here and tell me I don't know you because I haven't learned whether you brush your teeth with the water running or not. Celebrate the fact that I know the little things your other man missed."

I wave my hands in the air. "Luke, not every woman's epilogue includes a husband and three kids. I'm not in a rush to get married by 30. All I want right now is to read a good book when I want to, eat whatever I want without counting calories, have clear pores, have some peace of mind, and someday be a guest on *The View*. That's it. I'm not trying to change the world every day, and I'm not trying to let the world worry me." I push out a puff of air so heavy, I bet Luke can see it like cigarette smoke flying out my mouth.

"Right now, a life vest for me would be dumping a bowl of Cap'n Crunch in a spaghetti-stained mixing bowl and eating it dry, a mimosa, and laying up under my mama with my phone on DND. So, you could've kept all this. Except those olives. They're orgasmic." I grab one from the tray, pop it into my mouth, and slump back down.

Luke plops on his behind, both knees up. He leans back with his hands cupped over his face and lets out a cross between a growl and a moan. "Forgive me for not realizing that women don't appreciate romance anymore."

"I love romance. What I don't love is putting exclamation points where I still have question marks."

Luke slides over to me like Patrick Swayze is about to pull Baby from the corner in *Dirty Dancing*. "You take on the world without boxing gloves," he says. "All I'm asking is for you to lower your fists and let me fight for you. Let me help you. Let me protect you." He points across the hall, where I'm hoping Temper's resting well. "You don't have to go through any of this alone. All I want to do is take care of you."

"That's the problem. I'm tired of people using care as a weapon. Like without giving up my boundaries for you, I'm going to fail," I tell him. "And why are you looking at me like that?"

"Because I'm trying to find the woman I proposed to!" Luke hops off the floor, goes to the table, and snatches the open bottle of sparkling water. The sound of his chugging prickles my skin. He hunches forward, touching his knees, then bolts straight up. "None of this makes sense. You're probably the only woman who'd turn down a proposal this way. I pulled out my good moves. This feels like a bunch of excuses and bulls—"

A million responses try tunneling their way from the pit of my belly, but my ringing cell stops me. Without looking at the ID, I hit answer.

"I told you not to go back to Texas."

"Hudson?" His voice startles me. "Now's not a good time. I'll call you back."

"I told you," he slurs again. "I'm so sorry, JC. I didn't mean to do it."

"You're drunk. I'm going to hang up."

"It was an accident, JC. I'm so sorry." Seeing how shaken I am, Luke casts his hurt feelings aside and races over to me as I listen to Hudson sobbing.

"Do you want me to talk to him?" Luke asks. I shake my head and clutch the phone.

"What exactly are you sorry for, Hudson?"

"Your apartment," Hudson wails. "I didn't mean to do it . . . just went to get my stuff . . . I'll pay for it. I'll pay for it all."

"Stop talking in riddles," I yell. "Pay for what?"

"Your apartment, JC. It's on fire."

Well, there's one more thing . . .

TWENTY-FOUR

EVERYTHING I TOUCH turns to dust.

"It's gone," I whisper to myself. "Everything . . . gone."

I'm in a room away from Luke and Hudson because if Luke's choking Hudson like he promised me he'd do on the plane ride back to Cali, I don't want to have to testify against him.

Wading through the pile of rubble in what used to be my bedroom, I'm hoping that by the time I manage to summon enough strength to go back into the living room, I'll see Hudson's lifeless body buried beneath the ashes of what used to be my life.

"You're such a man that you burn JC's house down just because she doesn't want you anymore?" Luke yells while I waft through the mess on a dust cloud. "You're not a man. You're a punk coward who deserves exactly what I'm about to give him!"

Add that to the list of foul names Luke has called Hudson since we arrived. Thank God he flew back here with me. I'm too violated to function.

God never puts more on us than we can bear, I heard somebody say on the way here.

You know what? That actually doesn't help at all.

It didn't help when one of my Cox professors tried to fail me because the film I submitted for my final, *Code: Black*, was too radical. Didn't help when Temper quoted it at Daddy's funeral, just before she sang "His Eye Is on the Sparrow," when all I wanted was my father's eyes on me. And it sure as hell isn't helping when the last few months of my life have felt like I've been in a boxing match that I'm losing, and the ref refuses to call a draw. It isn't even a scripture. It's a cliché religious folk use to replace compassion. Say it all you want; unless you're the one bearing the pain, it's just words.

My tennis sink into the carpet, soggy from the ton of water it took to put out the fire. The footprints I leave behind are more solid than the stuff that survived the flames. Heading from the guest room I use—well, *used*, as a spare closet, I step over the purple-beaded gown with a thigh-high split up the right side and plunging neckline that I wore when I accepted the Best Director SAG Award for *Flogged*.

The night before the ceremony, I practiced controlling my face when I lost more than the acceptance speech if I won, so I'd lose with a smile. I learned that from all of Temper's trips to the Grammys. My acceptance speech was probably the worst in the history of the awards. Still, the media called my sincere ugly cry "endearing"; I made history and at least six best-dressed lists simultaneously.

I squat next to the platinum-framed cover of *Essence* of me sporting a kinky Afro that was so long and full, it covered up all my lady bits that the teeny gold dress I wore did not.

JC Burke: The Table She Made.

I study my contented gaze, coyly peering over my shoulder, gold lip gloss popping under the Galveston sun where the photo shoot was taken on the beach. Celebrity photographer Reynaldo Lumas was a pretty man who checked every box beneath "unprofessional" and had too many years over me to be flirting with me the way he was. Right in front of Hudson. Hudson hated how I flirted with Reynaldo's lens, but that cover was fire. And now the glass is shattered where Hudson stomped it with his foot—because that's what Hudson does. If you can't buy it, break it.

All of the material things that used to mean so much scream at me like spirits caught in purgatory. None of them ready to let me go.

The stench of smoke and mildew makes my stomach recoil as I tip through the destruction back to the living room. My feet don't feel like they're touching the floor; my mind's too jumbled to notice if they are. Somehow, I make it over to the ratty old forest-green and mustard plaid sofa I pulled all-night study sessions on in my dorm room at Cox. Ramen Noodles and generic brand crackers, bottled water, and Capri Sun, if I had a little extra change, got me through on that couch. So much sweat, slob, and tears soaked in that ugly chair. My last piece of *normal* before life changed. Now, it's nothing but memories and ashes.

"JC, you know I wouldn't do anything to hurt you on purpose," Hudson screams when I reappear. "You know I wouldn't!"

"That doesn't sound like an apology to me." Luke grabs Hudson by the shoulders, slams him to the floor, and kneels beside him. "How about you take the bass out of your voice and show a little humility to the woman whose life you ruined!" He reaches back a fist and pulls Hudson up by the collar of his white button-down, ready to pummel him again. Before he can make contact, I manage to make it over and grab him by the wrist.

"Don't." I don't yell, scream, or beg. There's barely enough wind in my lungs to speak.

At first, Luke scares me. I've never seen him so worked up like this. Veins in his neck popping, biceps pulsating, nostrils flaring. This is a man who wants to take something away from the person who robbed me. But I can't let him. I want Hudson to panic. To cut myself open in front of him, so he could see the gory remnants of every organ he poisoned inside me. I want him to feel lost, hopeless, and that death is the only relief he'll ever experience when he sees me living happily without him.

Pain surges through my side as it did when my cyst ruptured. Hudson didn't do me the honor of even worrying about me when he found out what happened; showing him wouldn't make a difference now. I'm the wife he screwed over before we took our vows.

And I want him to cry over me.

"Let karma handle him," I murmur.

The carpet slushes when Luke lets Hudson slip from his grasp, and his head slams against the floor. He strolls next to me and lays a hand on my shoulder, waiting for the signal for him to finish what he started.

Hudson scrambles to his feet. Luke clamps a bit harder on my shoulder to keep me in place. I need to feel Hudson's breath trickle down my face when he speaks. Need to inhale the scent that's kept me entranced for so long, even though the fumes from the fire are all I can smell. I want Hudson to feel me disconnect the IV that's been feeding us. I gently brush away Luke's hand and drag my feet over to him.

"Why are you crying?" I ask Hudson.

"None of this was intentional. You have to believe me."

"Tell that to the police," Luke jumps in.

I hold up a hand. "Out of all the things I hate about myself, what I hate most is that I love you so much you don't have to worry about me pressing charges. Because I'm not." I pretend not to feel Luke's shock boring into the back of my head. "Don't feed me whatever excuse you've come up with to justify ripping my life from under me because I don't care. I just want you to know that I'm done. With all of this." I cover my mouth and choke into my hands, then spot my legion of dragonflies on my arm. Protecting me.

"You don't have to do this," Luke says.

"You know what?" I face him with a cautious smile. "I appreciate you so much for coming with me and making sure I'm okay. I'm not even sure I deserve a friend like you."

"Hear that, my guy? *Friend*." Hudson takes the opportunity to regulate Luke to the zone on my behalf.

"You're the last person I need cosigning for me," I tell Hudson, then turn back to Luke. "Thank you, Luke, but I don't need permission anymore. From anyone. Okay?" The vein in Luke's neck protrudes; his eyes tighten. He rubs his fingers together like he's itching to put his hands on Hudson again but slowly inches an arm's length away to honor my request.

I face Hudson. "As ridiculous as it sounds, I needed this reset to happen. I'm not happy, Hudson. I'm not. But I've been too afraid to pull the trigger. I should be furious with you, but you set me free."

"But I'm telling you, I didn't do it." I hear Luke suck his teeth as Hudson squeezes out a fresh crop of tears. "Things will change," he promises. "I swear I'll be a man of my word about that from now on. I'll do better to love you the way I should have been doing a long time ago."

"Love can't be won through fear, Hudson." I press my palms into my eyes, then take them away. "I'm scared of who you are without having control over me. We've been fixated on each other without putting in the heart work. Look around here—look!"

Regret registers on Hudson's remorseful face as he does what I ask.

"There's nothing left. You made sure of that. Sure, a few things here and there can be salvaged, but the one thing that can't is this relationship. This isn't love. So, respectfully, I quit."

Hudson drags his weary eyes to mine as if I'm not the one who should be tired. "Quit what?"

"You. The film. The production company—all of it."

"You can't, JC! I won't let you leave me." Hudson takes a step forward, then stops when he sees Luke ready.

"Don't come near me," I hiss. "You gave me a gift; now, I'm giving you one. Start over, Hudson. Get a new narrative, learn how to be a decent human." I scan the length of his body, committing his jaunt face to memory. "When Luke and I walk out that door, you are not to contact me, my mother, Tati, Luke, or anyone associated with me. Don't DM me or even like any of my pictures on social media. In fact, unfollow me on every platform so you won't even be tempted. Because if you try to make any contact with me starting this very second, yesterday wasn't an accident. And I'll have you prosecuted to the fullest extent of the law. Understand?"

He doesn't, but doesn't say so.

"Now, please go, so Luke and I can sort through this mess, and I can restart my life."

"Jonica Burke, you're seriously not pressing charges on that man? Girl, you are better than me."

"Aren't you the same woman who's all right with the man who shot her coming up for parole because unforgiveness clogs your pores, *Pastor?*"

"Finish stretching, girl."

Izzy lifts a leg across the ballet barre in the therapy studio. She bends over it, stretching her side while I sit on the floor. Today's mood music, Michael Jackson's "Thriller." My current situation. "So, you have plans tonight for Halloween?" I ask.

"Only hiding out on the recliner, getting cozy with Netflix, and stuffing my face with the candy I pretended to buy for the kids," Izzy laughs. "You know, my typical Saturday night."

"Need any company?"

Izzy takes her leg off the barre and stares at me. "No trick or treating with the kids and *The Hottie Professor?*"

"*The Hottie Professor* helped me take care of the mess at my apartment, then stayed behind in California with his students for the film festival. Meanwhile, I'm waiting by the phone to see if they won."

"So, are you two . . ."

I shake my head. "We haven't talked about the proposal, and I'm not ready to commit to anything more than today. If it's not benefitting me, I don't want any part of it."

"So, being with Luke doesn't benefit you?"

I think hard for a moment, biting my bottom lip. "Luke's a wonderful man. Really, he is. The way he helped me through all of this . . . If I was a praying woman, he'd be exactly what I'd pray for." I wring my hands together and sigh. "The timing's just off. I don't want a partner when I haven't figured out my purpose."

"Makes sense. But don't you want to be there with Luke and the kids in case they win? I mean, you worked just as hard on the film as they did."

"Luke and Elaine have it under control. They don't need me there."

"You sure about that?"

I shrug off her question, extending my right leg to the side on the floor. I point my left foot next to the right knee and stretch my torso and arms over my leg. "I'll be much too busy crashing at Temper's, pretending not to be mortified that she insists on binding the devil to every child who knocks on her door tonight before she forks over the candy."

Izzy leans with her back against the barre and elbows propped on it and laughs. "And how is Temper feeling?"

"Worried about me, but that's to be expected. I'm trying to get her to relax so she won't have another heart attack, but that girl is hardheaded."

"Well, you did just lose everything in a fire that your boyfriend—"

"*Ex-boyfriend.*" I correct.

"That your *ex–boyfriend* set."

"Allegedly," I add on.

Izzy stomps over and plops on the floor in front of me. The messy bun piled on top of her head looks as frustrated as she is. "Cut the crap, JC. Your entire purpose for being here isn't to indulge in smoke and mirrors. It's to let out all that junk that makes you happy you lost what you did in the fire."

"All right," I concede more cheerfully than I intend. "I'm actually content. See, a wise woman once wrote, focus on the steps, and the dance will fall into place."

An easy grin stretches across Izzy's face. "You read my book."

I wink at her. "At the suggestion of said wise sensei, I'm relishing in my own power instead of wasting it on everyone else."

"And is this wise, gorgeous, obviously incredible woman the reason why you're dressed in all white every time I see you lately?"

I look down, admiring my two-piece leggings and crop top. "The book says there's always a flicker of light in the darkness. Since I had to start over, I've decided my wardrobe could lighten up a little." I match Izzy's smile with my own. "May I show you something?"

"Sure."

I slide the sleeve up my left arm and scoot close to Izzy so she can see my new ink. *Every Black Girl Dances.* White ink wafting through my dragonflies like clouds.

"JC, that's stunning."

"Thank you. I hope you don't mind, but your book is truly inspiring. It taught me that the only partner we need is purpose. I'm free to find mine finally." I let my sleeve down and release a puff of nervous air. "I'd love to turn it into a movie, Izzy. If you would let me."

Izzy's brows furrow. "Turn what into a movie?"

"Your book. I'd give you full credit, we can work together, and I believe you'll love my idea for the script." I take a deep breath and playfully push Izzy's shoulder. "I'm starting my own production company. I'm so in love with your brain and your beautiful words, Izz. If you'll have me, I want to bring your words to life on the screen."

I slap my forehead, trying not to giggle in Izzy's flabbergasted face. "Oh God, I totally botched this. I sound like I'm asking you to marry me or something."

"Oh no, it's not that. You caught me off guard. I totally wasn't expecting this," Izzy stammers. "But yes. Yes, I'll marry you. I mean, yes, let's make movies together!"

We stand, and Izzy pulls me into her arms, giving me the hug I didn't know I needed. I sink deeper in them, allowing myself to, for once, just be . . . until my cell sounds off.

"That's Luke," I explain and race to grab my phone from my purse by the barre. When I pull it out, I see he's video calling me.

"Hey!" Luke's flanked by Myzi and the rest of the Media Tech kids. "We won! We did it, JC! *No More Trauma*, first place overall, baby!"

"We did? We did!" I yelp. "I'm so happy for you, Luke!"

"Be happy for us," he says. "We couldn't have done this without you."

"Yeah, JC, this is all you. We love you!" Myzi screams into the camera.

"Hey, guys—how about a celebration dance?" Izzy turns up the music, and we start dancing circles around each other with Michael Jackson's "Thriller" blasting in the background while Luke and the kids dance along with us on the phone.

"So many bad things have happened, I knew it was time for something good," I holler over the music.

"It's time, honey. Just dance," Izzy says.

TWENTY-FIVE

YESTERDAY, A DRAGONFLY landed on my hand.

It was like heaven shifted just to remind me that I hadn't been forgotten.

"Oh my God, look!" I started to tell Luke, who was just a few feet away, taking my last box of supplies out of the trunk of my blue Classic Hardtop Mini Cooper. At first, I wasn't sure if it was real. I mean, dragonflies don't just land on people like that. But it was like the little guy wanted some alone time with me. The way he just perched on my skin was so strange, I let it be. He was letting me know that, yes, I'm on the right path.

"This is the last of it." Luke's brown Stacy Adams scrape the concrete as he strolls over to me, balancing the plastic gray crate on his shoulder. "You'd think a woman of your caliber would invest in something to drive that's bigger than a cracker box. I think I hurt my back getting all that junk out of your car."

"Well, a woman of my caliber has poured all her extra coins into funding *Black Dragonfly Films* and producing her first movie. So, until this lady's ready for otherwise, the change will be strange." I point at the crate. "And that stuff *isn't* junk. It's the start of my next chapter. Put that crate down. I want to show you something." Luke sets the box on the ground and stands behind me while I pull up what I want to show him.

I hand Luke my cell without a prologue and stay quiet while he reads, hoping that the sweat from my legs isn't sifting through the long, white-on-white polka dot chiffon high-low skirt wafting just below my belly button. The skirt's high enough to hide the scars from my surgery but just right to show off the *She Reigns* tattoo inked in yellow on my tummy.

"Read faster; it's scorching out here," I prod Luke as if he isn't burning up in the linen green Salisbury suit he's wearing. "August isn't too forgiving on my makeup or my armpits. We can't stand out here too much longer." I try fanning myself with my hands, which only makes the heat worse.

"You'll be all right. You're barely dressed." Luke nods to the teeny white crop top that wraps around my neck, crisscrosses my boobs in the front, and leaves nothing to chance in the backyard.

"You said I look like a goddess."

"Who said I'm complaining? I'm enjoying every inch of you." Luke glances up at me with a sly grin, then back at the phone, silently moving his lips as he reads. He does that a lot. Especially when he's really deep into the text, like he's doing now. He's proud. I can see it.

"This is amazing," he finally breaks the suspense. "*Every Black Girl Dances.* Director JC Burke's emotional journey is a stark contrast from her normal hood fare, but she manages to flawlessly transition from the tragedies that made her famous to capturing the triumph of the heart," Luke reads aloud. "It will be interesting to see how fans react to JC's departure from mainstream to indie art, but if they give it a try, they'll learn to celebrate and love themselves too." He hands me back my phone with a smile. "Wow, your first review as *you.* How does it feel?"

"It feels like . . .what took me so long?" My soft giggle disguises how serious I am. "But you know what? I needed to be sober in myself before I could've ever thought about pulling off something like this. All this time, I was trying to give a voice to everyone else when I didn't have one for myself. It just took going through a whole lot of hell to get to the happy, right?"

"At least now you know you never have to walk through hell alone."

I nod, slip a tissue from my white clutch, and dab the beads of sweat trickling out from my ballerina bun.

"When you walked into my life, did you ever think that 10 months later, you'd be the next Hottie Professor?" Luke asks.

"Not any more than I could fathom Tati being a mother— soon-to-be a wife, or that Temper would go into semiretirement to work with me at *Black Dragonfly*." I smile, reach out, and caress his cheek with the back of my hand. "Or that I would have you all to myself. But here we are. If I'm in some alternate universe or this is some crazy dream, please don't wake me up."

Luke feigns hurt in his eyes and grabs his chest. "What? You don't like getting to wake up next to me every morning?"

"Aside from your morning breath, I'd call sleeping next to you a blessing infinity. Even though Temper's not pleased about us *living in sin*."

"At least she's stopped laying hands on my face and screaming, 'Come out, come out,' every time she sees me," Luke chuckles. "And she only threw oil at me once during Tati's baby shower."

"Gotta love Temper. You know she loves you, though."

"I do."

I cup a hand over my eyes to shield them from the sun when I peer at the sign on the building. "You ready to take over as H.E.C.'s professor of film?" Luke asks.

"I still have two more weeks; don't rush me. But unlike last time, I'm ready for them. The question is, are the kids ready for me?"

"I know I am." Luke gives me a quick kiss.

"Now, let's get out of this heat and put this stuff in my classroom so that we can get to the premiere. Oh shoot, I forgot the skates."

Luke gives me a wink. "I already put them in the car."

"What have I done to deserve a man like you?"

"Just by being the woman you are." Luke kisses me a second time, picks up my box, and follows me into the building where my second career's about to begin.

Your movies would be better if you didn't have such a big mouth.

No one cares about your political views or race-baiting. Shut up and entertain us.

Your job is to make movies; no one cares what you think.

Why is it always about race? Be grateful they even let your black tail in the room.

That's what's wrong with Black folks who think they got a little power.

Somehow, the nasty messages flooding my emails, DMs, comment sections, and tweets since my split with Hudson became public manage to make themselves look even viler on Skateland's big screen. It's taken some time and a whole lot of dancing, but I'm numb to what *they* have to say about me now, even if my guests' stunned faces are shocked as they read in silence.

"The moral of this story is that people believe anonymity gives them power. I mean, why do we allow complete strangers to play on our insecurities and grant them access to our peace of mind? I choose not to protect them anymore. If I can't hide, neither can they."

I nod to the audio-visual worker, who's been waiting on my cue. Seconds later, the handles for my lovely critics pop up next to the colorful commentary they left for me. As soon as each name scrolls across, the guests cheer, with Temper being the loudest. She actually starts applauding until I raise a hand to get everyone to quiet down.

"Despite what you see up on that screen, today isn't about those guys because those comments brought out the lion in me. And the world's about to hear me roar!"

I dash to my right, where Izzy's standing with her arm around Temper, and haul her back center stage with me. "I am so blessed to have such an awesome woman by my side. Izzy Prince has taught me that following our dreams doesn't ruin our lives. It's not being brave enough to try that destroys us. So, we hope you enjoy the Parable premiere of *Every Black Girl Dances*, followed by the best skate party the South has ever seen!"

The lights go down, and I move out of the way of the screen as the credits start rolling across the title frame. **Produced by Jonica "JC" Burke.** As soon as I see it, my stomach drops to my feet, and my head feels light.

This is it. Let's see what you're made of.

Luke pulls me aside, lightly dabbing the mist forming beneath my eyes. "Is everything all right? I thought you'd be happy."

"Actually, I'm ecstatic," I choke out. "I'm just seriously overwhelmed right now. You ever have the wind knocked out of you because you have everything you've ever wanted?"

Luke confirms the feeling with a nod.

"That's where I am right now, Luke. I'm just really happy. Nervous too, but I finally believe that whatever's for me will find me."

"It already has, baby. It already has."

Luke wraps me in his arms and holds me close to his heartbeat. "For every bad thing that's happened to me over the past year, you've always been there for the good," I tell him. "I just want you to know I appreciate everything you've done."

"You don't have to thank me, JC. You're family. This is what we do." He pulls away and looks me in the eyes. "Don't ever forget, there's no next after me. We're forever." He leans in for another kiss when a woman approaches and taps me on the shoulder.

"Sorry to interrupt, but do you have a minute, Miss Burke?" she asks.

"Sure," I tell her. "Will you excuse us for a moment, Luke?"

"Got your seat reserved up front," he reminds me.

"Be there in a sec."

I escort the woman farther away from the guest area so that we can chat above a whisper. The end-of-summer Texas humidity has swelled her big, fiery curls; however, they look familiar. The oversized frames amplify her green eyes the way she takes up too much personal space instead of giving it. All of it seems so familiar.

"Do I know you?" I ask her.

"We've met once," she says with a smile. "A year ago, we shared a plane ride to Texas. I was heading to Plano to see my grandfather—"

". . . and I was incredibly rude! Oh my gosh, I'm so sorry." I extend my hand, and she shakes it like this is our first time meeting. "Jamaica, I mean, Jonica. Jonica Burke. It's so nice to see you. Again, I'm incredibly sorry for the last time we met."

"No worries," her saucer-sized eyes grow wide and bright. She still doesn't know how to respect a sister's space, though. "I'm Noel Martin, one of *The View's* producers."

"Excuse me? You're who?"

"I'm a producer for the television show, *The View*. You've heard of it, correct?"

If I had a drink in my hand, I'd have spit it all over sis's turquoise jumper. Better yet, let me get a drink so I don't pass out before I hear her out. With an index finger raised in the air, I dart past the soul food buffet straight to the libation station, where I can get a stiff one to calm my nerves. I gulp a shot of something strong, then down a second one before I finish swallowing the first.

I take a deep breath, smooth my clothes, and race back over to Noel like the effects of the alcohol aren't quickly kicking in. I'm tipsy but not drunk enough to miss this moment. I check my breath when I'm a couple of steps away since sis—I mean, Noel—seems to like standing close enough to smell what folks have eaten for lunch.

"Can you very slowly tell me what you're doing here?" I sputter.

Noel grins and rests a hand on my shoulder. "After our brief encounter, I started following you, JC. I have to admit. I was kind of ashamed that I had no idea who you were. I ended up bingeing your body of work and reading up on you. You are quite the influencer, and I'm a new fan, JC Burke." She cocks her head to the side and purses her lips. "Turns out our show's hosts are big fans too. And they want you to come sit at the table. I happened to be back in town visiting family and heard about your premiere, so I came to invite you in person. Are you interested?"

Yes, yes, a million times, YES!

My mouth is moving, but nothing will come out. This moment I've been waiting for my entire career, and I'm too stupefied to acknowledge this woman or tell her yes. Christmas came early for me.

Please, God. Loose my tongue!

"I, ummm, I—"

"You don't have to answer right now, but take my card and think about it." Noel digs inside her lavender clutch, pulls out a card, and hands it to me. You'd think it was in flames the way I cautiously accepted it from her. "Call me if you decide you'd like to take us up on the offer."

"Dragonflies," I mutter as Noel spins on her two-inch taupe heels to walk away.

"Dragonflies?" Her brows raise.

"See, there was this dragonfly that landed on my hand yesterday, and it just sat there, like we were engaged in this whole telepathic conversation, and dragonflies mean new beginnings and change and hope, and you're not following any of this, are you?" I stop to take a breath. "I must sound like a crazy woman," I chuckle.

"Actually, you sound like the perfect guest." Noel reaches out and takes my elbow in her hand, flashing a warm smile. "So, does this mean you'll accept my invitation?"

"This means there's no way anyone can stop me."

TWENTY-SIX

CAN WE MEET at Kline's Steakhouse? Tomorrow, 11 a.m. My treat.

Not going to lie; something about the last line of that text makes me feel like I'm about to get tricked.

Luke and I hadn't even been home an hour from the premiere when the text requesting an impromptu Sunday Brunch meeting came through my phone. Nerve. Unmitigated gall. Audacity. Whatever you want to call it, it's all LaDonna Sheridan.

Skye Falling, to you.

Luke strolls into our bedroom after he finishes shaving. Gliding all nonchalantly, as if he doesn't know that those ripples running down his bare chest are teasing me. Scanning the length of his sexy frame as he casually makes his way over to our bed, I can't help but think . . . *This is the man I get to wake up to every day.*

I'm not lucky. I'm loved.

"You sure you don't want me to go with you, babe?" He pulls our turquoise and silver comforter back and climbs into the bed, facing me. "I really should be there—you never know what Skye's up to."

"That's *LaDonna*, babe. You know that girl is reinventing herself." I finish plaiting my hair, then slip my gold hair bonnet on and slide under the blanket with my man. "I still can't believe what Skye's done to herself. No more lip injections or face fillers, she took out her fake behind, and had her breasts reduced. I have to admit, she looks really good."

"Not as good as my baby." Luke playfully flicks my nose, followed by a soft kiss. "I really wish you'd let me go with you tomorrow. You know, just in case."

"I'm not worried about Skye, and honestly, I doubt she's that concerned about me. On a confrontational level, that is." I lean in and steal another kiss. "Besides, I think she and I are long overdue for a little girl talk."

"I just wonder what she wants."

"Not trying to be rude, but I don't know, and frankly, I don't care," I yawn. "Can we not talk about the *Hudson* in the room? At least not for tonight."

"Hudson? What does he have to do with this?"

I smile, determined not to allow the ghost of boyfriends past to squelch the euphoria I've felt all day. Not when this has been the most incredible day of my life, without even having to get tipsy to be happy.

"Hudson has *everything* to do with that sour face of yours. He's not an elephant, but he's definitely in this room," I sigh. "He's doing his thing. On the comeback after his career took the hit from *Crack Dreams*, and I've moved on in the most glorious way. And you and I are doing our thing too. This was one of the best days I've had in years. Can't we just celebrate that? No drama, no controversy. I want just one day when my past doesn't have to come up every time my future makes a power move."

Luke shakes his head, his face a cloud of frustration and confusion. "I just don't want you returning to what hurt you, JC. Can't you see that?"

"Babe." I could stop right there, make it a complete thought. Preserve my energy for other things. But I can't leave this hanging between us. "Now you know the only reason you're concerned is because you think Hudson's behind Skye's invitation somehow. Not that I'm keeping up with those two, but from what I've read, Hudson and Skye aren't even working together anymore. And even if he does have something to do with this, I wouldn't care. Because I have all I need right here beside me."

Luke smiles. Exhales when I reach beneath the covers and stroke his bare thigh.

"I'm not worried, you know."

"I know," I confirm. "But in the back of your mind—even though you never say it directly, Hudson's looming. He'll always be the one who hurt me . . ." I remove my hand from Luke's thigh and rest it on his cheek, "but you'll be the one who revived me. Besides, he can't hurt what's already been healed. I'm healed, baby."

Reassurance rests on Luke's face. We silently exchange insecurities for confidence and inch closer to each other. He flips me over, pulls me into him, and wraps his arms around me. Rocks slow, recreates the rhythm we've come to revel in.

"I don't want to dwell in the past, okay?" I press harder into Luke's heated body. "Between therapy and you, I'm good. Seriously. I'm not accepting anything less than I deserve ever again. And no matter what happens tomorrow or who shows up, I'll always return to you."

"I'm so proud of you. You know that?" The compliment falls off Luke's tongue as if he hasn't uttered it a million times tonight. But it feels fresh every time.

"Thank you, babe. I'm proud of you too."

"Yeah?" his voice perks up. "Proud of me for what?"

"For being man enough to know that supporting me doesn't diminish you."

Luke's breathing quiets. I'm silently praying my compliment hasn't gotten lost in translation. "I don't always get it right, JC. And I won't. But as long as you're with me, hell just might be in trouble."

"Then let's fire it up, baby!"

Seated across from Skye in the restaurant of her choosing, I hardly recognize her.

The exaggerated extensions have been traded for a closely cropped fade that suits her high cheekbones. She's fully clothed; the emerald two-piece suit swaddling her new, deconstructed frame compliments her perfect shade of brown skin. Minimal jewelry and makeup, capped by the humble posture she walked in here with, captivates me. Skye looks nothing like the same woman without the enhanced features and body parts that made her famous.

Picking up the glass of water in front of me, I take a sip and set it back on the table. We've stalled long enough.

"Why didn't you tell me you were at the premiere, Skye?"

"LaDonna, please." Skye corrects me without a hint of aggression or delusions of grandeur she usually speaks in. Thank God that horrific fake accent is dead. "*Skye Falling* is attached to my mistakes. Now that God has helped me find myself, I want to live with and for the name He gave me."

I nod. "Respect."

This is the first time I've seen the natural brown eyes that are peering at me sans colored contacts. Skye's just as skeptical of the outcome of this meeting as I am. But she's also oozing sincerity.

"The last thing I wanted to do was ruin your day," Skye picks up where she left off, looking me up and down. What's that I spot in her eyes? Looks like a hint of admiration.

"My goodness, you have certainly reinvented yourself, JC. In the most fantastic way, I might add. I'm happy for you."

"Me? I'm sitting here in awe of you! You don't even look like yourself."

"That's because none of that was me," she says. "All that plastic I wasted thousands of dollars on, and I have nothing to show for it except footage I'd never want my children to see." The irony of what she says forces an embarrassed laugh from the pit of her belly. She fixes her mouth to apologize, but I wave my hand, and she stops.

I nod to our waiter, who mercifully brings the steak and potato lunches we ordered and sets them on the table.

"Is there anything else I can get for you ladies?" he asks, flashing the same courteous smile that hasn't dimmed since he seated us.

"Nothing for me," Skye says. "Are you okay, JC?"

"I'm dandy. Everything looks great," I chirp. "Thank you, sir."

Our waiter nods and strolls away, whistling as he tends to other patrons with the same chipper demeanor he's handled Skye and me with.

I pluck one of the buttered rolls stacked in the basket in the center of the table, break off a piece of the end, and pop it into my mouth.

"So, you never told me why you didn't make yourself known at the premiere. You didn't have to hide. I would have loved to have spoken to you, especially since you came all the way out here."

"Oh, I wasn't hiding," Skye chuckles, "but given our history, what was I going to do? Just stroll up to you and say, 'Hey, girl, hey?'" She follows my lead and grabs a roll for herself. "I know I haven't exactly exhibited as much in the past, but I have been known to display good manners every now and then."

"Noted." My steak and lobster look neglected; I stop playing with my piece of bread, pick up my fork and knife, and slice into the juicy red meat. I take a generous bite, and the savory goodness hits me all the way to my toes. This meat is well done, just like I love it.

"May I ask you something?" I question between bites.

"Of course! I invited you here to talk, so don't be shy." Skye digs her fork into her Cobb salad and spears a cluster of lettuce.

"Okay, in no way am I trying to offend, all right?"

"None taken in advance. Shoot."

I take a deep breath and exhale my apprehension without taking my eyes off the plate. "Not that I'm following you, but I've been seeing some things about you here and there on the 'net. You're so different now. Your physical changes, movie and television choices, and even your aura has evolved. It's like a complete transformation. Tell me, what prompted the evolution of LaDonna?"

"You," she simply says.

The loud clanking when I drop my fork on my plate causes some nearby heads to turn our way. Once they understand there's nothing to see over here, they get back to their own meals.

"I see you're surprised, but it's true, no matter how unbelievable it sounds. You're one of my greatest inspirations, JC. I'm just sorry it took so long for me to see that."

Skye goes back to chomping her food like this entire situation isn't strange. Neither the former Skye Falling calling me out as her muse nor Hudson inexplicably being hailed as the new face of *racial sensitivity* after releasing a documentary exposing his family's bigotry was on my Bingo cards this year, but here we are.

The earth has got to be spinning off its axis.

"How do I inspire you?" I want to know.

Skye sets down her fork, picks up her white cloth napkin, and dabs the corners of her mouth like a true Southern belle. She inhales, which I don't find a distraction for the first time because she's had the floatation devices she substituted for breasts deflated.

"Who wouldn't want to be like you, JC?" she asks rhetorically. "You've taken the worst Hollywood could give you, but you kept standing. All the hate you've gotten just for daring to be different? Humph, it couldn't be me." Her head shakes with regret. "You had a man, who had a woman on the side, who had another dude of her own because she only wanted your man for the clout she never got." She takes a deep breath and draws her newly thinned lips together. There's an apology lurking in her pensive glare, but not yet.

"I was so ugly to you, JC. We were all ugly to you. I wish I could take it back—"

"You don't have to." I reach across the table and lay my hand across hers.

"No, I do," Skye insists. "We're two women—*Black women*, fighting to find our way in an industry that's not always so welcoming to us. We never should've competed, we should have collaborated."

I was never competing, but okay. I'll let her have that.

"I don't know if you realize it," Skye doesn't wait for me to speak, "but that film Hudson made—*Race Baiting*—wasn't so much to share the lessons he's learned in Blackness and privilege with the world like he's claiming on his press tour. It's more of an open letter . . . to you."

"Me?" I draw my hand back, stunned.

Skye nods her confirmation. My eyes drop to her wrist, which has a chain link tattooed around it. Something I never saw during filming.

"Of course, Hudson's always going to be Hudson, so a fraction of the film was for money, but the strong public reception he's received and the bounce back is a bonus." She pauses to trace the tattoo that I haven't stopped gawking at. "The greater part of Hudson exposing the sins of his family was to apologize to you.

He felt so guilty about everything, JC. That much, I know. I think being unable to make things right with you took away a part of him. Ultimately, it's what came between us."

"So, that's what this is about? Hudson's not man enough to apologize to me, so he sends you?"

"Oh, girl, we haven't talked in months. Seeing his face reminded me too much of the child I never got to meet because Hudson thought it would kill his career." It's hard for me not to feel bad when I gaze upon the imperceptible cloud of loss hanging over Skye's head. I feel sorry for her. I do. Every one of us makes bad decisions. Whether we show compassion for somebody else is up to us.

"Hudson and I have made our peace, but he never got the chance to do that with you, JC."

I lean back in my seat, staring at the food that's gone cold by now. I pick at what's left of my bread, still wondering how I fit into Skye's new identity. "I don't hate either of you."

Skye bites her bottom lip and shrugs. "I know. That's what's drawn me to you. At least what I see of you in public. You've emerged, like a—"

"Dragonfly," I finish for her.

Skye laughs. "I was going to say butterfly, but all right. Anyway, after seeing all the public humiliation you've endured, then coming back stronger, wiser, and better than you've ever been before did something to me. It forced me to search myself. I went back to my parents, got in therapy, and started healing." She lays her hand across her chest and smiles.

"I don't want any parts of the old me anymore, JC. I'll be 35 in November, and I need something real in my life for a change. Holding the weight of all that fakeness was killing me inside. You showed me that it's okay to let go and start over. So, I'm starting over. And it's all because of you."

My eyes widen against my will, and I hear myself blurt, "Wait, you're 35?"

"I said 'almost.'" Skye rolls her eyes and laughs. "That's all you got from that?"

"Well, no. It's just that you're so naturally beautiful that I never would have known. The real you looks good on you, *LaDonna*."

"Thank you." LaDonna's shoulders rise with pride. "I feel much better, too. People hardly recognize me now, and I like that. Actually, I love it. That's how I was able to sneak into your premiere unnoticed. And it's why I wouldn't have been able to sleep at night until I made things right with you."

"Wow, I don't know what to say."

"You already have."

I take her hand in mine. The woman I'll give the respect of addressing by her birth name from now on. LaDonna. "You gave me something I didn't know I needed."

Her brows raise. "Closure?"

I shake my head. "No. I needed to know I was not crazy for refusing to be who they wanted me to be. For being myself. Thank you for that. I never thought I'd be happy to see you, but I am."

"I'm just glad you accepted my invitation. Girl, I thought you were going to cuss me out. That's why I sent a text instead of calling." She reclaims her hand and tosses her head back in a hearty chuckle.

"Tell me, did you enjoy the film, LaDonna?"

"Enjoy it? Girl, I'm crazy about it! I haven't stopped talking about it since last night." A sheepish grin crosses her face, and I spot a hint of the old *Miss Falling*. "Since we're good now, you think we might work together again someday?"

I don't even take a second to consider my answer.

"Probably not. But God still works miracles."

TWENTY-SEVEN

"DO YOU TAKE this woman to be your lawfully wedded wife?"

I never thought this day would come. That love would prove itself, even when it's denied. Sometimes, we search for love like we're on a quest to find the perfect bottle of wine. But what therapy's help me see is that love isn't about the tasting; it's about filling our glasses with what we want and spending what we're willing to invest in it.

These days, I only cry when I'm happy. Thank God I have so much to be happy about.

Moving back to Parable was the recharge I didn't know my life needed. The clean, country air alone is worth every breath I take. I don't miss my old life, not one bit. My latest movie made me a bigger celebrity director than all of my previous films combined. One reviewer said, *"We all knew JC Burke had this in her; we're just glad she decided to let herself in on the secret."*

All right, as good as this feels right now, I'm not going to do it. I refuse to cry! Not today. No matter how bad my eyes are stinging, I paid too much to let this fabulous makeup go to waste. Besides, I don't want to look like a raccoon on one of the biggest days of our lives.

"I do."

The bass in his enthusiastic response snaps me out of my daydream. I do that a lot these days. Drift off, thinking about how it felt like I was the universe's pot to piss in at one point, but now I realize one thing. Whatever our "*it*" is, it will never be done until we go through it.

We try to cry and scream our way out of life, but life's more stubborn than we are. And if we're going to be mentally fit, we've got to face it, no matter how bad it hurts. Just like the end of a movie, the pain has to stop. It's just a matter of time before the credits roll.

"Do you take this man to be your lawfully wedded husband?"

Not yet.

Elaine designed the most stunning work of art I've ever seen for the dress. A nontraditional, V-neck, white and ivory boho, cap-sleeve dress made of tulle and lace that dips to the floor and does not have a train. Straight out of a Shakespearian film. The chapel's sickeningly exquisite and big enough to hold the 300 guests who piled in to witness the happy couple become one. There are sunflowers everywhere, including the end of each pew. The front of the chapel is stacked with ivory and pink candles; the rest of the décor is a faint pink and rose gold. Everything's perfect. But it's just not for me.

My forever is for the man who deserves it. *Someday.* Don't get me wrong—I'm not saying Luke doesn't deserve the best of me, because he does. In the midst of constant changes and pivots that I wasn't anticipating, he's been my rock. A king, really. One who reminded me what hope looks like when you find it again.

"*I can't believe Pops made it all the way down to Westbrook Road,*" Luke said as he slid off his shoes and plopped on our bed several nights ago.

"*Seems like you're just as tired as him.*" I scooted over to where he sat on the edge of the bed and massaged his shoulders. "*I finally got Elaine to go back to sleep. She feels awful about this, babe. She couldn't eat until you found him.*"

Luke swiped his hands over his face and groaned. *"It's not my sister's fault that Pops left while she was resting. Chemo's been knocking her out. I can't believe the cancer came back."* He smashed a fist into his open palm. *"Eff cancer, man!"*

"Hey, hey, hey. She's going to be okay." Luke's jaw tensed, tightening the nerves throughout the rest of his body. *"Look at me."* I gently cupped his chin and turned his face to mine. *"Elaine's going to beat this. She's done it before, and she'll do it again. And all of us, we're going to be just fine. You hear me? We're going to make it."*

Luke pressed his forehead to mine, breathing in the air I gave him. *"I love you so much, JC. I hope you know that."*

"I do, babe. I do."

Maybe I'm more ready to be a wife than I thought.

"Really, Axel? You're just going to spit up on godmommy's wedding suit like that?" The wedding party and guests burst into laughter as I hold Tati's son away from me.

"Give him to me," Tati's mother, Mama Ko, rushes from the front row and grabs her grandson out of my quivering hands.

"Wait, Mom," Tati screeches, "it's almost over. Give us just two more seconds."

"My boy needs to be cleaned," Mama Ko insists.

"Just hold on, Mom. Our entire family needs to be together, including Baby A," Tati hisses. She turns to Temper, who's officiating the ceremony. "You think you can hurry this thing along so our family can be joined together?"

"By the power invested in me, I now pronounce you man and wife," Temper spits as fast as she can. "Adam, you may now kiss your bride."

The hysterical laughter turns to cheers as Tati bends down, takes Adam in her arms, and dips him for a long, passionate kiss. The history of their brief lifetime together passes before they finally come up for air.

"Ladies and gentlemen, I present to you, Mr. and Mrs. Adam Nation," Temper shouts over the screams and catcalls.

"We did it," I whisper to myself. Then out loud, "Oh my God, we did it, Tati! We're married!"

"No, ma'am!" Temper taps my shoulder. "*She* did it. *Tati's* married." She fixes the collar of the pale pink Victorian dress Tati requested she wear for the nuptials. "But if you and Luke are ready, we can do a two-for-one. What do you say, Luke?"

Luke and I lock eyes. A sly grin turns the corners of those sexy lips to the sky.

"Congratulations, Mr. and Mrs. Nation!" Luke hollers.

"I can't believe your mother let us get out of the chapel without getting hitched," Luke says. "I really thought she was going to handcuff and lock us inside until we said, *I do.*"

"Just be thankful Temper hasn't been working out like she used to. She almost caught the tail of your tux when we were racing out the back door."

Luke squeezes my hand as we make our way down the River Walk at Parable Park. The sun's hinging between dusk and daylight; the natural light we're losing is giving sweet relief from the heat. At least baby Axel did me a favor by spitting up on my dinner jacket. The pearl-studded bustier is much cooler to wear outside.

"You think Tati's going to be upset that we skipped out on the reception early?" Luke asks.

I shake my head. "I'm going to tell you what Tati's been telling the internet trolls since they started dogging her relationship with her new husband: *Do what makes you happy.* And what makes me happy right now is sharing space with you." I raise the hand Luke's not holding, revealing a bottle of Dom I swiped after the couple was toasted and the guests were on round eight of the Electric Slide before we tipped out. "This makes me happy too."

"You are trying to get blitzed, woman." Luke's boisterous chuckle scares the family of ducks passing by.

"Just trying to be happy, my guy. Just trying to be happy."

We reach the end of the walkway and stroll toward a cluster of picnic tables in front of a small pond. I sit at the table while Luke pulls out his cell. By the time I pop the top and turn the bottle up to my lips, Tevin Campbell blares through Luke's speaker, asking, "Can We Talk." Luke extends a hand to me and helps me up from my seat, wrapping his arms around my waist. I wrap mine around his neck. We rock back and forth, allowing Tevin's buttery falsetto to dismiss the sun and summon the moon.

"Myzi says you killed it in class this week," Luke informs me. "She said something about loving how you're exploring films that don't make you feel like you need therapy when they're over."

I angle my head to look into his eyes and laugh. "Yeah, well, sometimes we can all use a break from reality. These last two films I worked on taught me that. I don't feel heavy like I did before. You had a lot to do with that."

Luke stops swaying and feigns surprise. "Me? I didn't do anything."

"You've done more than you'll ever know." I softly take his bottom lip between my teeth, then kiss him full on. "Thank you for giving me a home, Luke."

"It's not like you didn't have a place to stay. Temper has plenty of rooms."

"Stop playing. You know what I mean." I lay my head on his chest, and we begin to sway again. "This has been some year."

"Just so we're clear: you moved back to Texas, became a teacher, released a film that smashed at the box office, killed it on *The View*, and did something no other woman has ever managed to do."

"Really? What's that?"

"You captured *The Hottie Professor's* heart. I've never been in love before now, JC. And I appreciate you for showing me what love is."

"You gave me room to love myself first, and that's all I can ever ask. I love you too."

We dance in silence until the end of the song, but Luke clutches me to his chest, even after the music has stopped. Finally, he pulls away, and we walk back to the bench and sit.

"What's next for us, JC?"

"I'm not really sure." I take another swig of wine. "Being in therapy's shown me that I don't have to have it all figured out. Not today, not tomorrow. Not even next week. I don't have to be controlled by people's expectations of me or the schedules and standards they try holding me to. The only boundaries I'm worried about are the ones I create for myself."

Luke nods. "So, where do I fit in?"

"Exactly where you are right now. Beside me. Growing together." I lean in and steal a kiss that's so hard and strong, like I've been deprived.

"Until then, we dance."

ACKNOWLEDGEMENTS

My parents, Robert and Billie Rigdon. It's because of you that I'm not afraid to dance the way I want. Thank you for being the constant in my life, always encouraging me to follow my dreams, in my own way. I love you!

My dear friend, LaChelle Weaver – you are such a light, wonderful friend and talented author! Thank you for lending an ear when I was tossing this book around as an idea. I truly adore you.

Aunt Joyce Crockett-Hamilton, I love you and thank you for being so supportive of all my endeavors!

Our "baby girl" Sharbra Harris, you are more than enough. It's time to dance...

To my publisher and acquisition editors, Shawanda "NTyse" Williams and Kreceda Tyler – all I can say is, WOW. When you first accepted a meeting with me, I had no idea it would turn into this blessing. I appreciate you so much for giving a platform to myself and other authors to flourish. I can't wait to see what's next for Black Odyssey, this has been an incredible journey!

My husband, Cedrick Johnson ("Hershey"). Through all the losses, wins, and uncertainties, you've consistently supported my creative risks, waited patiently, listened, contributed, encouraged, and helped me to FLY. You are my biggest cheerleader, and I love you so much! You're my partner and my best friend . . . and you got next, baby!

And to some phenomenal women whom I watch from afar, but glean so much from: Jacquelin Thomas, Cheryl Polote-Williamson, Victoria Christopher Murray, Cherie Banks. I love watching you all dance!!!